GOLD RUSH

GOLDEN OMEGAVERSE
BOOK ONE

R. L. RANDOLPH

Cover image: *Spray of Flowers and Ferns* by **Titian Ramsay Peale** (date unknown)

Image sourced from the National Gallery of Art

Editing by: DerpyWickedFox Editorial

For the ones who can never choose.
You don't have to.

PLAYLIST

A NOTE

This book contains sensitive content.
This book takes place in a version of our current world where every person has a secondary designation: *alpha, beta,* or *omega*. If you're unfamiliar with the omegaverse, there is a guide specific to this world in the back matter. The guide contains no spoilers, and is meant to provide further context.

You can also view the content warnings and spice list for a better understanding of the content included in this novel. These are all in the back matter.

PART ONE

CHAPTER ONE

JUNE

Today is not my day.

I can barely tolerate the airport normally, but as I stare at the red text on the departures board, my stomach churns and my palms sweat.

My flight from New York to London has been delayed *again.* I wanted to fly out of DC — it was the closer option to my Virginia apartment but Janet, my literary agent, asked if I could come to New York City, just for a last minute meeting before my European tour.

"I know you hate it in the city, Juniper, but we really need you to sign the rights agreement."

So I agreed — it was the only polite option, even though this building is an overstimulating hell for my anxiety. Bright lights, loud noises, mixes of perfumes, and chemical enhancers — all creating a volatile mix in the air that makes me want to walk away from my gate and say *fuck it.*

I can't though. Tickets have been sold, readers are excited, and I'd have to be lying dead in a ditch to disappoint that many people.

Chewing on my lip, I glance up at the board again, watching the numbers flash. I don't know why they keep pushing it back, but the sheer number of hours I've spent both in this wretched city and this chaotic airport is starting to make my skin crawl. I operate better at home, in my tiny apartment I've lived in since college, with my creature comforts of shitty take-out and a litany of romance novels lining the second-hand shelves.

There's three separate waiting areas at this gate, and from my seat at the very back, I can see them all.

The primary one — full of chairs and people and bags scattered — looks like every other airport gate I've had the misfortune to be temporarily stuck at. There's enough space not to feel like you're sitting on top of the next person, but not enough to truly *spread*. I have my carry-on between my legs, my arm hooked around it as my eyes land on the priority sections.

One is entirely for alphas — mostly in business, because who else has the time to accrue enough airline miles to be a priority boarder? The section isn't *as* busy as the beta section, but it does look comfortable. The seats are a little more plush and there's a beta attendant flitting around serving drinks.

The same cannot be said for the rest of us, we get questionable water fountains or overpriced bottles from the convenience stores.

To the right, though, is a partition. I've never been at a major airline's gate that had one before. The screens are semi-transparent, separating the seats from everything else and giving the illusion of calm and privacy from the bustle. It's only for packs, or bonded omegas and their alphas.

I'd *kill* to be around the corner right now, not listening to the beta woman next to me bitch into her phone about the flight delay.

She stands, and with her comes a cloud of perfume enhancement spray. Her natural scent is almost sticky, clinging to my nostrils and punched up with the chemicals, turning the floral notes into something near-noxious. It's like being showered in faux rose water. I turn my head, my eyes watering as I let out a little breath, flexing my fingers and readjusting in my seat.

Betas don't have as strong of scents as alphas or omegas. The natural pheromones are subtler, but there are products that claim to make a beta's scent as *alluring* as other designations.

It never works. Everyone ends up smelling like cheap body spray, which is *great* for anyone with sensory issues — like me.

I sat away from the gate for that very reason, even though I'd prefer to be closer. It's not like getting on board any faster would make a difference, my ticket is still economy — and I highly doubt any of the alphas are going to glance twice at a beta woman sleeping on a balled up sweater as a pillow in the back of the plane.

The chatter of people talking mixes with the smell of half-burnt bagels from the kiosk down the wide hall and the passengers around me. There's a bitter scent lingering, and I briefly wonder if the combination of smelling it and burnt toast means my anxiety has finally decided to kill me via stroke.

Leaning into my own arm, I sniff my sweater. I've been anxiety-sweating since I left the agency offices this morning. The last thing I want is to be yet another person adding to the noxious mix. If my flight is delayed anymore,

I'll be going straight from the damn airport to the bookstore.

And I'd *really* like to sleep.

"Could you grab me a fizzy drink?" A woman drops into the vacant seat next to me, bringing with her a cloud of blueberries. I blink, glancing to the side as she smiles up at a tall, lean man with a crop of red hair.

"Are you nauseous?" He eyes flare wide, concern evident as he reaches for her.

The woman next to me leans back, making a face. "Actually, I'd like you to leave me *alone* for five seconds, but sure, if it helps — I'm nauseous, go get me a fizzy water."

The man stares at her for a beat, a mixture of amused devotion lifting the edges of his lips before leaning forward and pressing a kiss to her dark-skinned forehead. "Brat." He hums the word softly and affectionately. When he pulls away, he glances down at her. "I'm going to find Quint — he might be able to get us into the pack seating."

The moment he's gone, the woman glances at me, her brown eyes bright.

"Well, you're probably going to hate me for saying this, but I'm glad this flight was delayed, it took us *forever* to get through security. I'm not surprised the pack area is full-up." Her British accent is light as she smiles at me, her lips pulling up at the corners, smooth brown skin flawless.

"Oh." I glance at her, not expecting the immediate conversation. "Yeah, it filled up quickly."

I've been here *way* too long, and watched the entire three seating areas slowly become more and more crowded. I didn't *need* to leave the offices so early, but with the delays it's turned my *semi-unreasonable* anxiety-fueled early arrival into an hours-long wait. I settle on the simple words, because nothing is worse than a stranger trauma-dumping their anxieties on you in a public place, my voice softer than the omega's.

She's beautiful. Her long black hair in a low ponytail, not a bag in sight — which makes sense, if she has a pack, they've probably taken care of it all for her.

She won both the genetic *and* the biological lotteries.

The omega shrugs, looking over at the gate. "I like to leave early, but you know the lines here, even with express. My alphas all have different passports, it makes it a bloody nightmare to get from point A to point B. Hopefully they'll let us on soon."

"Well, regardless, you'll have first dibs." I try for a reassuring smile, but it feels unnatural. The omega looks back at me, her brows drawing in tight and I flounder for a moment. "Because your pack will board first?"

She pauses, and for half a second I think she almost looks startled, like she thought we were talking about two different things. After a delayed second, she tilts her head. "Yeah, packs board first." Her hand drops to rest on her stomach, flat under a bulky crewneck emblazoned with some rugby team. "People always think omegas have easy lives — useless shit about how we all get lucky to find alphas to settle down with, but if you turn on the news, you'd be clued in that is *far* from the truth."

Embarrassment pangs through my chest, and mild confusion. She keeps including me in her statements, like we're not perfect strangers stuck waiting at a glorified bus stop. My brain reels, trying to grasp at some kind of topic.

"I saw the reports about the blood testing breakthrough this morning." Blurting the words, I stumble ahead. "They found traces of golden blood in a fourteen year old lupus patient. Apparently her designation hasn't fully emerged, but they were looking for experimental treatments. I don't like to think about how young it starts — how they don't have a choice almost from the word go."

My words die off, hanging in the air.

No biologist has figured out *why* omega blood is golden-hued. And I've never seen it before, as a beta with standard red blood. Designation detection blood tests are run yearly from puberty onwards to check that no previously-assumed betas show signs of a different designation. For alphas, it's silver-hued blood, slightly luminescent like an oil slick.

It presents a unique set of challenges. Omegas who need blood transfusions can really only take them safely from universal alpha donors, with bonded alphas being the safest option. Society and medicine have intertwined themselves, with most omegas predisposed to chronic conditions or illnesses.

Omegas don't have the option of deciding their own future. The designation is increasingly rare, and parents or guardians take over the decision-making for their omega children, setting them up with designation centers that will help the omega choose alphas to bond so they're cared for the rest of their lives.

"I heard about that." The omega next to me jars me out of my thoughts, her voice lower. "Doctors always want to test for designations earlier and earlier, but they never seem to care as much after we're older — unless you're pregnant. Then there's a vested interest, of course." She gives me a chagrined look, her hand on her stomach shifting slightly.

Her alpha's overprotective behavior suddenly makes a lot of sense.

I don't know what to say, and as I settle on the obvious — a *congratulations* — she squints.

"I don't know how betas stand it. These lights and smells give me a headache." The omega shifts in her seat, groaning slightly. "Forgive me, I totally forgot to ask — what's your name?"

"Oh it's —"

One of the gate agents crackles over the intercom, interrupting me mid-sentence. *"Thank you for your patience, at this time, we'll be allowing priority pack boarding."*

"Oh!" The omega pops out of her seat as another man appears. He's *massive* — muscles stacked on muscles, stocky with a wide smile on his face. Undeniably alpha, but he looks like a giant teddy bear. "We're in luck." The omega glances at me, smiling wide. "Maybe I'll see you on the plane with your pack?"

I open my mouth, startled all over again, but her alpha adjusts the bag slung over his shoulder, talking first. "Ol and Quint are coming. You ready to head home?" He slides an arm around the omega's shoulder and she leans into him, her smile gentle.

"Mhm." The omega waves at me as they head around the throng of people who've been waiting *hours*. "It was nice meeting you!" She joins up with two other alphas at the gate, one of them — a blond — handing over their boarding passes before they're all ushered to board.

I sit back in my seat, biting my tongue as my brain reels.

She thought *I* was an omega like her. Suddenly the entire conversation makes a hell of a lot more sense, but I can't fathom why she even made the assumption in the first place. I've been sitting alone for hours, shoved at the back of the seating arrangements, with no sign of a doting alpha or bond mark.

Maybe omegas don't have it all. Being born and almost immediately told you're biologically weaker is bullshit. Not to mention the expectation to find an alpha and marry them, just because society doesn't want to recognize someone can be chronically ill and still an active member of the world. But fuck, if I don't want the other perks, the world adjusting to *their needs*.

The fluorescents above me crackle, making me nauseous, flickering as the gate agents welcome the single alphas to board. One golden-sheened bond away from being the world's priority.

My head aches as I slump in the uncomfortable seat, waiting for final boarding like the rest of the betas sitting in economy.

I THROW up the *second* I unlock my hotel room, barely making it to the toilet before the soda and crackers from my flight reappear.

It was a *nightmare*. Someone in front of me had a toddler that was old enough to know better than to scream and thrash for four hours straight, leaving a nap impossible. And the guy next to me smelled like cleaning products and chemicals — I'm not sure who he thought he was going to attract in the back fucking row of economy with his faux perfume, but it only made the mounting nausea worse.

A migraine tagged along with me when I left the airport, an unwelcome passenger as I drop my single carry-on onto the little luggage bench inside the room, digging out my phone from my pocket as it rings.

I don't know why I look at the caller ID expecting my mom — she never calls, she's too busy going to "charity" events with Dad and chatting to other betas who pray and hope they'll have an alpha or omega kid they can pair off, because *"God put betas on this earth to help alphas find their single, perfect omega. Packs are ruining the god-honored sanctity of bonding."*

I moved out for college and haven't looked back.

The ID, instead, reads *JANET* in all caps, and I answer my agent as I suck in a long breath.

"Juniper?" Janet's Queens accent is thick. "I saw the flight finally landed, did you get to the hotel safely? The bookstore confirmed the signing for tomorrow evening. I told them you would be there, rain or shine."

"Awesome." I move over to the bed and drop down onto it, holding the phone to my ear while I attempt to sound chipper, even though I feel like I've been run over by a kitschy red double-decker bus. "I'll be there, I'm meeting a friend in the hotel bar tonight and then getting some sleep."

"Okay," Janet's voice is a little softer. "Just remember, it's only a London signing, and a couple in Manchester and Brighton, you'll be back by the end of the week."

I breathe out softly, feeling a smile tug at my lips. For as punctual and stern Janet is, she's a total mother hen. She's been my literary agent since I was fresh out of college, a cool six years ago at the ripe age of twenty-two. She's fostered my career as much as I have, helping my little contemporary romance debut grow to the point that readers even *want* to come see me in London of all places. Even while feeling like garbage, gratitude fills me.

"Thanks for calling to check on me."

"Of course." She's back to business in a flash. "Go have *one* drink, then go to bed. Agent's orders."

I laugh, pulling the phone away after saying goodbye and looking down at it. My cell is four years old, my old laptop is still sitting on my desk inside my apartment, and yet, somehow, in the past week, I've found myself signing a multi-million dollar deal to sell the film rights for my first book.

The Pack and I has gained so much traction in the last six years, it makes my head spin.

Flopping on the bed, I finally suck in a deep breath and then glance at my phone when it buzzes *again.*

> **MICHAELA**
>
> I'm at the bar! I got away early, don't rush.

The text makes me smile. An old friend from one of my first creative writing classes — Michaela — was in London and saw the signing announcement. She said she couldn't make it tomorrow night, but offered to meet for a drink if I had the time. I think she's working as a copywriter at a PR firm handling sports teams these days.

I sit up, pushing back errant strands of my auburn hair as it frizzes in front of me, sending a quick reply.

> **ME**
>
> Just got to the room, I'll be up there in five.

I take five minutes to throw myself into the bathroom, scrubbing my teeth twice to get the taste of bile out of my mouth, swearing off actually consuming anything alcoholic tonight. I don't drink often — I've never really subscribed to the Hemingway-adjacent lifestyle other authors do — and my stomach is still churning so horrifically, I can't fathom anything but water touching my lips.

The harsh lighting in the bathroom highlights the slight sweaty sheen to my pale skin and the redness in my flushed cheeks. It's not... great, but I can pass it off as harried and wind-swept. I deem myself presentable *enough*, tugging the sleeves of my sweater down and smoothing out the front. The rumpled outfit screams that I've been on a plane, but I snag my phone and purse instead of digging for something better from my limited options.

In the hall, I rush toward the elevators, narrowly missing one of the two as the doors shut and send it up. Groaning, I stab the button again, watching the other light up, coming from the ground floor. Smoothing out my hair again in the warped reflection of the closed doors, I mentally pep talk myself.

Michaela was always nice. We sat next to each other for the entire semester and kept tabs on each other until we grad-uated. Then she did *congratulate me when I published my debut novel. Just because we've not seen each other in years doesn't mean the conversation will be awkward. We could talk about the weather. We could talk about...*

I look to the side at the windows overlooking the busy London streets, dappled with rain, my brain immediately supplying how fucking awkward the chat with the omega in the airport was.

We can talk about the weather. It might be less painful that way.

The elevator dings and I jolt away from my reflection as the doors slide open.

I barely glance at the two men inside, standing near each

other and as I step in. As I reach for the button, one of them also moves forward.

He's slightly taller than me, maybe a few inches, with the richest, dark skin I've ever seen. His brown eyes are soft, his lips pulling into a smile as he motions to the buttons, voice deep and accent distinctly American. "What floor?"

I flounder for a second, opening my mouth, then look at the buttons quickly, seeing the rooftop is lit up. "Actually, it's already pressed. I'm good." I shuffle back, keeping my distance from them and giving them their personal space, but I can't resist a glance at the man's companion.

The other man is a couple inches shorter than the first — almost in line with my own height — tanned skin at the junction of his neck and shoulder scarred in a round silver-toned bite, only exposed because his long brown hair is pulled away from his throat, tied into a loose bun.

An alpha and his bonded beta.

The first man returns to his side — strength in his narrow shoulders. He bends his head and says something, and the other man looks up with a grin, shrugging.

I look away, pressing my lips together, glancing down at my phone. There's no doubting the dark-skinned man is an alpha. He radiates power in the small space of the elevator. There's a light fragrance in the air, sweet like chocolate covered oranges I've indulged in around the holidays. The numbers ding as the elevator rises and rises, and just as it nears the final five floors, there's a metallic CLANG as it grinds to an unexpected halt.

CHAPTER TWO

JUNE

I FREEZE, clutching my phone in my hand as I stare at the doors, willing them to open.

It's only a little hiccup. A small glitch and the doors will mistakenly open on a floor.

This elevator is not stuck.

"Oh god," I squeak the words, pressing against the metal wall. The two men look over at the panel in alarm before the first one, the alpha, moves forward and jabs the button for the rooftop.

The second man, the beta, looks over at *me*. His eyes rove over me as I suck in rapid breath after rapid breath, before he mutters, "Hey, it's okay." He moves closer and I glance up, making eye contact with him, feeling my heart pound in my throat, a rapid beat that makes the nausea come back full-tilt.

I shake my head, whispering, "It's going to move right? We're not stuck? Please tell me we're not stuck."

"Uh..." The alpha glances at us, then he turns and jabs the button for the emergency alert.

My stomach drops out of my body and I crumble to the floor, sucking in a wheezing breath. First trapped in an airport, then trapped in a plane, and now a tiny fucking elevator. I don't know what past transgressions I did to deserve *this*.

"Whoa." The beta drops down onto one knee in front of me. "Hey, it's going to be fine." He touches my arm, his voice soft. "Bennett will get them to restart it or... however elevators work."

I bury my head in my hands, sucking in a breath, squeaking out, "Sorry, I'm fine."

"It's okay if you aren't." The man next to me is quieter as his hand on my arm moves back and forth. I can feel the heat from his palm through my sweater, calm, warm, reassuring on a baser, instinctual, level.

It grounds me and I lift my head, glancing up. His soft smile is a little devastating, it's so pretty. He flashes me straight, white teeth, his light brown eyes pinched at the edges in concern.

"Really." His hand on my arm moves slightly, his thumb rubbing fabric. "It's okay if you're not okay. Is it... the elevator itself? The small space?"

Bennett, the alpha at the buttons, makes a surprised noise when the speaker in front of him crackles.

"This is maintenance. It looks like you're stuck between floors." There's a light whine of feedback before the disembodied voice continues. "I'm going to send a guy to reset the systems and if it doesn't work, we'll call fire and rescue."

I hunch forward, my stomach rolling again. The speaker crackles off as Bennett mutters, "Real fucking helpful." He turns, his eyes widening as he looks down at the other man and... me, a mess on the dirty elevator floor, heaving in panicked breaths every half second like a gasping fish.

He frowns, bending down in front of us. The beta next to me readjusts, leaning his back against the elevator wall as he stretches his legs out. His hand is still on my arm, and it's a comforting kind of weight as the guy's alpha eyes me, his expression torn. "They might reset it and get it started again."

The thought makes me groan, dropping my head down into my arms, mumbling into them, "What if they restart it and the elevator plummets to the first floor? And then we all just..."

I taper off, my brain supplying the helpful image of a stick figure version of me splatting on the ground into a pile of goop, the fiery remains of the elevator unhelpfully blowing said goop to the sky. There's no funerals to be had for goop.

"Well, that's not a helpful thought," the guy next to me mutters, his tone dry. I glance over at him and he smiles, his lips twitching, like he's privy to the wildly unlikely goop-scenario playing in my mind. "Is that how elevators even work? What if they do restart it and we're up at the bar with no issues?"

I stare at him, my eyes narrowing. "I don't know. I'm not an expert on elevators, hence the sheer panic. What if they can't restart it and then they have to call the fire department?"

"What if the firefighters come immediately because it would be absolutely devastating if three of the hottest people currently in London died in an elevator related accident?"

"I—" I bark out a laugh, leaning my head against the wall. "What?"

"Seth's good at saying things that should be left as inside thoughts." The alpha sinks to sit in the center of the elevator.

Seth shrugs, leaning his head against the wall, a little smile still on his lips. "I know I'm hot, I know you're hot." He eyes Bennett, effortlessly flirty, and the alpha leans back a little, his lips pressed together, glancing off to the side. Seth's gaze darts over to me and I flush, head to toe, my thin sweater suddenly warm in the tight space.

Don't think about the walls caving in right now.

"I'm flattered." I pull my knees to my chest, clearing my throat.

Seth smiles. "And also no longer panicking."

He's annoyingly *right*. My breathing comes a little easier as I shoot him a disgruntled look, my mind whirling as the entire elevator jolts again.

"Oh my god." Jerking, I grab onto Seth's arm, my other hand over his on my sweater, clinging to him as the lights flicker. There's another metallic screech and I press closer to him, over my embarrassment and instead choosing to embrace the abject terror of death by elevator. His alpha — Bennett — leans forward, his body moving to cover both of ours, one hand bracing on the side of Seth's neck, holding him in place. The other lands so close to me that the air charges — but there's no touch accompanying it — just the awareness that his protection extends to *me*, not just his bonded.

There's a wash of perfume, and my mind feels fuzzy, like it can't function with the combination of smells. It's not in the unpleasant way of chemical mixtures from the general public — this is bone-deep, like my body is reacting to them before my mind can. Seth's body tucks closer to mine in the way only someone does when faced with unexpected chaos.

Together, the three of us are a bundle of limbs, like I'm not a perfect stranger to them.

The entire box shakes before it starts to rise once more.

"Sorry about that, folks." The voice over the speaker sounds embarrassed. "Someone stepped out for a smoke and accidentally hit the emergency brake. You should be moving again."

Bennett's face tilts, his head directly between mine and Seth's. This close I can *taste* his natural perfume, a burst of citrus, like zesting an orange, or the spray of juice when your nail breaks the skin. My head spins as I stare up at the stranger, sucking in a deep breath. Everything is sweet, and it takes me a second to recognize the other scent as fudge, warm and gooey. It all almost has a layer of *extra* sugar over it — and Bennett suddenly leans away, standing firm and tall above us, hands extended.

Seth rises first, taking one of his hands, before he turns his attention to me. Both of them help me up from the floor and I shuffle back a half-step, feeling flushed as I tug on my sweater, my palms sweaty.

This elevator is too small, too warm.

"Thank you." I throw the words at them. I feel like I'm swallowing spoonfuls of honey.

Bennett's eyes linger, his lips parting before the elevator jolts to a stop. I stumble slightly, looking up as the doors open to the rooftop. We couldn't have been stuck for more than ten minutes, but there's a group of people standing in front of the elevator, multiple hotel staff members with wide eyes, and then two men, one white, and one Indian, who push through the crowd.

"Are you both alright?" The Indian man grabs Bennett

the second he turns, and I slip past them, looking away as the white man checks them both over frantically.

My eyes catch his for a moment, but I tear them away the second I hear a shout. "Were you *stuck* in there? Are you okay?" Michaela grabs my arm and drags me to the side, her eyes wide.

"It's okay." I find my voice, putting my back to the chaos, sucking in a breath. "I'm okay."

Michaela shakes her head at me, squeezing my arm. "You look rattled. Let's get you a drink." She grabs my sweater, tugging me forward, throwing over her shoulder. "You smell *really* good, are you wearing a new perfume?"

"WE'LL MAKE sure the queue is tidy and then come get you for the signing." The beta bookseller gives me a faint smile before shutting the door to the back office.

I feel like I haven't been able to function in the last forty-eight hours. It's been one thing after another. Michaela and I had a couple drinks, and I relegated myself to a half glass of white wine and salty french fries, trying to keep my nausea at bay as she peppered me with questions about the "*alphas in the elevator.*" When I told her I was certain one was a beta, like us, she shrugged.

"*I mean, there was some...*" She makes a face. "*Tension when the doors opened. Or did nothing happen?*"

I laughed at her and said nothing happened — even though I felt eyes on the back of my neck the entire time I sat at the bar.

And then I took the elevator down to my floor, showered,

collapsed into the hotel bed — and proceeded to toss and turn for the next eight hours, unable to rest even though I was exhausted.

When I did drift off for a couple hours of sleep this morning, my dreams were weird, flashes of hands on my arm and voices telling me it was okay. I'd woken up nauseous with another headache developing. So, in desperation, I'd ordered the too-expensive room service breakfast, picked at it, and tried to linger in my hotel room as long as possible before coming to the bookstore.

It's been a long day.

Rubbing my forehead, I crack open the seal on the water bottle left for me and take a long drink, draining it as I go over everything that I just said to the group of readers. There was a short question and answer session that everyone sat down for, with a few people asking about my next release, and any news on the rumors about the movie rights. While I wasn't *legally* allowed to say much, I did tease it a little.

But I'm tired.

I set out to become a writer because I wanted to create stories. It's so rewarding to be able to communicate and meet readers, but it drains me to constantly be '*on*' all the time. I don't want *anyone* who takes their time to come meet me to walk away ever feeling like I wasn't fully present, but it takes a lot of my energy to keep the smile plastered on my face. It's the entire reason I've never done a huge tour, even though my publisher had requests for appearances two releases ago.

"We're ready for you, June!" The bookseller pokes her head back in and I stand up, smiling immediately and smoothing out my outfit before going to rejoin the throng of people.

The line moves quickly after I get seated and greet the

first person, personalizing the girl's paperback and sliding a bookmark into it for her with character art on it. *The Pack and I* was an underdog, but publishing really enjoyed the contemporary twist on pack romance. It's not like I have any experience with alphas and packs, but I had the idea in college to write about an omega who wanted to get her education *despite* the world around her encouraging her to get married, bonded, and skip it. It never made much sense to me that an entire designation are told they should only aspire to find a partner, or partners.

Omegas, as a designation, aren't common. Betas make up a good sixty percent of the population, with alphas being a solid thirty. And in the romance world, most books are written by betas, for betas. I reached out to a few omegas I knew in my introductory lit classes when I started developing the book and after talking to them, I decided to just go for it.

I never expected that a random daughter of a Hollywood director would read it this past summer, years after its release. Suddenly, I found myself in talks to sign the film rights away to my story about a young omega getting a law degree and finding herself in love with three alphas.

I've heard from readers through the years that the story means a lot to them, and it's what drives me to do these events in the first place, even if they do make my skin crawl.

The lights overhead are the kind of bright white that all shops tend to have, and as they buzz, I smile up at the reader in front of me. Her eyes are wide, her thick London accent making it hard for me to keep up with her string of words. "It means a lot to me and my sister, so if you could sign it for her — for Chey — I'd really really appreciate it."

"Of course." I pick up my pen and write FOR CHEY

with a flourish, adding the tagline I put above my signature, *FIND YOUR HAPPINESS*. At the bottom, I sign my pen name — June Wald.

As I look up to hand it back to her, my eye catches on a man at the front of the store. He lingers against the front display window, in a bulky jacket, with the hood partially up, and my chest tugs uncomfortably as one of the other booksellers approaches him. They exchange words and the man tugs a piece of paper out of his pocket. I glance to the side, looking for one of the other booksellers, when a stomach cramp rockets through my body. It's startling enough to make me suck in a sharp breath, blinking rapidly as the pain roars through me like I've been stabbed.

I double over in the chair, groaning a little as the reader in front of my table gasps. The bell to the store jingles, but it's dull in the back of my senses as I hold onto my torso, riding out the pain, nausea crawling up my throat, the burning of bile chasing it as I shiver out of nowhere.

"Are you okay?" The reader whispers the words as I hold up a hand, trying to fight back the mortification of feeling *this* sick in front of the end of the line. I was *so* close to being done with the night and able to go back to the hotel before my train ride tomorrow to Manchester.

There's a sudden smell, sweet and herbal, and it's not unpleasant, but it comes out of nowhere. I suck in a breath, fighting off tears as the cramping starts again. The smell turns slightly bitter.

The sound of a book hitting the table startles me and I look up at the girl in front of me. She couldn't be more than a couple years younger than *me*. Her eyes are wide and sympathetic as she steps closer, her voice soft. "Oh." She looks over her shoulder at the man with her. "Brian —"

His brow pulls together, his nostrils flaring as he looks at me. There's a silver bite mark on the girl's wrist where her oatmeal colored cardigan is pushed up. He's bulky, and eyeing the reader in front of me warily — as warily as he's now looking at me.

"I'm sorry, excuse me." I push up from the chair and turn, running toward the office. I only make it partially down the hallway before I take a hard right to the single person bathroom, locking the door behind me as I drop in front of the toilet, throwing up the remaining food on my mostly-empty stomach as I shake with chills.

My mind *spins*. I've barely had any food in nearly two days. There's no way it's food poisoning, and normally my generalized anxiety doesn't cause this level of severe symptoms. It could be a virus, but it's been so back and forth, I feel like I'd have more consistent symptoms. And there's not a chance in hell I'm pregnant, not only have I not slept with anyone in over a year, but I've had an IUD for three years because my periods started getting worse after college.

The doctor I have back home pushed it off as a sign I probably needed to settle down, because the second best thing in the world, after a pregnant omega, is a pregnant beta — on the off chance *another* omega could be brought into the world.

I have no interest in children, thus the stalemate of fake hormones to curb the bad periods and self-imposed celibacy.

As another cramp hits me, I curl up on the floor, squeezing my eyes shut as I smell that same sweet, herbal scent — like someone is holding a warm mug of tea up to my nose with honey mixed into it.

My heart drops as there's a knock on the door.

Most designations present around eighteen, a few years

after puberty to let the hormones settle, but not *too* late. It was a big deal about a decade ago when an omega emerged at twenty-five — because clearly it was *so* old. How dare he have a developed frontal lobe before picking alphas and forging bonds for life? Everyone seemed to be alright with it when, only a year later, it was announced one of his new bonded — a female alpha — was pregnant. I can't imagine a female omega getting off that easy.

Sweat beads on my brow and I stare at the toilet, my hands shaking.

I turned twenty-eight last month.

There's no way.

"June —" The voice of the beta bookseller is soft. "Um, we sent everyone away, but there's... Well there's a reader out here and she says she can help and we didn't know — but my colleague, um, James, he's an alpha and well, Julia's boyfriend is an alpha here too and they both say they can smell you —"

I push up, closing my eyes as I try to get my shit together. I drag myself over to the door, unlocking it and easing it open a sliver.

The reader from before stands in the hall, her eyes wide. "I don't know how to tell you this, but I think you're an omega. I think you need to go to a Designation Center, *right now.*"

Fuck me.

CHAPTER THREE

JUNE

"I apologize, Miss Walden, we normally..." The director of the London Designation Center shuffles her papers, looking down at them with wide eyes. "Well, we normally deal with the *parents* of the omegas who seek our services."

Because most omegas aren't seen as legal adults in the eyes of any government. Because most omegas have their *ownership* transferred from their parents to their first bonded alpha after being bitten. Because omegas should *not* be a nearly thirty year-old woman, sitting in a tiny room functioning as a doctor's office as a beta doctor eyes her like a medical marvel.

The blood sample in front of me is still wet, as is the tip of my pricked finger. Red blood oozes out, but when it catches the light there's a golden shimmer to it that can't be faked.

I'm an omega.

There's a stack of pamphlets next to me, all in bright, cheerful colors, meant to... I don't know — lessen the blow of being told you're a second-class citizen? One of the titles is *SO YOU'RE AN OMEGA: WHAT TO KNOW ABOUT YOUR FIRST HEAT* and the sheer *concept* of a heat makes me want to start hyperventilating.

Biologically the differences between omegas and everyone *else* are that, for some reason, they often have a fertility spike anywhere from three to four times a year, following a cycle. It happens in all omegas, regardless of their gender identity, and the symptoms the pamphlet clued me onto included: shivering, shaking, vomiting, nausea, stomach issues, headaches, sensitivity to sounds, smells, and lights, increased libido, and overall increased fertility — among many, many other possible symptoms.

I've already been shuffled back and forth to multiple rooms in the center, constantly aided by one of the workers. So far, I've not seen anyone other than betas — and I'm assuming it's because they don't know what to *do* with me. Designation Centers are glorified office buildings at the end of the day, they're neutral places for omegas to meet alphas and packs — not house newly emerging freaks of nature.

All the rooms smell sterile, like they've been sprayed with hundreds of layers of disinfectants. The doctor already told me that my natural perfume is soft — its honeyed tea scent following me every time I enter the room. Though it's bitter now, leaving a bad taste in my mouth as I stare at the organizer in front of me as she looks up from her stack of papers.

"I'll be *right* back, Miss Walden." She's out of the door before I can ask her *why* she's leaving again, and I look over at the doctor, exhaustion making me sink back on the table.

The doctor glances at the door before stepping forward, giving me a concerned look. "I'm not sure what they're going to be able to offer you here. I don't think they expected anything like this to occur." Her accent is soft, tone almost motherly as she looks me over. "I'm really concerned what this level of stress will do to you, biologically."

I blink at her, "I need..." I trail off, shaking my head, "I need the truth, I guess. What am I supposed to *do*? I'm not taking my birth control out." It was the first suggestion from the center's coordinator and I balked at the other woman like she had three heads.

Because telling me I'm about to be incredibly fertile, suggesting I take out my birth control, *and* meet with total strangers who will sleep with me during the week I'm out of my mind — that sounds like my own personal hell. I actually think I'd take a thousand airports over that.

The doctor glares. "No, you are *not*. I have no authority to remove your birth control, Miss Walden." She looks at me seriously. "And neither does anyone else. You're lucky, this is the same dosage we sometimes put omegas on. It shouldn't affect anything with this heat, other than keeping you safe from pregnancy. The designation breakthrough happened because the hormones were unprepared to manage it, and it wasn't combined with blockers." She clears her throat. "Don't let a single person at the center insist that you need to remove it, or a *pack* for that matter. You have the right to your own choice."

My heart clenches in my chest as I nod at her, glancing at the door. Someone mentioned alphas, *packs*, because if I go into a first heat without an alpha nearby to help ease the symptoms, it could cause irreparable damage. The high temperatures begin to wreck omega's immune systems and bodies if the heats aren't tended to by an alpha — thus the need for at least *one* alpha to be with an omega during each heat cycle.

Most of the Designation Centers function as glorified matchmaking services. Very few are funded privately, most receiving grants and government assistance to provide services that keep a list of alphas and their scents for new omegas to look through and find a match. What no one ever said to *me* was that most alphas pay to be listed with the centers, keeping a subscription in hopes one day they get a call that an omega is interested to meet them.

Because while alphas don't have heats, or anything that would make them a burden to society like omegas are — they *do* have an innate urge to take care of others. It's why so many of them find themselves at the top of businesses or people of status. Alphas, unquestionably, function as *leaders*, even if all of them don't have personalities suited for the roles.

I signed two sheets of paper when I walked into the center — one non-disclosure agreement confirming I refused to have my information given out to any of the press currently knocking on the center's doors, and one waiving my permission for the center to run the necessary tests to figure out *why* this was happening.

The doctor in front of me frowns. "I need you to know that—"

The center coordinator chooses that moment to reappear, looking *slightly* less harried than before. Half a step behind her is another woman, her silvery blonde hair pulled back in a high ponytail as she holds out a cup of coffee to me. I take it eagerly — I'm not sure what time it is exactly, but I've been here for *hours* and no one will tell me when I can go back to my hotel room.

"Miss Walden." The coordinator smiles at me, but there's something slightly *off* about her expression. "I'm sure this has been a very *chaotic* evening for you, but I'm afraid I'm going to have to be the one who breaks this news."

Staring at her, I clutch the coffee a little tighter, acid on my tongue as I glance at the other three women in the room. "What news?"

The coordinator's smile falters, just a *bit*. "Because you're not technically an omega who falls under the protections set forth by any of the country's governing bodies... because of your... age," she clarifies with a wince. "I'm afraid I can't let you access our paid database of alphas, packs, and scents." Her lips press together, back into the same faux smile. "You are both not a client, and have no authorized guardian who can facilitate the meetings."

The lid pops off the rim as I squeeze the cup. "I'm sorry?"

The coordinator glances to the side, looking at the woman next to her before looking back at me. "Well... you really shouldn't *exist*, so procedures don't exist for you."

"Okay." I swallow, exhaling with a little, hysterical laugh. "Okay, I'm just going to go back to my hotel—"

"Miss Walden." The coordinator stops me, her eyes wide. "I'm sorry, but you also can't do that. Or fly back to America."

I blink as my hand shakes.

"This close to a heat, an omega is legally prohibited from air travel, at the risk of sending an alpha into a rut. It's a great risk to anyone you might come into contact with." The coordinator winces. "And your hotel has contacted us and said they are no longer comfortable having an omega stay in a room as they don't have the proper ways to accommodate a guest with your needs."

The unspoken words float in the air — the hotel can't risk legally having me stay — if I go into my first heat, it would cause utter chaos for their other guests.

"So..." I stare at her. "What the hell am I supposed to do?"

At this, she forces another smile. "I am making the executive decision that you can stay here, *temporarily*, until I'm able to contact some packs in the morning who might be willing to waive their prior age ranges and meet with you. All packs, currently, have only agreed to meet with omegas under twenty-five."

Because twenty-five is the oldest omega to ever emerge. Except for me.

"And I can't leave." I say the words softly, my eyes falling on the doctor.

The doctor shakes her head. "I would be concerned about your safety if you were to leave this facility without a proper place to stay."

It feels like my world comes crashing down as I sit on the little table, clutching the coffee so hard that it spills over the edge, the lukewarm liquid dripping down my wrist.

"Can I..." I look at the coordinator. The last thing I want is to meet with strangers, to be... paired up with *strangers* before I go into a heat where all I'll want is to be *fucked*. "Can I think about this?"

She balks. "Your first heat should hit in two weeks. You don't have *time* to wait, Miss Walden."

"What about suppressants?" I grasp at straws, looking over at the doctor.

She shakes her head at me. "Since you are experiencing

symptoms, they likely wouldn't do anything. I'm sorry, Juniper."

I close my eyes for a moment, feeling a wave of exhaustion hit me as I nod. "Okay." Licking my lips, I look over at the coordinator. "Can I... Is there somewhere I can lay down for a while?"

Her expression softens a little. She nods, moving to the side as the other woman with her opens the door. "You can stay in my office, I have a couch in there."

It's better than nothing — which, coincidentally, is my only other option.

SOMEONE POSTED about my signing on social media.

It's a call from Janet that wakes me from a fitful sleep on the office couch two and a half hours later, sunlight already streaming in through the transparent curtains, the sound of London's morning traffic filling the space. She's *frantic*, but I answer her questions as best as I can. At some point, someone must have brought my suitcase in — because the single carry-on is sitting against a wall, everything I have with me in a foreign country as I tell my agent that yes — my designation emerged late, I'm an omega, and no, I have no idea what the *fuck* I'm doing about it.

I've already texted my parents multiple times, but when I finally get off the phone with Janet, there's only a single text from my mother that makes my nausea and headache return tenfold.

MOM

This is embarrassing, Juniper. Please stop texting me, you were born a beta, and you're too old to be behaving like this for attention.

I don't know why I expected anything else, but it still hurts.

A knock on the door startles me, and the same blonde beta from last night steps in. "Hey, I wasn't sure if you were awake." She shuts the door quickly, coming around to lean against the coordinator's desk, chewing on her bottom lip. "I'm Laura, normally I do whatever Denise tells me to — but last night I..." She shakes her head, staring at me. "I'm sorry, I just couldn't even fathom being in your place. Are you okay?"

It's a loaded question, and it makes my throat tighten as I sit up and push my slightly greasy hair back. I regret not taking a shower yesterday before the signing, because now that I don't have access to one, I keep thinking about how nice hot water would feel.

"Honestly?" I look over at her. She's slightly rumpled and it makes me feel better about my own shitty appearance. "No?"

Laura nods. "Okay, what if I said that Denise *just* left, but I have some files of the alphas who might want to meet you. Would you want to look at them? I can get them right now and maybe you won't have to spend another night in here."

I glance around the office and then nod. "If they're my only option, then yeah."

She perks up and then slips back out. I hear her heels clicking quickly before she returns, a small stack of file folders in her hands. There can't be more than thirty files, nowhere near what I expected, but still — they're *options*.

Laura sits on the couch next to me and then hands me the top one, her voice soft. "I might have met some of them, I can tell you if they seemed nice?"

The kindness in her voice makes my eyes sting as I nod and open the first folder.

THE SUN IS ALREADY STARTING to go down as we near the end of the pile, and it's only taken this long because Laura stepped out and came back with more files.

There's three stacks, one of potential alphas who are in town and willing to meet short notice, one stack of files I've not looked at yet, and the stack of strangers I don't want to meet. I've tried not to be picky — since I can't really afford to be. The information packets are full of things I would never have expected, from who employs the alpha, to a little scent card in a sealed packet that I can open and take a whiff of.

The swirling scents have given me a headache. So many of them smell so strong. One alpha's scent was bad enough I gagged and pushed the file into Laura's hands just to get it away from my nose.

She's been beside me most of the day, even when Denise came into the office with an armload of files and a quiet comment that *these* were the only alphas or packs willing to meet with me. I don't think a simple thank you will be enough to either of them, but I've tried to say the words multiple times today.

I caught a glimpse of myself in the bathroom mirror

earlier and wanted to fling myself out a window. My hair is a greasy mess, the makeup from my signing all wiped off between getting to the center and sleeping on the couch, and the nice trousers and blouse I'd worn last night are beyond creased. I finally gave in and changed into clean leggings and a sweatshirt, even though I want a shower.

I close the file in my lap and shake my head, putting it in the stack of other rejected options.

Beside me, Laura hesitates with her hand on the next one, sucking in a little breath. "Why don't we slip out?"

"What?" I look over at her, raising an eyebrow. "I thought I couldn't leave."

"Well" — she glances at the door — "security change should be happening soon, and we could use a side door and go to a cafe like... two blocks away." Her words are rushed. "And I'm kind of worried if you don't eat something other than the vending machine snacks, you'll start to throw up again." I survey the wreckage of chip bags and cans of soda, all plain because it's the only thing I've been able to keep down today.

Looking back at Laura, I nod quickly. "Okay, cafe, let's go."

She darts out of the room and then comes back with a spray bottle in her hands. Lifting it, she presses the nozzle, dousing me in a continuous stream that makes my eyes water. It's like being covered in window cleaner — mixed with bleach. The moment she steps back, she inhales deeply. "I can't smell your natural perfume. This should last us long enough to get there and back."

I trust her, because she's my only option, and throw on my jacket before following her out of the room and down a flight of stairs, sliding out a side door after her keycard unlocks it. Reporters have apparently been camped out at the front of the building all *day*, just hoping to get a glimpse of me, or have Denise answer questions about the '*old omega.*'

I try to ignore the unflattering name as I hustle to keep up with Laura, talking quietly as she navigates the sidewalks of London. "I think we can expect you to meet with two or three packs in the morning, maybe you can stay with one of them through this first heat and then go home?"

I did manage to get a representative on the phone from the American Embassy earlier, who confirmed that legally they couldn't risk moving me out of the country until the heat passes. I feel like everyone is treating me with kid gloves — telling me in no-uncertain terms that making my own decisions is not an option anymore.

She tugs open the door to a little cafe and I step in, inhaling the smell of coffee and pastries, my stomach immediately growling.

Laura looks back at me, her lips twitching. "Order what you want to go. We'll get back before anyone comes looking for you."

I flash her a chagrined look before stepping up to the counter. The door said the cafe is closing in only twenty minutes, so I feel a little bad as I scan the remaining fresh options, trying to find something that doesn't make my stomach full of potato chips churn.

The bell on the door behind me chimes and I feel the chilly wind as it ruffles my hair.

"We'll find you someone decent from the stack of packs." Laura's voice is soft as she looks at me. "I promise. There are a lot of alphas who don't want something traditional."

I point to a pastry quickly, wrapping my arms around

myself as I order a hot tea from the barista. Nothing that comes to my mind seems like the appropriate response to her statement. Of course I'm not a traditional option — I'm nearly thirty, don't want children, refuse to remove my birth control, and have no interest in sleeping with strangers for a week.

So I say nothing and step back to give Laura some room.

Only, the second I do, I crash back into someone *else*.

Something rattles as it drops to the floor. "Whoa." The voice is familiar, and olive-tan hands grab onto my arms, steadying me as I fumble and whirl around, looking at the man behind me. I glance down, taking in the bag of coffee beans before looking up again, unable to comprehend it as I blink.

It's *Seth*. Elevator Seth. The Seth who sat on the floor with me while I had a panic attack two nights ago. The Seth with a bite mark on his shoulder — only his alpha is nowhere to be found as he stares at me, his hazel eyes wide.

"I — You —"

His hands are still on my arms. Their warmth seeps through my coat, my sweatshirt, searing into me as my brain ceases function. I flush and the spray has no hope to combat my body's reaction.

It's pure biology.

Home. An instinctive, bone-deep feeling settles in my chest as our eyes connect. It's like I've known him my entire life — but this is only the second time we've ever crossed paths.

His brown eyes widen as my perfume blooms in the small cafe, the smell of honey and tea curling around us. I'm rewarded with the parting of his full lips as a whiff of chocolate fudge comes from him, overpowering the other light scents clinging to his clothes.

Seth blinks as Laura grabs my shoulder, her voice tight. "Let's *go*."

I stumble to the side with her, taking my tea and pastry as she shoves them in my hands.

It's terrifying — concerning — how much I want to *stay* when he looks at me, his voice croaking, "Wait —"

Laura tugs the door open, dragging me out of the cafe as he stares. She pushes me a few paces down the sidewalk. "Thank *god* he was only a beta, we need to get back before any alphas smell you." Her eyes scan the road, frantic and on-edge, and I almost feel bad as I look over my shoulder, contemplating running away from her.

The cafe door is shut, and a part of me prays for another glimpse of the man — *only a beta* — that I just left behind.

CHAPTER FOUR

SETH

I LEAVE the cafe with a bag of coffee beans and a sense I just let half my soul walk away.

Which is weird, because my actual soulmate, Bennett, is the entire reason I went to buy coffee in the first place. We ran out this morning. Last time the pack was in London, collectively for business, we drank it all. I was already grabbing snacks for movie night and the cafe was *right there*. It made sense to go in before they closed — except now I feel like it was meant to happen.

I'd know that face anywhere.

The same woman who was trapped in the elevator with us two nights ago. The same woman who stepped into the small space, with dark auburn hair swept back, a mess of waves, clad in only a pullover sweater and a pair of leggings. I'd felt my entire life shift when she'd pressed against the wall after nearly touching Bennett.

Unlocking the door to the townhouse, I let myself in, shaking my head. I never even got her *name*. Neither of us did. And I *know* Bennett has thought about her, how could he not? How could either of us leave that elevator without thinking about the random beta who'd smelled like fresh honey and was terrified she was about to die?

I'm very glad we didn't die — but also, I'm wondering if this is all some weird fever dream, because that was the *same* woman and she sure as *shit* wasn't a beta.

She looked worse tonight, her hair stringy and hanging limp, her eyes wide with dark circles under them — but it makes no sense because she looked around my age — and thirty year old betas don't suddenly wake up with an entirely different designation. I don't think anyone has ever had their designation emerge after twenty-five, it's unheard of.

The woman with her mentioned something about packs when I walked in, and I'd not thought anything of it, but now my mind is doing what it does best — sprinting ahead with no fear of falling.

Wandering into the living room after dropping the coffee beans onto the kitchen counter, I make my way over to Bennett on the couch, throwing a sack of snacks onto the coffee table before dropping down next to him.

"You okay?" My alpha looks down at me, running a hand over the back of my neck, his thumb brushing the edge of the silver bond mark he gave me on my throat. His skin is so much darker than mine, but it looks damn good as a thrum of desire pulses through our bond. Bennett's eyes are soft as he takes me in. "I felt something weird in the bond while you were out."

Sinking into the couch, I tuck my forehead against his chest and ignore Theo as he leans forward to rifle through the snack bag. I just need a second — a moment to inhale Bennett's thick orange perfume, feeling righted by the way he hums and leans closer, inhaling the side of my neck.

"You smell so good." He whispers the words and my heart lurches as he runs his hand down, over my chest. "You didn't miss anything, we haven't started the movie yet."

"It's supposed to be garbage anyway." Theo tosses a piece of candy into the air and then catches it, looking over at the pair of us. His smile is teasing as he takes us in, his huge body overtaking the chair he's lounging in. "Should I leave you two alone? Or join?" He pauses, then his brows pull together, inhaling slowly. "Damn, Seth, did you buy scent-enhancing spray? I can smell sugar all the way over here."

I pull away from Bennett, reeling. I'm losing my fucking mind, because normally beta scents are so soft they don't alert *two* alphas to them — especially not when it's a casual bump against someone else. Otherwise the world would never function.

Bennett starts to laugh, but something on my face makes him stop, frowning. "What is it?"

Theo gives me a weird look. "What happened when you were buying snacks?"

Pushing up from the couch, I shake my head. "I'll be right back — I need to shower." It feels wrong to have both their eyes on me when I know it's *her* on my skin, causing the reactions. She didn't ask for that — and I shouldn't have the image of her stuck in my head while I slobber over her like a pervert.

Bennett is only a step behind me as I head toward the stairs. Gripping the handrail, he touches my back, his voice softer. "Hey, I'm sorry. What's going on?" His concern is evident, a soft nudge in the bond.

The bite on my shoulder itches as I shake my head and look down at him on the stairs. "You're going to tell me I'm crazy." We talked about her — that night — after we got home and Arin set off for Paris. Bennett's voice had been barely a whisper when he admitted his first instinct was to protect us *both*, not just me above all. The bond should have made him grab me first when the elevator jolted, but instead he'd thrown himself over both of us.

Bennett looks up at me, his hand sliding over my side. "Lay it on me."

"I thought I saw the beta — but she's not a beta — from the elevator."

He blinks. "What?"

"She was at that coffee shop — you like their light roast." I stare down at him, my throat feeling thick as I run over the moment in my mind again. "I stopped to get you more and she was just... *there*. But she didn't smell like a beta, Bennett, and the woman she was with had a jacket on from the London Designation Center. They were talking about finding her a pack."

Bennett moves up a stair, joining me on the second floor. He's slightly taller than I am, and I lift my chin as he looks down at me. "The smell on you?"

"I ran into her." I glance up at him. "Or, well, she turned around and ran into me." Bennett leans in closer and breathes in. I see the second the perfume registers in his brain. His long, lithe body goes still, a predator reaction to the scent of prey. All the muscles in his body tense, his hand steadying himself by grabbing my hip.

When he opens his eyes again, they look slightly haunted. "No, that's not the smell of a beta."

THE SUN STREAMS through the window over the breakfast nook when I step into the kitchen the next morning. I washed her scent down the drain last night with some scent-cancelling body wash and Bennett didn't comment on it when I rejoined him and Theo for our movie.

Bennett moves around the counter, spooning coffee beans into his grinder when I walk in. From the corner, Theo points at the TV visible through the archway to the living room.

"I've never fucking heard of anything like this."

I turn, and there she *is*. The photo is of her smiling, her eyes soft as she looks up at someone clutching a paperback to their chest.

"The author's signing was cut short two nights ago. Reports say that the nearly thirty-year old suddenly displayed signs of illness, and while the readers waiting in line were ushered away, multiple sources say that she perfumed, emerging as an omega almost five years later than has ever been reported."

My blood runs cold, knuckles tightening as I grip the edge of the marble counter.

"As for official comments, June Wald's agent said this morning, '*My client, June, experienced something unprecedented during Monday's signing. She's currently dealing with this matter privately with help from the Central London Designation Center.*' We can confirm that designation centers only provide emergency aid to omegas."

Before I can think about it, I whirl and grab my keys from the hook near the front door. Bennett and Theo both give me a weird look as I do.

"What's going on?"

"I met her." I shove my phone into my pocket. "Last

night — but not just then. She was in the elevator with Bennett and I." I look up at them as Theo freezes with his cup of coffee nearly to his mouth. The set of his shoulders are tight as my eyes flicker to Bennett, pleading, but my decision is already made.

I think I made it last night before the other woman dragged her out of the coffee shop.

"Last night she ran into me, that's who you both smelled."

"What —" Bennett looks back to the TV, then at me again. "What are you about to do?"

I step back, shoving my feet into my shoes, shaking my head.

"Seth." Theo's bark is harsh. "Where are you —"

"I have to go." I look at Bennett, praying he understands the tangle of emotions through the bond, the feeling that if I don't leave *right now*, I'll be making a huge mistake.

I've always been an impulsive person, but it's always paid off. I'm hoping now is no different.

CHAPTER FIVE

JUNE

THEY'LL HAVE to air out the meeting room behind me because one of the alphas smelled like motor oil and wet cigarettes. I didn't know that a large portion of being an omega was just praying that anyone who gets near me doesn't fucking *reek*.

The man next to me falls into step as I head toward the bathrooms. After last night's cafe debacle, I told Laura to go back to her flat and get some rest. At least *one* person dealing with all this should have a shower and a bed.

Meanwhile, I spent the morning taking a sink bath, trying to make myself presentable for the alphas who were in town and agreed to meet with me.

It's been nothing short of a disaster.

The first alphas I met were two men, friends who stuck together and formed a small pack. While each of them were nice, one smelled like spring onions, and the other freshly cut grass. It wasn't really my *favorite* in the files that I combed through yesterday, but I wanted to at least try. When I stepped into the room, both of the alphas had visibly deflated at seeing me, and even though they were polite, I could tell there was no attraction from any of us.

I cut the meeting short and let them go on their way. As much as I can't stand the thought of multiple meetings, I can't help but feel a pang of sympathy for the alphas who keep walking in hoping to meet their soulmate, someone they want to bond immediately, and instead they get... me.

Splashing water on my face, I stare at myself in the tiny bathroom mirror, chewing on my red and raw lip. I tried to smooth back my hair, but it makes it look even worse. The unwashed state is bordering on fully unkempt, and I tried to put my blouse and trousers back on this morning, only for the trousers not to button from being bloated.

I feel like shit, and I look like it too.

I can't even force a smile as I wipe my hands off, adjusting the only sweater I have, the one I wore on the flight over and in the elevator. Wearing it, once again, over leggings, just makes me look sloppy. *No one is going to want you.*

My heart lurches as I step back out, the beta representative waiting for me as he grimaces and nods toward another room. "This one next, Miss Walden."

Someone from the American embassy contacted me this morning, but legally, I'm barred from travel until the heat passes. They gently encouraged me to find an alpha, or pack, that will take me in. I don't really relish the thought of staying with strangers while I'm out of my mind, begging for sex, because the pamphlets Denise left for me made it sound like I won't even be lucid, just horny.

Not terrifying at all.

The embassy representative at least clarified that the London center is on the hook for helping facilitate *something* for me. Even if all the alphas keep wrinkling their noses when I enter the rooms. Denise told me this morning to be *calm* because stress makes omega perfumes smell *off* apparently.

I feel so hopelessly alone in all of this.

As I cross the walkway open to the main lobby, I hear arguing. A man leans over the reception desk, long hair pulled back into a bun as he plants his hands on the surface.

The receptionist stares. "Sir, you are a *beta*, you cannot submit a pack into our files without an alpha's approval. That's not how any of this works."

"I know but my alpha is on the way, okay? My partner will sign, I just need to see her."

The sound of the man's voice makes me stop, clutching the glass railing as I stare.

"Juniper."

I jolt, looking to the right as one of the alphas from before steps closer. She's slighter than me, an inch or two taller too, with lean muscle cording up her arms. She and her pack were nice this morning, but I could tell that there was no pull from any of them. They were going to be my option if I only needed a place to ride it out. I'm bisexual — the gender of the alphas never mattered anyway, and her pack was pleasant enough that I didn't feel like I'd be in danger staying with them.

The alpha keeps her distance from me, a soft frown pulling her features down. "It's probably going to be difficult to find a pack this short notice, but I wanted to give you this." She holds out a card, and I lean forward, taking it from her. Her voice softens. "It's a heat help center, if they... let you out of this place." The alpha looks around. "You might consider it."

"Thank you." I pull the card to my chest, a small lifeboat as the commotion in the lobby gets louder.

"This place lacks what you *need*." The female alpha takes a half step closer, her gaze serious enough that it makes me focus. She has so much power in her mere presence, it makes me want to listen, to *stop*, and heel. "But you don't *have* to pack up, regardless of what anyone here says. There are plenty of omegas who wait to bond until later in their life, no one speaks about them. They want to focus on the ones who '*find their dream scent match*' at eighteen." Her head tilts. "Take care of yourself, please — and go with your instincts, they exist for a reason."

I open my mouth to... I don't know. Thank her again? Confirm that I won't just *settle*, when the man below us slaps his hands onto the desk.

"I'm *not* leaving until I see her."

I look down just as he tips back, his head lifting, his tanned skin washed out under the harsh lighting, his chest heaving as he breathes in. I grab onto the glass railing to keep myself upright as a Black man walks through the front doors, his gait long and gaze furious as he brandishes a piece of paper.

I know them.

"I hope you know what you're doing, Theo is *furious*."

Seth snags the paper from Bennett and pushes it across the desk. "File it and let me see her."

The card in my hand flutters to the floor as I forget all about the alpha next to me, turning sharply and running toward the stairs, taking them two at a time. The security guard at the bottom gives me a wide-eyed look, but doesn't get a chance to stop me as I run directly toward the reception desk.

Seth looks up sharply, and all the tension in his shoulders sag as he pushes away and meets me halfway. His hands rise, hesitating before he touches me, his voice soft. "This is going to sound insane."

I stare up at him, my heart pounding, the feeling from last night hitting all over again as we look at each other. "I don't think it will."

He nods, his lips parting before he steps closer. "I don't even know your name."

My resolve crumbles as I feel his fingers tighten on my shoulders, so right, like they've touched me a thousand times before. "I'm June."

"June."

The way he says my name is so quiet, a mere whisper as his eyes flicker over my face.

I can feel eyes on us and glance to the side, catching the gaze of his alpha — Bennett — and I step back, pulling into myself as I realize how it must look. He's *bonded*, they're *together* —

Seth steps forward, then follows my eyes. After a moment, he looks back at me, like he's taking me in, or afraid I'm not real. "Where have you been staying? Is there somewhere we can talk?"

I open my mouth, startled by the questions, when Bennett walks over. My brain feels sluggish because he's so *undeniably* alpha. Even in the open lobby, I feel overwhelmed by the heady citrus scent rolling off of him, mixing with the smell of fudge coming from Seth. I feel a flush creep up my cheeks as Bennett's eyes look me over, his mouth pulled into a soft smile.

"Hello again."

"Hi," I breathe the word, glancing away only to get

caught in Seth's gaze. I fumble, tugging at my sweater, realizing it's all they've ever seen me in. *God, they both must think I'm a disaster.* "I've been staying here." Clearing my throat, I look between them. "I can't go anywhere else. But maybe we can go upstairs to one of the meeting rooms."

Seth nods rapidly, stepping closer and sliding a hand over mine. His touch makes me release my sweater, his smile encouraging. "Let's do that. Let's go talk, June."

"Okay." I suck in a breath and move to turn, seeing the startled representative that's been dragging me around all morning halfway down the stairs. Just as I open my mouth to explain, I feel a warm hand against mine, palm to palm. Seth's fingers intertwine with mine.

I look up at him, slightly startled, but his smile is easy. "Lead the way."

I tug him up the stairs beside me, brushing past the representative and taking the room I *know* is empty. It's the same one I just left, and still smells vaguely of oil and cigarettes, but Seth doesn't blink, and neither does Bennett as I take a seat, reaching across the table for the abandoned paperwork and shoving it toward them. "The center keeps asking people to fill this out, I think it's so —"

Seth takes one look at it and then sits down in the chair next to me, scooting it closer. "I'm going to be honest, I don't give a *fuck* about paperwork."

"Seth," Bennett mutters his name, but it's almost laughing as he takes the seat behind him, angling it out, not even glancing at the form.

Seth grabs my hand again, squeezing it. "Are you okay? You didn't look okay last night." His warm eyes rove over me again and I feel bare as he lingers on my sweater and leggings.

My lip wobbles as I whisper. "Uh..." *Why is this so hard? Why do I want to burst into tears because he actually took a minute to notice?*

His eyes widen, and in seconds his arms are around me, halfway out of his own chair. Seth pulls me into a tight hug, covering me in him, grounding me while simultaneously keeping me from falling apart. "Sorry if this is weird," he rambles in my ear, squeezing me. "I just... it feels right, please don't cry."

And it does feel right. In the strangest, biological way, when I sink into his touch, my brain quiets, the anxiety gripping my chest loosens its hold. I close my eyes, wrapping my arms around him as I mumble, "I'm sorry the last few days have been a lot and... and..." I hiccup, trying to sort through the onslaught of emotions.

He leans back just enough to touch my cheek. "And this feels right, right?"

I nod.

"You're coming home with us." His expression grows serious as he turns his head, looking back at Bennett. "She's coming home with us." The alpha watches, something gentle in his eyes as Seth says, "Throw however much money at this that will get her *out* of here."

Bennett frowns as Seth leans back. The beta's touch lingers on my hands, squeezing them both as Bennett asks, "Have they really kept you here?"

"Yes." I chew on my lower lip, pausing when I taste blood. At this rate I'll have no skin left on them. I force myself to stop before giving them the condensed version of what the doctor said, and then the hotel, and the embassy. The more I talk, the more the two men in front of me look... angry. I finally taper off, my voice quieting at the end. "I've been sleeping in the coordinator's office down the hall for the last two nights."

A low whine builds in Seth's throat and he drops my hands only to shrug out of his jacket. He leans forward to wrap it around my shoulders without preamble, his head jerking to the side as he looks at Bennett. "*Fix* this."

"Done." Bennett stands, running a hand over his short hair, barely longer than a buzz. He reaches out, squeezing Seth's shoulder as he passes us, and I turn toward him, leaning unconsciously forward as his scent follows him. Inhaling sharply, I close my eyes for a moment, the citrus invading my senses.

The room is quiet until I open my eyes again.

Bennett looks down at me, his expression unreadable. "Will you?"

"What?"

"Will you come to our pack house?" He hesitates. "We're not forcing you into anything, but you deserve to be treated better than this — better than whatever they've tried to convince you is *acceptable*." He surveys the bright conference room, and I wonder if he knows — if he knows I've been sleeping on a couch, that the lights are buzzing too loud, that the world is too *much*.

His lip lifts in a little snarl.

"Because this *is* unacceptable, June."

I wring my hands together, Seth's jacket draped around my shoulders. "Is it... only you two?"

"No." Seth grabs my hands again, stopping me from wringing them. "No, Arin and Theo will be there too, but it'll be okay. I promise. They'll like you." His smile is soft, gentle. "We'll get you home, you can sleep in the guest bed, and then we can go from there, okay?"

Swallowing the lump in my throat, I nod, not under-standing the why, but knowing *deep* in me that I can trust them. They've already proven it once, even though the elevator wasn't a *real* threat, and they're still strangers — something in the back of my mind — in my hindbrain, the deep biological part that is all primal instinct and gut reac-tions — makes me whisper, "Okay."

Out of all the alphas and the packs I've been shoved in front of — none of them have made me feel like this. None of them have been Seth and Bennett.

Seth's smile widens. "Good. We're going to take care of you."

CHAPTER SIX

JUNE

THERE's a sleek black car waiting outside the Designation Center for us, and I don't know if it's their personal valet, or a rental. It doesn't matter, in the grand scheme of things, because the second we step out, there's a barrage of camera flashes and people *screaming* questions at me.

Seth's hand on my back is the only stability I have to get from point A to point B. Bennett takes up the rear, snarling something at a man behind us as he puts my bag into the car, and then we're in the backseat, two bench seats facing each other.

The flashes cut off when the door slams shut.

Denise seemed *thrilled* for me when I left the conference room to find her and Bennett in the hallway. Seth had touched my back while Denise looked up at Bennett with wide eyes, and, I don't think I imagined the way Seth's fingers flexed, almost possessively as he moved us toward the alpha. I didn't mind, a small part of me was on board to squish the alpha between the two of us so no one else would look at him.

I'm not blind — Bennett is *handsome*.

Regardless, no one stopped me from leaving, but they also didn't stop the rush of reporters ready to pounce. I've sold enough books to know what comfort looks like in knowing my rent is covered, but never enough to be subjected to the brunt of public speculation.

The roar of voices dies down as I sit in the back of the car, running my hands over my arms self-consciously as Seth's jacket hangs over my shoulders. He glances at me, then shifts closer. "You'll like our townhouse. Arin found it and we all have our own space. There's a guest room on the second floor across from mine and Bennett's room."

"Thank you." My eyes fall on the aforementioned alpha across from us. "I really appreciate —"

"You don't have to thank me," he cuts me off quickly, but gently. He adjusts, like he's keeping his distance as he glances out of the window at the reporters, frowning. "I... I don't think I knew how *bad* those places were."

Seth scoffs. "Downright fucking inhumane." His hands move, and then he pulls his jacket tighter around me, flashing me a smile. "You're lucky I didn't run after you last night."

A flush rises on my cheeks. "I don't think they would have let you in after hours."

Seth's answering grin is downright naughty. "Probably not, but I could have caused some chaos."

I laugh, my lips twitching as I try to fight the smile. It shouldn't be this easy for him to get a reaction out of me, but each one seems to spur him on.

He leans in closer, his grin growing. "I mean big, *huge* commotion." He nudges me. "I'm talking throwing rocks through those glass walls at the front — who the fuck puts that much glass all over a building meant to keep a low profile, anyway? Stupid."

I laugh harder, shaking my head at him. "I don't know, but the main office had street facing windows. That's all I've heard the past two nights — traffic. And it was so *bright*," I whine the last word, thankful the car interior is darker.

"That's a crime." Seth looks down at me. "I can't believe they'd risk your beauty sleep like that. It doesn't seem to have affected you though."

Scoffing, I lift a hand, pressing it against my cheeks, worried that they're bright red. For a moment Seth's gaze flickers down to my lips. The car suddenly feels no bigger than the eye of a pin. His lips part, his tongue appearing as it runs over the plump flesh of his lower lip, and my breath catches as his hand moves, knuckles brushing my cheek.

Then he just pushes my hair back and tilts his head, his smile goofy, the tension breaking apart. "What do you want for lunch? We'll order something to eat after you get settled."

I sink into the car seat, unable to stop smiling at the man next to me as he goads me into admitting I've had a diet entirely of vending machine snacks for two days straight. The car slows to a stop and Bennett climbs out first, turning immediately to offer me a hand.

It shocks me, but as I glance up at him, I recognize the same look of surprise — like he didn't even know he was going to do it himself. On auto-pilot, I reach out and take it. The slide of my palm against his sends sparks up my arm, like a continuous zap of static electricity.

Bennett's grip tightens and he *pulls*, our chests touching as I'm suddenly upright on the sidewalk, my head tilted, staring at him wide-eyed as a rich, deep vibration travels from his chest all the way down to my hand and up my arm.

He's *purring.*

Even though I've never heard the deep, contented sound, my body reacts, preening like he's just given me a deluge of compliments. An alpha's purr is supposed to comfort stressed out omegas, or show their pleasure with something — like their bodies can't possibly contain their emotions, whether to comfort or to endear.

And he's purring because he's touching *me.*

All too quick Bennett steps away. My mind spins as his touch falls away and my bones near-ache from the sudden separation as he steps to the back of the car. I watch as Bennett tugs out my suitcase from the trunk as Seth joins me outside the car.

Seth ushers me up a paved pathway as my eyes rise and *rise,* taking in the white townhouse.

I can't tell exactly how many levels it has, but it must be at least three. My brain struggles to act normal as it catalogues the fact they own a home minutes outside of Central London, multi-storied on a quiet stretch of equally luxurious residential properties. The front garden looks professionally manicured with a small stone path on the side that clearly leads to a garage.

I can't even fathom what a place like this would cost.

Before I can even guess a number, Seth tugs me through the front door. Inside, the marble floor lining the foyer sparkles, stairs leading up, hallways creating offshoots — it's too much to take in. Seth points out the front rooms quickly — a kitchen, a small living room, a hallway to the back, the mention of the garage — and then he moves us toward the stairs that shoot up to the next level. As he tugs on me gently to get me to follow him, he glances back, his smile wide as he motions to a door on the next level, barely letting me take in the polished wood finishes.

"Bennett and I are in here, and this" — he opens the door across from his and Bennett's room — "is the guest room — your room." Seth motions me inside, flipping the lights on. "The bathroom is through there, if you want to wash up."

I stop in the middle of the room, spinning in a little circle, my head whirling with my body. The walls are a light gray, cool-toned and simple, with a plush bed against one wall. Seth lingers near the door to the hall, looking over at me.

Opening my mouth, I try to formulate an appropriate response — but he only reaches out and takes my hand again, squeezing it.

"Why don't I order our food and let you settle?"

Nodding slowly, I lick my lips as he lets my hand go, making a beeline for the door. This is all too much — too fast — he can't just *leave* when he's the only reason I feel *safe* for the first time since leaving my stupid apartment three days ago —

"Seth, *wait*." He staggers to a stop as I stare at him, my heart going wild. I clear my throat, trying in vain not to break down in front of him, putting all my gratefulness and over-whelming emotions into my voice instead. "Thank you for getting me out of there."

Reality crashes down as he hesitates. His long brown hair is slightly unkempt, falling out of the bun on his head, and he levels me with a look that has my stomach flipping.

"My biggest regret is leaving that bar without your name and number. My second biggest regret wasn't stopping you before you left the coffee shop. Luckily, the universe decided to give me a third chance — and I'm not stupid enough to waste it, June. Go shower, unpack, do whatever you want to do, and I'll order you food and see you downstairs when you're ready."

I let out a surprised breath as he shuts the door behind him, leaving the room.

The *relief* hits me — of being clear of the center, at the fact there is nothing expected from being here, that I can *breathe* — all my emotions come crashing down. Tears well, overflowing as I break, covering my face with both my hands as I just *feel*. I'm not even sure it's enough time for Seth to have left the hallway, but I don't care.

I step over and throw the lock on the door for my own peace of mind, before fumbling with my phone, Seth's jacket still on my shoulders as I plug my charger into a socket. The bathroom is spotless when I walk in, and I turn the shower knob to scalding hot, staring at the bottles of scent-canceling shampoo and body wash sitting on the tiled bench inside.

I'll try to reach out to my parents later, but right now I don't have the energy. I want to tell them that I can't fly back, that I'm not lying, that I need *someone* to give me an ounce of guidance — but it doesn't matter anymore.

It was enough effort to gather my things and leave the center. The downstairs receptionist stopped us before we walked out so I could sign more paperwork, all while telling me that one pack cancelled on seeing me and someone else called claiming they were my brother, insisting on a meeting — but I don't have any siblings. *Bullets dodged.*

The hot water helps me feel human again as I put myself back together, taking time to scrub the shampoo through my hair, lathering up the body wash. It takes my own scent with it down the drain, but it also clears the mix of other smells from the center. I glance at the bottles, wondering if Seth put them here — and how he had the time, but I try not to linger on it as I dig through my carry on, an oversized fluffy towel to my chest. It's shockingly soft, but, not only that, it's big enough to cover all of me, from my full chest to my wide hips.

I ignore the clothes I packed with the intent to look nice at my signings and go straight for the only other pair of leggings I brought with me. Shimmying them over my ass and hips, I shove my sweatshirt over my head.

My bag is woefully empty. The pile of clothing left absolutely pathetic, stranded here until I can figure out what to do — or until someone, somewhere, decides it's okay for me to travel home.

The nausea returns with a vengeance, my stomach roiling as I wrap an arm around myself.

A light knock on the door makes me flinch, before Bennett's voice carries through the wood. "The food is here, and it's hot. Seth wanted me to offer to bring it to you — but I think you should come downstairs."

I turn and eye the wood separating us, chewing on my lip as Bennett spurs forward.

"I know this all is probably overwhelming, but you can eat with us." His voice softens. "Just consider this your new hotel. Everything else can be figured out tomorrow, after you have food and rest." He pauses. "I..." There's a soft thunk, and I swear it's the sound of his forehead hitting the door. "I don't feel *great* that I had to sign you out of that place. I want you to know that. You're not... mine now, or Seth's — so please don't think that. He did this because... well, Seth just *does* shit sometimes. But please feel like you can just *be* here. There are no expectations."

I scramble forward, saving this painfully awkward alpha

from himself and unlock the door, opening it. His head jolts, looking down at me with wide eyes. They're brown, but unlike Seth's light brown eyes, Bennett's are deep, beautifully dark.

"I don't know why I'm surprised you were listening to me make an idiot of myself."

"Like you said, we don't have to hash it out now, we can just eat."

He nods slowly, pressing his full lips together as he stares at me. Bennett doesn't move, his eyes flickering over my baggy sweatshirt and leggings, catching on my wet hair. "Yeah, we can just eat."

My stomach flutters. He's not the first alpha I've seen today, but he is the first one to make me feel like I'm not a disaster. His expression isn't one of pity, it's layered concern and something more simmering under the surface.

"I kind of have to leave the room to go downstairs."

"Right." He jumps back, clearing the doorway before stumbling to the side and motioning sharply to the stairs. "Food's this way — kitchen is — I mean Seth showed you that and we don't *eat* at the table — but —"

I press my lips together, trying to hide my laugh as I ease the door shut behind me. "But the food is downstairs."

"*Yeah.*" He runs a hand over his head again, sucking in a quick breath.

I turn and slowly start down the stairs, his tread echoing behind me as he makes a small embarrassed noise. *At least I'm not the only catastrophe here.*

CHAPTER SEVEN

BENNETT

I'm an idiot.

Scratch that — I'm an idiot *alpha* who can't stop staring at the pretty omega sitting next to my pretty beta on *our couch*, eating chicken strips and french fries while Seth tells her stupid stories of our time in business school.

Her auburn hair is wet, and the moisture has it curling in soft waves around her face as she tips back on the couch and laughs at something Seth says. Her pale cheeks have two bright spots of red on the apples, holding color as she grins at him. It's a marked difference from how she looked when we walked into the center, and it makes my heart jerk as I stare at the pair of them.

She's still a little hesitant, almost pulled in on herself. The sweatshirt she has on swallows all her curves I saw and felt briefly in the elevator. There's something about June that makes the alpha inside me pace, like it's caged. My hindbrain screams to protect her as much as I want to protect and keep Seth happy. But the urge toward Seth makes sense, because he's my bonded — maybe all of these feelings are just because she's an omega.

It doesn't matter anyway, because I'm a colossal idiot who could barely ask if she wanted to come downstairs to eat without making an even bigger fool of myself. I just didn't want her to think that she... *owed* us anything. The mere idea makes me half-nauseous. The center already made me fill out three forms that stated I was *'taking responsibility of her'* — like she's not a grown woman.

It's bullshit, and it wasn't their call. It was *hers*. She made it abundantly clear to Seth and I that she wanted out of there, and I wasn't about to leave her, so I signed the stupid forms.

Dark hollows rest under her eyes, but the smile brightens her face as she turns and tilts her head at Seth, muttering something as she eats another french fry. Seth pushes his hair back, one arm on the back of the couch as he leans closer, murmuring back. He's always been a terrible flirt, and I've never minded it. If he didn't make the first move, then we'd never have bonded — and the perk of sinking my teeth into him means that he's *mine*.

But I can also feel the hum between us, the curiosity and the pull he has for her.

I don't know why I did it — but the moment the elevator started moving again, I felt like I *had* to protect them both in case something happened. Seth always makes fun of myself, Theo, and Arin for pulling *alpha bullshit*, but it's instinctual, primal.

I never expected to see her again. I never thought the elevator was anything more than a fluke, the sweet smell of honey and tea lingering inside it from some omega who'd come and gone.

But I've smelled it multiple times here and *now*. The strongest was when Seth made June laugh in the back of the car. I had to hold my breath because it coated the inside of my mouth and crawled under my skin, seeping into my bones.

I shouldn't *want* someone this much. Seth and I have been happy for years, but watching the two of them laugh and talk, like they're old friends, feels *right*. The feeling that this is meant to be, that all roads led to here, hums in my chest, seamlessly filling a spot that I didn't even know was empty.

Theo's home, but the fucking asshole hasn't even been out once since we all walked in. I caught a whiff of his scent near the guest room before I knocked on her door, but I can't figure out why it was there. Arin's taken care of too — I left a message for him and he immediately sent a surly text back that he'll be home from Paris no later than tomorrow night.

June covers her mouth, yawning as she shifts, holding her plate in the air with a tired smile. Seth grabs it, his voice softer. "You're probably exhausted."

"M'fine," she slurs her words, blinking at him slowly, her expression tender.

Whatever it is about Seth — it makes her softer around the edges. I get it. He's the kind of person who could make friends with a brick wall. He lures you in, offering his heart and soul from the first moment, and he *means* it. There's no ulterior motives with Seth, he just *is* and it makes him easy to love.

"I'll put it up." I jump, grabbing both of their leftovers.

Seth casts me a look, grinning as June adjusts on the couch. I turn, but it's not fast enough, and I catch a whiff of her hair, her *perfume*, clouding the close space and making my brain fog. I can taste the honey on my tongue as I ram my shin into the coffee table and full-on flee to the kitchen.

It barely takes a minute before Seth follows, shaking his head as he wraps his arms around me from the side. I groan softly, turning my head and tilting it down. He's only an inch or two shorter than my five-ten, and it makes him the perfect height for me to bury my nose in his throat, inhaling deeply just to smell his fudge-coated perfume mixed with *hers*.

"I've never —" I bite out the words, my throat working to verbalize them.

"I know." Seth kisses my jaw, his hand resting on my breastbone. "She's tired, I think she's still trying to adjust to the fact she can sleep in an actual bed tonight, instead of being shuffled around like fucking cattle."

Anger radiates from him and I press my lips against his temple in response, my voice soft. "Take care of her." That surprises us both, and I pull back, looking down at him. "It seems like she trusts you, and I don't want to overstep..." There's no telling what other interactions she's had with alphas through the years. Some of the worst men think being an alpha means they've been given a free pass and the power to do whatever they'd like.

Seth cups my face, his voice serious. "You won't. Arin won't. Theo... might." His eyes narrow, but then he shrugs. "But he's a dick on a good day. We'll cross that bridge when we get to it."

Oh to be as blasé as Seth about the future.

"Yeah." I swallow, glancing at the doorway to the living room. "I never expected... I mean it's the smell and..." My words catch. We've been together for almost five years, and before that we knew each other in college. He *knows* me, as much as I know him — but this is such an unknown I feel like I'm reeling to keep my head on my shoulders.

"Are you having a crisis over this?" His eyes twinkle, teasing.

A crisis? No. A realization? Yes.

"No, just realizing some things."

Seth tilts his head, frowning softly. "About...?"

"Not about *us.*" The growl slips out as I cup the back of his neck, holding him as I force his head up to look at me. "I thought you were *it* for me." I feel my brows pinch as I try to find the right words. Every prior relationship in my life has been initiated by the other party, from school-age crushes and dates, to Seth — I don't normally see the signs myself until the other person is too tired of waiting for my oblivious ass to catch up.

But with *her* —

Seth leans up and brushes his lips against mine. "Oh, babe." He pulls back. "You and I both know that things can change in an instant."

They can. They have — like the night we went out for a business dinner and I ended up with a lapful of the beta in front of me, his hands on my head as he kissed me senseless to make sure I knew what I'd been missing.

I exhale softly. "Yeah."

"Ride the wave." He pecks me again, then pulls back, untangling himself as he nods toward the doorway. "I'm going to go convince her to take a nap, at *least.* I'm worried she's going to pass out sitting up." He takes a step back, then flashes me a smile. "One day at a time — one hour, one minute, one second, even."

My heart tugs, reaching out to his via our bond. The

strand between the two of us is as strong as it's ever been, a hum that echoes with love and understanding. I shake my head. "Go." After a moment, I hesitate. "If she…"

"If she needs anything, I'll let you know, *alpha*." He grins — *tease* — and then he's gone, leaving me reeling while I try to figure out if I can have my cake and eat it too.

CHAPTER EIGHT

JUNE

I'VE BEEN SLOWLY MIGRATING CLOSER to Seth as the afternoon grows longer and the light through the windows dims. I'm so tired, and I think he knows because he hasn't said anything as my head has sunk back on the couch, curled into the soft fabric. It smells like oranges and fudge, but crisp and clean too — like rain and mint.

It's *comforting*, and it's echoed in the way Seth smiles at me, the way Bennett looks over at the couch occasionally, his eyes catching mine. I'm too sleepy to feel self-conscious, but the third time I jolt awake after accidentally nodding off, Seth leans over, his hand sliding over my arm.

"Time for bed, let's get you upstairs."

I don't fight him. I just fall into slow steps with him as we make it up the stairs and in front of the guest room. He leans in and pushes my hair back, his voice soft as he glances to the door across the hall.

"I'm over there if you need *anything*, okay?" His eyes search my face for a moment, and he must see something he approves of before he steps back. "Do and use whatever you need, the townhouse is yours."

"Goodnight." Bennett flashes me a smile before he disappears with Seth.

Slipping into the guest room, I shut the door behind myself only to lean back on it. A tight coil wraps itself around my chest, making my breathing quicken as I try to wrap my head around being here — around what's happened. Panic rears its ugly head, savoring the fact I'm alone again and creeping up my throat.

On autopilot, I force myself to let go of the door and do tedious tasks; brushing my teeth, checking my phone, and then crawling into the plush bed.

The sheets are cool on my skin, and smell freshly laundered too. Turning my head, I bury it in the pillow, willing my eyes to droop, for the feeling of security and sleepiness to finally win out, but nothing happens.

My heartbeat is loud in my ears as I chew on my lower lip.

It's just a temporary solution for a lifetime problem, no big deal. I mean, so I'm an omega and a very nice beta and alpha have suddenly taken me in.

At some point in the spiral of thoughts I slide out of the bed and start to pace.

It's not like it means anything. Bennett said it didn't. And I trust him. But why do I trust him? Why do I trust either of them so much already? What about the other alphas?

Stopping short, I suck in a breath as I wrack my brain to remember the night of the elevator incident and the two men that waited for Seth and Bennett after we all made it to the rooftop. But the memory is murky, I really only remember the urge to look back at them, not to go with Michaela to the bar.

Shivering, I pull my sweatshirt closer, glancing at the door. One of the alphas is in Paris — Arin, Seth said his name was — but there's one *here* and I've yet to see him. There has to be a reason for that, right?

Easing the door to the guest room open, I pause, listening to the quiet of the townhouse before I slip out into the hallway. I feel like I'm doing something wrong, but I feel restless, an itching under my skin as I make it to the stairs and turn to continue up to the topmost floor.

There must be a window open because the second my foot touches the top landing, I'm hit with the smell of rain. My eyes run over the decor in the dim light, catching on a small sitting area with a loveseat in front of a picture window overlooking the street below. The road is dappled with rain, cast in a yellow light. Running my hand over the furniture, I sink down onto it, staring out the window, watching the drizzle.

My heart crawls up my throat, sitting on my tongue as I try to get comfortable, sucking in deep, slow breaths. A counselor I saw when I was still in college used to say that breathing was the first step to avoiding a panic attack — she always gave talks before finals, and I quietly took note.

I don't really remember a time in my life I didn't feel anxious, where my body didn't seem to quite fit my skin. My parents have both always been the type to say that the feeling of discomfort is *just in my head* like that isn't the root of the issue. I saw a therapist for a while, off and on after I finally moved away from home, but I always felt like such a burden. There are other people in the world dealing with so much worse than me complaining about the fact I feel too nervous to leave the house sometimes.

Regardless of everything I've tried through the years to manage the anxiety, I've always felt *off*.

I guess there was a reason all along.

Pulling my knees closer, I rest my chin on them as my throat tightens. My tour is cancelled — there's no way I can continue to the other stops right now. When my parents finally *do* reach back out, I have to figure out a way to tell my mother that I'm not only still in London, but in the house of a pack — the very thing she's adamantly against.

But wouldn't so many betas kill to be in my position?

For as much as alphas and omegas are the *other*, the outliers, I know there are so many betas in the world who hope desperately for either the power or the security that comes with being *more*. But all I feel is trapped — suffocated.

This isn't what I wanted, none of this has ever been a part of the careful plans I made for myself. I was going to finish my next manuscript and Janet was going to sell it for me. I was going to sign the rest of the film rights over, pocket some money and maybe finally move out of my little apartment — maybe even invest in real furniture instead of hand-me-downs.

Fat tears roll down my cheeks as I reach up and scrub at my face, curling up into myself as I sniffle and suck in breaths, knowing it's bordering on hyperventilating, but unable to regulate it. I stare at the street, willing it to be enough of a distraction.

There's no use, I'm going to sit in this strange home and lose it, once again an embarrassment who can't even function like a normal person.

There's a soft creak of floorboards and my heart stops.

I jerk, holding my breath as I look around the upper floor.

A man steps out of the left hallway, and I scramble up from the couch, wrapping my arms around myself, conscious of my pajamas.

He's partially in darkness, but I can still see the way his bare chest jolts with his inhale of a breath. His body goes rigid, and my eyes flicker over his skin, almost entirely covered with tattoos, thick and black against his pale, stocky torso. His stomach is rounded, like mine, but unlike mine, I can see the muscles corded under his skin, layers of muscle and fat working together to scream two things: *strength* and *alpha*.

This isn't Bennett, familiar and strong in a way that oozes kindness. It's not Seth, approachable and instinctively *safe*. This stranger is broad, thick, and almost threatening with the way he stands so stock still, like moving to breathe is even a measured motion.

I freeze with him, snared, too scared to back away and too nervous to open my mouth.

After what feels like forever, he speaks in a growl.

"You should *go back to bed*."

His voice is dark, deep, and *rough*. It's so harsh, like he's holding himself back from saying something more, but the unspoken words float into my brain. *I interrupted him. I upset him.*

I flinch toward the stairs, my brain working overtime to process the involuntary movement to follow his order. It's a *bark*. He *barked* at me and I'm powerless to do anything but listen, wavering as I keep my stare on him, my feet edging me toward the stairs.

"*Go.*"

The single command is powerful, and I scurry away, back down the stairs as my heart pounds. Confusion and alarm hit me as I comply — I don't like that I'm suddenly this beholden to a stranger's request, and I stop at the bottom of the stairs, jerking my head to look up at him.

The alpha is *huge*, silhouetted above me at the top of the staircase.

"Go to sleep, little omega."

My eyes feel heavy as I take a step back, ducking my head and running into my room, slamming the door behind me and locking it. I barely make it into the bed, between the covers before my eyes slip shut.

I wish the light had been brighter upstairs. I wish I'd been able to see him. I wish I remembered his name. I wish I could fight the futile wave of exhaustion as it crashes with the alpha's command and sweeps me away, forcing my body to sleep, his harsh voice ringing in my ears.

CHAPTER NINE

THEO

I SHOULDN'T OPEN *the door.*

But I want to. It's begging me to.

Because I know that behind it is the answer to why there's been soft laughter drifting up from downstairs since this afternoon. Behind it is the *omega* that Seth and Bennett brought home even though Arin isn't here.

I've been hiding.

I don't want to see them — any of them.

My fingers curl over the doorknob, forehead resting on the wood as my ears pick up the soft sniffling. She's crying. She's outside my door and she's softly sobbing on my couch while Seth and Bennett are asleep on the floor below us.

I turn the knob quietly, and pull the door open, only to get hit in the face with the sweetest smell — thick sweetness, dripping and mixing with the herbal smell of tea, like a warm mug on a rainy morning. It makes my head spin as I stand still, letting it wash over me.

I should've bought that scent canceling spray.

I put the scent canceling wash in the guest room, but

either she didn't use it, or it doesn't work, because the moment my brain adjusts to her perfume, it's picking through it. I smell the slight bitterness in it, the *hurt*.

And she is just sitting there, in front of the windows, staring at the darkened street.

She's *gorgeous*. The dim light catches on the red in her hair, making her stand out like fire in the dark. Her jaw and face are soft, rounded, her torso swallowed by a big sweatshirt. I can't see anything but her knees up to her chest and her head resting there, but I'm suddenly certain the rest of her is just as beautiful.

And she looks so sad.

The urge to comfort her hits me, and I fight it, choking to hold still, forcing myself not to make a sound. I *never* wanted an omega. I've spent my entire life putting myself as far away from any possibility of crossing paths with one as humanly possible.

And now there's one in the *fucking* house.

Anger sears through my body, clearing my thoughts as I shift.

The floor creaks under me and she jumps. Her perfume sours, the sweetness turning sickly, *wrong*, fear tanging through the air and slapping me across the face. My hindbrain scrambles, telling me to fix it, but I tense all my muscles, doubling down.

The bark comes out, low and harsh, and she reacts before she can even think about it. It leaves me with a sick feeling as her eyes widen and she scrambles away from me, fear in her gaze as she clings to the stairs and fumbles to leave.

Good — if she's scared of me, she won't get near me again.

Just like my mother makes sure to avoid my fathers.

"*Go.*"

She runs from me, and I feel like my body is being cleaved in half. The urge to not let her out of my sight brings me to the top of the stairs, and I stare down in a daze as she wavers, looking back up at me. One more command and she tucks her chin, running away for good.

I stand there until I hear the door to her room slam shut and the lock click.

Not hers. The guest room. The guest room door slams.

The internet said that scent-cancelling products would make the adjustment easier on a new omega, because smells were too overwhelming to them. But what about me?

I lick my lips, tasting the sweetness in the air, assaulted by the burnt, acrid smell of fear tinting it.

She can't stay.

I can't fucking do this.

CHAPTER TEN

JUNE

ALL MY CLOTHES SMELL.

And it's not in the new *"I'm an omega now and hyper-sensitive to scents"* way, it's more in the *"I only have three outfits and they all reek of body odor"* way which is infinitely worse.

I survey all my clothes sitting on the bed; a pair of trousers and a skirt I packed to wear with my two blouse options, a travel outfit, and then an extra pair of leggings, which I'm currently wearing, a sweatshirt, and a sweater. There's also a pile of underwear off to the side, because even though I overpacked, per usual, I'm nearing the end of my clean options.

Stepping back, I tug at my sweatshirt and go over to the door, opening it slowly, hoping I can catch Seth and ask to use the laundry — wherever it is in this massive place. But when I look into the hall, the door across from me is open, and voices carry up the stairs.

I adjust my hair and slip out of the room, glancing down at myself again. The clothes I'm in will have to do.

As I reach the bottom step, the conversation becomes loud enough I can make out the words.

"I think it's a good idea."

"Of course you do, it's *your* idea."

Seth and Bennett bicker lovingly, and it tugs a smile from me as I ease forward.

"I'm sure Arin will have something to say about all of this, about *her*."

The third voice makes me freeze. It's dry, but deep and rumbling — the same one that barked and put me to sleep last night. And now, standing here, I recognize an unfamiliar scent curling around me, filling the foyer and my lungs.

Petrichor.

The townhouse has a mixture of smells — Seth's perfume is like fresh fudge, and Bennett's alpha scent is crisp, ripe oranges. But this smell is the same one I thought was an open window last night — and makes the candle I have back home on my nightstand look like a poor imitation.

It's soft, rich, and fragrant. The smell of fresh rain wafting off the damp ground. The sun is shining through the windows on the front door, casting little rainbows on the marble floor — and I know, without a shadow of a doubt, that this is the big alpha's perfume.

My heart lurches as I refocus, realizing that he's still talking.

"It's a pack decision, and you went behind our backs and did it anyway, Seth. You invited a stranger into our home, an *omega*, and you expect me to... what? Pack up and suddenly want an extra person around? Someone who is biologically predisposed to be a burden, demand attention, and expect to be catered to? Fuck that." His snarl sends a shiver up my spine. "You better not bite her, Bennett. She's not sticking around, and Arin will make sure of that. She's not welcome, and I don't want her here."

The words hit me like a slap across the face.

My eyes sting, and I fumble back, turning on instinct to go get my bag. I'll take my chances at the center. I'm not staying in a place that has someone so vehemently against me — even though we don't even *know* each other. I deserve *better* than this.

But my toe catches on the stair runner, because of course it does. Pain pangs up my foot as I grab onto the railing, my knee slamming down onto the stairs as the kitchen goes dead silent.

"June."

Seth's voice is upset, just behind me. I blink rapidly, trying to reorient myself, refusing to look at him until I hear other footsteps.

"Come eat breakfast." Bennett's request isn't a bark — but it is firm, making me hesitate as I finally glance over my shoulder to see Seth standing wide eyed, Bennett behind him. Something unspoken passes between the three of us. I wasn't supposed to hear any of the conversation, but it doesn't change anything for the pair.

I don't feel the knee-jerk reaction to comply like last night, but I'm *tired*, and I want to relent. I want to walk over to them both and let them take care of everything, of *me*. I don't want to fight, I don't think I have it in me.

Seth edges closer. "Please?"

I waver, and in that split second, *he* appears.

In the light of day, the other alpha is even larger than I remember. His bulk spans across the archway to the kitchen, in a pair of plain sweats, and a dark t-shirt stretching across his chest. It exposes the tangle of tattoos I saw glimpses of last night, snaking up his arms, covering his pale skin, and winding up under his clothes. His arms cross over his chest, making the muscles flex as his jaw tightens, his blue eyes narrowing on me. His hair is blond, a stark difference to both Seth and Bennett, with stubble along his jaw.

He's got more than a few inches on Bennett, and between that and the bulk of him, he overtakes the space. I don't *know* if he's the prime alpha of this pack, but I could believe it if he was. Some alphas are just stronger, and natural pecking order means that in packs, there's always an alpha above all the others, the decision maker — the prime.

The alpha's face pinches, and I shrink back, feeling myself cave in at his dark glare.

"Theo." Seth turns sharply, his shoulders squaring. "Don't be a jackass, apologize to —"

"No." His voice holds no question, his eyes flickering over me. "Why should I apologize to the stranger who hooked you and got a free night with a rich pack?"

I stare at him, acid in my throat.

Bennett's growl is low. "Theo, what the *fuck*?"

"You both *left* and came back with a stranger who could be here for *any* reason —"

"What the hell is your problem?" I snap the words, and the big alpha — Theo — turns his attention from Bennett to me, his eyes cutting me to the quick.

"I know you're not stupid, you clearly know I was trapped in the designation center until I happened to run into Seth again. Stripped of my *rights*, stranded in another country, told I couldn't *leave* —" My voice breaks, emotions bubbling up as I struggle to fight back tears. This isn't the *time.* I can't be overly emotional, I'm supposed to be able to express myself — not prove his point.

Theo takes a step forward and I jerk away, raw fear shooting through my veins. I don't know *why* he's getting closer, but everything in me says to stay away. My perfume sours in the air, filling the space with utter terror as my first thought jumps to him hurting me. He stops short, and for a moment, I swear I see him pale, like the fear jars him as much as it does me.

"*Enough.*" Bennett barks the word, striding forward and breaking the tension. Then he's in front of me, blocking my sight line of Theo. He wraps a hand around mine, loosening my grip from the railing and pulling me down a step, his voice softer. "Did you hurt yourself when you fell?"

"No." I hate how small my voice sounds.

"Oh, come *on.*"

"Leave." Bennett's head whips around, snarling at Theo. In the second he looks back at me, he softens again, guiding me off the stairs, his eyes flickering down to my leggings and my feet.

Theo recovers quick, quipping, "I would, but your new charity project is blocking the stairs."

"Fuck off." Seth shocks us all as he snarls the words. It doesn't have the weight of an alpha behind it, but it does quiet Theo — finally. Seth isn't cautious as he shoves Bennett's hand off of me, wrapping his entire arm around my shoulders and turning his head, dipping it down and whispering, "There's breakfast, let's get you a plate. Come on, June."

As he pulls me into the kitchen, my eyes catch on Theo, the alpha glaring at us, at *me*, at Seth's arm on my shoulders — until Bennett snaps at him to move. I don't see where they go, but I can feel both of the alphas watching until Seth and I disappear into the kitchen.

He makes me a plate, and I eat, gearing myself up to ask about the laundry room, trying to figure out if I can look up the heat service the alpha at the center recommended. *I shouldn't have dropped the card* — I can't stay here, and it was a bad idea to agree, even for one night.

"I think we should get out today." Seth glances out a window at the bright street, "It's nice for once." His eyes find mine. "As long as you're feeling up to it."

My brain stops, then I nod slowly, covering my mouth. "My agent sent me an email this morning and asked if it would be possible for me to make it back to the bookstore and finish signing the stock. I ran out toward the end of it, I think it's less than twenty copies."

His expression is soft. "Sure, finish up your food, and we'll head out."

THE BLACK CAR pulls up in front of the bookstore after a short twenty minute drive. I still feel like I look awful, but Seth assured me twice before we even left the townhouse that I didn't. As I climb out, I glance back at the beta, my hands going instinctively to my sweater.

"I'm worried I smell."

He glances at me, then slides an arm around me, pulling me closer and inhaling my shoulder. I flush as he hums, "You do, but it's *really* fucking good."

I shove his head away half-heartedly, grumbling as I

trudge toward the door, thankful I called ahead as I step into the bookstore, Seth's laughter following me.

The owner — Penelope — looks up from behind the register and visibly jolts when her eyes connect with mine. "June!" She rushes out, wrapping her arms around me. She talks as she steers us toward the back room. "I couldn't believe it when my booksellers told me what happened at the signing, and then you were on the *TV*. James is barely twenty and when I hired him he wasn't even an alpha yet, but he said he knew immediately and had to clear everyone out."

I flinch, giving her a sheepish look as I glance at the small stack of books, embarrassment wrapping itself around me. I should have held it together and finished the signing — all these people were *waiting* to meet me and I ruined it. I ruined their experience.

Seth's hand barely brushes my back, lingering as Penelope quietens and glances between us, quickly excusing herself and slipping out of the office.

As I take a seat and pull the books closer, picking up the signing pen, my heart clenches. I let so many people down and caused so many issues, she probably lost sales, I probably lost readers —

"How mad at me would you be if I bought all your books and read them?"

Seth's voice drags me out of my head. He flips open the cover of *The Pack and I*, fluttering through the first few pages and flashing me a smile, his eyes twinkling.

"I wouldn't be mad." I look down at the books, opening the first one and signing my name quickly. "Just mortified." Pushing it to the side, I take the next one. "Don't get me wrong, I'm really grateful for everything but..." I pull the pen back after signing the second book, afraid to leave an ink blot as my mind spins.

He puts the book down as my words die in my throat.

Seth's face falls slightly, holding his hands out in front of himself in a pleading gesture. "I know I don't think shit through. Bennett can attest to that — but what I *did* was see you that night in the elevator and think, '*Wow, this* woman.'" His voice sounds wonderstruck as he stands on the other side of the table. "And I kicked myself for not talking to you more than just assuring you that the stupid piece of shit elevator would start again. And then in the coffee shop — I wanted to stop you — stop the beta you were with — just so I could actually *talk* to you."

Seth shifts around the table, swallowing as he bends down next to my chair, tilting his head to look up at me. "When I saw you on the news, I knew that I was finally getting my chance. I didn't think, I just acted." He reaches up, touching my hand, unconsciously making me release the death grip on the pen. "And maybe that's insane, it all sounds like it is when I say it out loud, but you can't sit there and tell me that there isn't a part of you that recognizes me, a biological part that..." He shakes his head, searching my face.

My lips part, my throat tight. "I'm scared."

His entire face crumbles, his eyes softening as his hand slides to cover mine, his tawny skin soft against the back of my hand. "I'm not going to do anything you don't explicitly tell me you want. I'll move every damn person out of the townhouse and leave it to *you* if you want that. Every single decision is yours to make."

I reach up with my free hand, rubbing my forehead as it aches, my chest tightening. "I refuse to table my entire life because society decided to put brakes on an entire designation. I'm not going to kick you out of your home — but I — I can't *go* — and it's just because —"

He shushes me, taking the pen out of my hand and standing up. Seth drops it to the table and then cups my face, looking down at me seriously.

I swallow, my throat convulsing as I struggle to reconcile the man in front of me with my desire to just *run*. I don't want to deal with any of this. I don't want to make decisions. I don't want people telling me what I can and can't do. I don't want to feel this gnawing wrongness in my body every time I'm awake.

Everything is simpler when I stay home, when I'm safe and it's quiet.

"Maybe this is easier to manage when you're raised for the slaughter." My voice is soft as I stare up at him, thinking of the young omegas, the ones who have families who prepare them, who tell them what to expect, who don't spend their entire lives telling their children that designations like alpha and omega are for people meant for more in life.

"I'm nothing special." *I don't deserve his kindness.*

Seth winces. "June."

"How would you feel if you suddenly woke up one morning as an omega?" I shoot the question at him without thinking, then pause, frowning. "Don't answer that. I bet Bennett would just make you pancakes or something equally, stupidly, perfect."

Seth's lips twitch as he laughs, bending down. I freeze as he nears me, but his head swerves, lifting so that his lips press hard against my forehead, kissing me as his thumbs stroke my jaw. "So, lunch after this? You seem hangry."

I grumble at him, but there's no ire behind it. I can't

muster it, not when his lips are so soft against my skin and his touch eases the frantic feeling in my chest, the rabbit-heart urge to run.

He pulls back, giving me a dopey smile before he flops into the chair next to me. I glance back at the books, picking up the next one and scribbling my name as there's a knock at the door.

One of the workers from the night of the signing eases it open, looking in at us, her eyes flickering from Seth to me. "I'm really glad you're okay." She swallows, her eyes widening as her coworker appears over her shoulder.

He's overwhelmingly alpha, and bounces on the balls of his feet as he looks into the room.

"Did you tell her about the call?"

The girl frowns, glancing back at him disapprovingly before her eyes dart back to Seth and I. "Someone called us and asked if you were rescheduling, but I told the guy you hadn't set a date yet. Penelope will coordinate it with your agent, and I'll make sure the few people who we had to..." She hesitates. "Well, who had to *leave*, I'll make sure they get their copies." She motions to the books in front of me as I mechanically sign them.

"I don't think the guy was someone who even had a ticket." The alpha behind her pipes up again and Seth's shoulders tense an almost imperceptible amount. I probably shouldn't be watching him close enough to even *notice* that.

The guy rambles on. "I was at the front of the store when Mary said you were sick or something because some guy walked in and wouldn't show me his ticket for the event, he had a letter and was being weird — I had to kick him out, and I think it was *him* —"

"*James.*" His coworker cuts her eyes to him, hissing his name in warning.

I finish signing the last book, pulling my hand away as I try to smooth over the chaos. "I don't mind rescheduling, I know it was inconvenient for everyone —"

"But it can wait." Seth looks over at me. "You can talk to your agent about it."

I glance at him, then pause. The memory of the alpha bookseller and the sound of the bell above the door makes my skin prickle as I whisper, "Yeah, I can wait."

The girl in the doorway nods. "You should. There's a lot of weirdos out there." Her eyes linger on Seth before she flushes and looks back at me. "It's probably safer if you're settled in a pack — uh, not that all omegas need one but —"

"It's safer though." The alpha behind her nods rapidly. "I knew a guy who would chase down omegas, bite or no bite at uni. He only stopped when another alpha threatened to kill him for hitting on his omega."

Seth scowls as my stomach sours. Pushing up from the table, I force a polite smile at the two workers. "I'll have my agent contact Penelope when I know more about my schedule. She's going to ship some bookmarks over to go in the leftover books."

They thank me, shuffling to the side as Seth's hand finds the small of my back, his head bent as he whispers into my ear. "I know it's not my designation *or* my place, but I don't like the idea of you being anywhere without..." He hesitates as we step out of the bookstore and I squint up at the cloudy sky.

"A bodyguard?" I look up at him, his nose nearly brushing mine as the line between his brows smooths out.

He smiles. "No."

I glance back at him as he opens the car door, tilting my head, amused. "What, then?"

His lips twitch. "A me, honestly."

The laugh bubbles up as I climb into the car, followed by him only a second later — Bennett was right, he says everything he thinks, but there's something so open about it. There's comfort in knowing Seth is utterly transparent in his affections.

CHAPTER ELEVEN
JUNE

I HAVE no idea how I ended up in a clothing store.

One second Seth and I were in the backseat of the town car where I finally found the courage to ask about the laundry room, and in the next, the car was stopping on a street row full of shops. Seth dragged me into one of them, and now I'm *here* and there's a very chipper beta associate fawning over me and showing me rack after rack of clothes in my size.

I didn't even know I *could* buy things off the rack in London.

I've always been above the standard size range in stores, but this one has a plethora of options, from jeans and trousers to shirts that actually encompass the expanse of my chest.

It helps that the other workers are *eating* up Seth's presence. He waltzed in with all the confidence in the world, and I don't know *how* he manages to command a room so well.

"What about something like this?" The associate helping me holds up two different options of pants, and I consider them. One is a tighter pair of jeans, while the other pair of trousers look similar to the loose fitting ones I brought from home.

I nod toward the trousers, reaching out to touch the fabric on instinct. They're *very* soft. "I like these." Reaching for the tag to see what the damage will be, I startle when the associate jerks them away.

"Sorry, your boyfriend said not to let you look." She gives me a sheepish look. "I'll just go put these in the fitting room."

She scurries off as I turn my head slowly, eyeing Seth on one of the couches outside the fitting rooms. *Boyfriend.*

He raises a glass of complimentary champagne at me, his smile easy. "When do I get a fashion show?"

I scoff, striding over and plucking the glass from his hand, pointing it at him. "You..."

He leans up, his perfume washing over me. It's light, but *rich.* I once went to upstate New York for a writing retreat and there had been a candy shop that made its own fresh fudge, filling the air with the smell of sugar and cocoa. It comes off him in waves, sweet and decadent — *dangerous.*

My eyes flutter as I try to control myself, and Seth only grins even wider.

"Me?" He reaches out, sliding his hand over mine. "Yes, June? What were you saying?" My name on his lips is sinful, soft and whispered, full of promise.

I stutter as his warm fingers ease the glass from me. "Um..."

He beams, taking his champagne back and downing it before nodding behind me at the fitting rooms. "Go try on what you like. Indulge me." Flushing, I stand over him for a moment. His hand brushes my hip, his head tilting as he looks up. "I *want* to do this for you."

"Okay," the word escapes. I extract myself, stepping back so I'm not inhaling lungfuls of him as I bite my tongue. "We're still getting lunch, right?"

Seth leans back on the couch, lounging like a king. "Yes, I got us a reservation around the corner. Don't rush. They know me, and our table will be there when we get there."

I cast him one more look as I back up, pressing my lips together and trying to hide the thrill that gives me. He took care of it. There's no reason to hurry — and my eyes flicker around the store, at the other racks I've not even glanced at yet. I *could* buy things here — a piece of two at least — with how well my book sales have been this quarter.

I've never indulged, but there's something about Seth that makes me *want* to.

I LOSE COUNT of how much I try on and how often the associate comes into the back with new items. There's a rack that's been filled, emptied, and filled again near the mirror where I've been surveying myself. Beside it is a small pile of clothes I genuinely like, and that got nods of approval from Seth when I stepped out and showed him.

He'd bitten his fist when I'd walked out in a pair of jeans that hugged my hips, and a cranberry red v-neck sweater made of cashmere. I'd laughed all the way back to the fitting rooms.

Touching a brown dress on the rack, I stare at it, uncertain. The associate brought it to me and I scoffed because *when* would I need a dress this nice? It has a fitted bodice and puffed sleeves, which I'd never pick for myself. But the color is deep, almost mahogany, and I find myself pulling it off the hanger before I fully realize it, sliding it over my head and glancing at myself in the mirror.

It *fits*, and it's beautiful.

If the tour wasn't on hold, I'd wear it in a heartbeat. The fabric drapes perfectly, skimming my hips, giving me a silhouette that screams quietly luxurious. Even without shoes on, it looks like it belongs on me.

My heart tugs as I smooth my fingers over the dress, knowing there's no way I can get it home without ruining the fabric. The thought is sobering — all of this is so temporary. My first heat will hit, I'll make it through it — and then what?

I'll be able to book a hotel, or fly back home. This time will fade to a memory of the two weeks I spent in a townhouse in London with men who doted on me.

My eye is drawn to the bodice, hugging my chest and showing off my cleavage, just enough to be tantalizing and flattering. Pulling my hair to the side, I reach back, trying to get to the zipper so I can at least *see* it fully on, but my fingers fumble, unable to reach it. There *are* pockets though, and I grin at myself in the mirror, sticking my hands into them experimentally.

It would look really nice with a gold necklace. I can't lie to myself. Extracting my hands, I skim my collarbone, picturing it — the life I could have in *this* dress, with the man outside.

It would be beautiful too. Life would be full of moments like this, full of dresses and dinners and smiles exchanged. It would be *full* of laughter — I just *know* it would, because already my heart feels tethered to Seth, our souls recognizing each other.

I've always wanted more. More from my parents who have been so focused on others their entire lives — whether that's believing in a god who ordains designations as better than others, or themselves, trying to make connections and friends they feel are worthwhile and powerful.

Seth's attention feeds a part of my brain that can't help but preen. I don't know if I should be upset or not that I'm so easily swayed — maybe the other alpha, Theo, is right. Maybe I'm only a silly omega, a stranger getting swept into a lifestyle I'll never be a part of.

I smooth the dress down self-consciously, hearing my mother's voice in the back of my mind.

"Betas like us aren't meant for the things the world gives alphas and omegas. You've never been small, Juniper, you've never been meant for anything more than what you are. You'll do well to remember your place. No alpha is going to give you a second look when they have a prettier, petite omega out in the world, meant for them."

It's biology. It's always been — but now, more than ever — I understand the difference.

But she was wrong.

I *am* an omega — I could be meant for more. I could deserve it.

There's a sharp inhale, and I whirl, the skirt flaring out as I stare straight at *Bennett* as he lingers in the doorway, in a pair of navy trousers with a white button up. His hands clench next to his sides as I'm hit with the vibrant smell of freshly peeled oranges, the citrus scent overpowering and potent.

He stares at me, sucking in a breath as his shoulders square.

"I—" Fidgeting, I turn around quickly, facing the mirror again. "I can't reach the zipper."

"I'll do it." His voice is deeper, huskier as I watch him stride toward my back in the mirror. He slows to a stop, his dark hand grazing the brown fabric. It disappears behind me, and I'm rewarded with the warmth of his fingertips as they glide over my bare spine as he grasps the zipper.

My skin burns, goosebumps rising as he eases the zipper up. My heart roars in my ears as the dress comes together.

"There's a clasp." His voice is soft, ragged as the pads of his fingers brush my neck, pushing baby hairs away as he hooks the dress shut.

His head tilts in the mirror and I watch, holding my breath as he bends down. His nose barely brushes my exposed throat — but it's enough. My perfume *explodes*, filling the fitting room area with the rich, sugared scent of honey, a tang of herbal tea undercutting it, mixing with the smell of citrus — reminding me of quiet early mornings, curling up with a good book in a comfortable seat.

Bennett's head dips closer, and then his nose *is* touching me, right at the junction where my neck and shoulder meet. Vague memories of scent marking blink through my brain — when alphas want to make sure others can smell them on an omega. His eyelashes flutter in the mirror, his pupils wide as they rise, meeting mine.

"You look beautiful."

I flush, my cheeks bright under the lights as I look down, fidgeting with the skirt. My fingers grab handfuls of it, crushing the expensive fabric. "Thank you." I laugh nervously. "I don't have anywhere to wear it. It's silly — I shouldn't get it."

"Buy it." His firm tone makes me look back up sharply. "I'll make sure you have somewhere to wear it."

The heat from his body, from his gaze on mine, makes my brain fizz as he reaches around, touching my wrist. I let go of the fabric immediately as his fingers slide down, over my hand, his voice raw. "Juniper —"

I shiver, my heart ricocheting in my chest. Is it *always* going to feel like this? I was nervous around the alpha in the bookstore this morning, but this... is something else. This makes me want to shed my own skin and crawl into his.

Bennett opens his mouth.

"Oh!" The associate from before skitters to a stop, staring at us. She takes a step back. "The dress fits! Good!" She hesitates, looking back, "I — your boyfriend said to wear something you'd like so I was coming to take the tags off."

I shake myself out of the haze as Bennett steps away. The crowding presence of his scent fades enough that I can think, and I turn, giving the associate what I hope is a grateful look.

"I'll just wear the jeans and the cranberry sweater out, if that's alright?"

"Yes." The associate rushes to agree. "Let me take their tags and go ring it up. Will you be taking this dress?"

Bennett answers before I can. "Yes." He dips a hand into his pocket and pulls out a black card, motioning it to the associate as his eyes move back to me. "Ring it all up on this."

My skin prickles as she takes his card, and then Bennett touches my shoulder. He turns me, sparks dancing across my body as he mutters, "Let me unzip you." His fingers deftly unhook the top of the dress, and then slide the zipper down, exposing my skin again.

Swallowing, I glance at us in the mirror, muttering, "Thank you."

He nods. "I'll —" He clears his throat. "I'll be out with Seth, he invited me to lunch —"

"Okay." I interrupt him. "I'll be right out."

He all but runs from the fitting room and I make my way over to the pile of clothes, slipping off the dress to let the associate take it. She hasn't blinked at my bra or underwear this entire time, but as I reach for the jeans, she glances at them.

"You know, I think we have a selection of intimates in your size — if you'd like to see them."

I look over at her and pause with my hand on the jeans, then nod. "Yes, please."

She flashes me a little, almost knowing, smile before taking the dress and rushing off.

In less than fifteen minutes, I step out clad head to toe in new clothes. Thanking the associate over my shoulder, I pause, realizing how quiet the store is, raising my eyes to see Seth staring at me — unabashedly, with Bennett next to him. Seth's mouth hangs open, and I flush at his expression of hunger as I step toward them both.

"I thought this would be more appropriate for lunch."

"I'm definitely hungry."

"*Seth*," I laugh, letting out a little squeak as he reaches out for me, sliding his hand over the arm of the cranberry sweater, caressing the soft fabric and *me*. His brow furrows, and then he leans in closer, his lips twitching as he inhales.

"You smell like oranges, June."

"I —" I flush even more, clearing my throat as I look down at my outfit, catching Seth looking between Bennett and I.

The alpha makes a strangled noise, turning. "We should go, so we don't miss the reservation."

"Hm." Seth slides his arm around me, bending his head and inhaling again. "I'm going to have fun breaking the two of you. How do you feel about Italian food?"

"I like it."

"Good, because that's where we're headed."

Bennett looks back at us, his eyes soft as he takes in Seth's arm around me, opening the door for us with one hand, and holding my myriad of shopping bags in the other — like it's the most natural thing in the world.

CHAPTER TWELVE

JUNE

SETH ORDERED us all lunch in flawless Italian, and I found myself sitting between him and Bennett at a table outside, enjoying the soft breeze as they chatted about the liquor business they apparently share.

And for the first time in my entire life, I felt like I *belonged*.

Bennett left us after lunch. Seth spent the rest of the afternoon dragging me around London to stores I've never even heard of, like a furniture store with a *huge* comfy leather chair that caught my eye.

By the time we made it back to the townhouse, I could feel myself dragging. I rallied my energy to shower, but now that I'm in my — suddenly clean — pajamas, I'm wide awake, staring at the ceiling of the guest bedroom.

The lingering happiness from earlier has soured. My parents still haven't contacted me, and I don't think they care. Janet said to take time off in her last email, that we'd iron out the details after the heat is over — but with nothing to occupy my mind, it's spiraling.

Seth and I walked in earlier as Theo was disappearing up the stairs. My eyes snagged on the large alpha immediately, his back ramrod straight, stalking away from us. I think he hates me — he wouldn't even look back even when Seth called his name.

What he said this morning was cruel, especially since I'm only trying to navigate this as best as I can without putting myself at risk — but maybe there's a kernel of truth to it. Maybe I'm taking advantage, maybe I should have told Seth no today, maybe I shouldn't be looking at Bennett so much.

But I don't have the luxury to pack my things and leave.

My phone lies discarded beside me as my mind spins, tabs still open from the research I did ten minutes ago about omegas and heats and emerging. Most of the forum posts are from omegas, barely eighteen, navigating it with other teenagers. There's nothing from adults suddenly thrust into this — raging emotions, symptoms that make a period look positively *fun* — the sheer thought of the heat I'm racing toward makes my throat close.

There's really only two options: go through it alone, or be okay with Seth... and maybe Bennett's help.

Someone posted a list of recommended toys, including knotted vibrators and thrusting dildos. I'd thrown my phone down after reading someone saying that she *still* couldn't do it without an alpha next to her, the pheromones and the alpha's scent helping ease the anxiety and panic attacks from feeling unwanted.

Seth and Bennett are in a loving and committed relationship. Who am I to get between them? How much of this is just hormones and biology?

Scrubbing a hand over my face, I sit up, my stomach

rising to my throat as I crawl out of the bed and slip out of the bedroom, the hallway and the stairs quiet. I make it to the kitchen and drink a glass of water before I hear movement down the hall and freeze. I shouldn't be out again — Theo could come around the corner and bark at me. I shouldn't be awake or making a nuisance of myself.

Hurrying to put the glass up, I slip into the foyer and stop short, seeing a pair of loafers near the front door, and a light on at the end of the hall, just past the living room. There's a door open too — one that Seth didn't show me on his brief tour, and I take a step toward it, hesitating.

I don't *want* it to be Theo, because he'll snap at me. It's stressful, on a biological level, like my body is rejecting itself because I've disappointed an alpha with garbage opinions.

I ease forward, lingering just outside view of the partially open door, waffling. Before I can make a decision, an accented voice barks from inside. "Bloody hell, Theo, *just come in.*"

I jolt, stumbling forward. Grabbing onto the frame to steady myself, I stare wide-eyed at the man behind a desk.

His head jerks, black hair a tangle of ruffled curls as it flops over his forehead. Deep brown eyes dart up to me, just as wide as I'm sure mine are, his mouth opening amongst a scattering of a light beard. A tanned hand raises, adjusting his glasses on his broad nose, his features distinctly Indian as he freezes.

"You're not Theo —"

"I'm sorry —"

We talk over each other and I immediately go quiet. My heartbeat pounds in my ears, my mind working overtime to catch up with what I already know — this is the other alpha and the last member of Seth's pack.

His nostrils flare, his hand dropping away from his glasses. "The omega." It's barely a whisper, and I don't think he means for me to hear it as I skitter back.

"Wait" — the alpha holds up a hand — "it's alright." He stands quickly and I suck in a breath, watching him rise and *rise*, so tall and a little gangly. I'd have to see him side by side with Theo — but I'd swear he's even taller than the big alpha, lean and muscular, his suit rumpled.

He raises his other hand, holding them palm out like he's trying not to startle me.

"Bennett called while I was in Paris. I got home earlier — I thought..." He pauses. "I thought you'd be asleep, or upstairs."

His thick British accent wraps itself around me as I chew on the inside of my lip. "I was thirsty."

The alpha frowns, stepping carefully out from behind the desk. "That's okay, you should make yourself at home." His eyes catch on me, scanning my sweatshirt and leggings. "Where are my manners?" His eyes soften. "I'm Arin. You can come in — if you'd like to. You can leave the door open if that would make you more comfortable."

My fingers cramp on the doorframe, and I slowly unclench them, taking him in. He's handsome, even in clothes that have clearly been worn for a while. He shuffles, then pulls his suit jacket off, his tailored button-up tugging around his shoulders as he throws it over the edge of the office chair.

I wet my lips, stepping forward and glancing around the office. Full shelves, a small couch, it's very plain but clearly well-used and high quality. "I'm sorry — I —"

He looks back at me, tilting his head as he does. "I can hear your heart racing." It misses a beat as he sucks in a breath, his shoulders sagging. "Is it me? I'm sorry if I'm making you nervous."

"No." I stumble over the word, staring at him. He's so unthreatening, it's unthinkable. "Well —" I catch myself as he looks at me seriously, like he's worried I'll lie to appease him. "I don't know." Everything feels new and scary, a stark difference to the feeling of warmth and rightness with Bennett or the toxic sparks with Theo.

This is *heavy*.

Arin nods, and I nearly step back when he approaches me. I don't get more than half a step away before his scent washes over me with his newfound proximity. It's harsh and spicy, a burning bright mint. The clean smell all over the townhouse reorients itself in my brain — not the sign of a clean house — but instead *him* hanging on every surface, taking space up in my brain without me even realizing it.

I try not to fold in on myself, but I fail, wrapping my arms around my torso as he slows to a stop in front of me. Arin stands for a moment, unmoving, until a low, soft rumbling sound fills the air between us, steadily growing in volume.

I blink in surprise, looking up at him as he purrs.

The tightness in my chest loosens, unfurling the small *omega* feeling, the insecurity that I'm weak, susceptible, unwanted.

His brown eyes snare mine, his voice soft despite the purr radiating through his chest. "Why don't you start with your name?"

I glance down, unable to take his eyes on mine, finding his socked feet instead. He must have come in straight from the airport. I'm the reason he had to cut a business trip short.

"Juniper."

"Hello, Juniper."

A shiver crawls over my skin at the sound of my name on his lips, and I glance up again, watching him from under my lashes. Compared to the brief moment Bennett purred, this is different, steadier and soothing. This isn't a surprise to him — he's *consciously* purring for me and the sound is deep, like a hum resonating from the center of his chest.

There's a cautious, but kind smile on his lips, juxtaposing the messy, scruffy shadow on his jaw and cheeks.

"Can I help you, Juniper?"

I open my mouth, closing it almost immediately before nodding.

He steps closer, and then he wraps his arms around me — not tightly, but firmly. The effect is immediate, his purr radiates through him and into my body, the scent of his perfume stuck on his clothes, saturating them — sinking into *me*. A sense of serenity drags me under, like blowing out a candle flame, dousing the fear and anxiety in my chest.

I turn my head on instinct, burying it into his chest, my eyes burning before tears overflow, a sob wracking through me.

Arin makes a little sound as his hand lifts, stroking the back of my head, running over my hair as he hugs me. The last week hits me like a truck, the impact making me feel off-balance. He doesn't waver as his arms become the only things keeping me upright.

"My youngest sister emerged early as an omega. She was barely seventeen." His voice is gentle as he guides us both over to the couch between two bookshelves. He keeps me in his arms as he sinks down, arranging me until I'm tucked against his side, partially in his lap.

"There's five of us, if you can believe it. I'm the second

oldest, and all of them are girls." His fingers card down my hair, then brush over my shoulders, rubbing them as his chest continues to rumble. "My older sister, Theresa, is a beta. Then there's me, the only alpha, then the twins and my youngest sister are all omegas." He laughs softly, shaking his head. "I was the only one home when Vera started showing signs, and she had a breakdown. It's not funny, but she was convinced it meant I'd drag her down the street and drop her off at the nearest center like she was some used clothes at a charity shop."

Arin's hands pull me closer and my nose finds his shoulder, inhaling in small bursts, sniffling as I sink into him.

He sighs, and his head turns, tilting down toward me. "I didn't, to clarify. I gave her a hug, purred for a bit until she calmed down, called Mum and Dad — who rushed home —" He squints, his gaze faraway. "This was thirteen years ago, she's five years younger than me, so you and her are probably close in age." His eyes refocus. "She's been with her pack for the last decade, one of them plays rugby, he's a good guy."

I watch as his glasses dip, slipping on the bridge of his nose. His hand stills on my back, applying the slightest pressure before he moves it, touching my cheek and using his thumb to wipe at the tear tracks.

"It's a lot. That's all I'm saying — it has to be." Arin's eyes search my face. "Whether young or old — that's a lot of pressure for a person to suddenly have on them, especially with no support and in an unfamiliar place." He frowns, his thumb touching under my eye. "When did you last sleep a full night?"

I pause, feeling like I can't lie to him. Something in the back of my brain won't *let* me. "Before I got to London, over a week ago."

His eyes flash, anger, sadness, disappointment, then he readjusts us, pulling me closer without a struggle. Arin snatches a thin decorative blanket off the back of the couch and settles it over both of us, pressing me against his chest as his purr grows louder, almost like it's being forced out.

"Close your eyes."

I peek up at up, inhaling the minty scent, my nose burning as I nod and sink into him, resting my head against his thrumming chest and heart. Unspoken words hang in the air: *is this okay? Are you comfortable? Will you rest?*

I let them all fade as I wrap an arm around his torso, my eyes drifting shut as I murmur, "Thank you."

His hand rests on my back over the blanket, his tone even. "Don't make me command you to sleep."

Unbidden, a little smile tugs on my lips — wouldn't be the first time.

The hum of his purr surrounds me, the warmth radiating from him getting trapped by the blanket, creating the perfect cocoon to sink myself into. My mind goes quiet, blissfully silent as sleep sweeps in before anything can interrupt it.

CHAPTER THIRTEEN

ARIN

THE OMEGA IS in my arms.

I smelled her the second I walked into the house, but nothing prepared me for how much *more* she is. My expectations were set by Bennett's periodical updates — first it was that Seth made a knee-jerk decision, then it was that *Bennett* had gone along with it, and finally it was that Theo was acting out — which is to be expected.

The text is seared into my brain.

BENNETT

> Seth ran into the beta we were trapped in the elevator with. She isn't a beta. She's at the house with us because the designation center was mistreating her. You should come home.

I'd tried to wrap my head around cutting my work short to come home to a stranger, but somehow now that I'm here, I'm not upset by it.

How could I be?

She — *Juniper* — is in my arms, practically lying on top of me, her soft body melting against my own. And she's all curves, pliant and thick, her weight resting against the side of my body, warming me from the inside out. I've never had a difficult time making my designation work for me — strength helps when I'm keeping my body fit, power keeps eyes on me while working, scents and heightened senses clue me in when deals might sour, and the few times I've had to purr to curb Theo's tangled thoughts all came naturally. It didn't take any effort for the rumble to fill my chest, to wrap my arms around her and let her sink into me, to find *safety*.

I just hadn't expected it to be *her* in the doorway. I've grown so used to Theo seeking me out the moment I return home after traveling, trying to channel his anxious alpha energy into *something*. He fights his designation, but I've spent my life making it work for me.

When she'd stumbled in, the sweet smell of her perfume acrid with stress, soured and frantic — I *knew* I could help. It was unthinkable not to.

Bennett didn't have to verbalize that she doesn't have anyone. It's clear. He never would have brought someone back to the townhouse if there wasn't a reason, and now with her pressed against me, I *know* why he made the call without mine or Theo's input.

How could someone see you and not want to give you the world?

I lift my hand, stroking her hair. It's red in the dim light, reflecting the lamp I didn't turn off, casting shadows on her round features, full lips, and little button nose. She's *beautiful*, and in sleep, her perfume smells like honeyed tea, wrapping around me, near intoxicating as it drips down the back of my throat, soothing me as much as my own scent seems to have soothed her for the time being.

Never in my life have I smelled a perfume so distinctly *home*. I learned all about scent matches after emerging as an alpha, but no one told me that it was an instinctual *'when you know, you know'* sensation. Other people have appealed to me through the years, but never like this, never to the point where my fingers want to dig into her skin, to hold her against me and never let her out of my sight for the rest of my paltry life.

Mine.

I sink back into the couch, wrapping both arms around her tightly. It's chaste, compared to my raging hindbrain. It's never had this reaction to any of the casual partners I've taken through the years. None of them were ever omegas though, and it adds a layer of... *more.* My limbs feel heavy as I make sure she can't move in the night without me knowing.

Most omegas I've met have already been bonded to the packs I help purchase property. They're quiet, shy, like her, but smaller, shorter, thinner. Her thick thighs press into mine and I close my eyes, breathing in deeply, willing my body to behave as she breathes out softly against my chest, humming in her sleep as she adjusts, pressing more of her body into mine.

Maybe I can just let her rest for an hour or so, then put her to bed and figure out the next steps with the entire pack in the morning. I already know what Seth and Bennett will say — but I'm not going to disregard Theo's discomfort, that would be a misuse of my power.

Her hair is so soft.

The thought trickles in, my hindbrain fighting against

my better senses and winning. I inhale deeply, smelling her perfume, her skin, *her*. It takes all my effort to simply tuck the blanket closer, cupping the back of her neck gently, keeping her stable so I can make sure she gets as much rest as she needs.

CHAPTER FOURTEEN
JUNE

THE BED IS much *firmer* than I remember.

I shift sleepily, inhaling the smell of breakfast mixed with overpowering mint. My eyes flutter open, taking in the long, lean torso of the *man* under me. The same one that talked me down from panicking last night. There's a drool spot on his shirt where my cheek is, and I jerk, feeling his hand tighten on my shoulder, keeping me from flying off the couch.

We're both covered by not one, but *two* blankets.

He blinks owlishly up at me behind askew glasses. "Morning."

I flush, sitting up a little slower and both the blankets fall onto the floor. Reorienting myself, I rub my face, clearing the crusty pieces from my eyes, the skin slightly swollen from crying last night. A whiff of chocolate comes off one of the blankets, and I turn toward it, closing my eyes as my heart flutters.

Seth was in here.

"Come on." Arin sits up, long limbs hanging as he gives

me a small smile. "Let's see what Bennett made for breakfast."

I stagger upright, wanting to give him the space to stand too, but all it does is immediately remind me of how *tall* he is. The sheer height of him makes me feel like an ugly duckling, scrambling to keep up as he walks out of the office with me hot on his heels.

Arin steps into the kitchen and I peek around him. Bennett moves back and forth between two sections of countertop, mixing ingredients for pancakes. Seth leans against one side, stealing a kiss every time Bennett walks by.

The beta perks up immediately, his smile widening as he looks between Arin and I.

"I couldn't figure out why your room was empty... then I came downstairs." Seth shoots Arin a look. "I told you to stop sleeping on that couch with only that decorative blanket. It's not warm enough."

Arin coughs, glancing to the side as he runs a hand over his mussed hair. "I'm... going to get out of these clothes. I've had them on since yesterday morning." As he turns, his eyes catch on me, lingering. "I'll be back for breakfast. Eat something, Juniper."

I open my mouth, but nothing comes out as he slips past.

Seth pushes off the counter, walking toward me. I flush as I glance up at him, barely having to move my eyes to do it since we're so even-matched. He touches my jaw, a line appearing between his brows. "Are you okay? Your eyes are puffy."

Rubbing them self-consciously, my heart tugs uncomfortably. The fact he even *noticed* makes my mind spin, my throat feeling suddenly tight as I inhale shakily.

His frown deepens, and then he wraps his arms around

me, pulling me into his chest, smelling of oranges and choco-late. Just as I have the thought, he laughs softly and mutters directly into my ear. "You smell like mint tea, like Arin coated you in his scent overnight."

From behind us, Bennett clears his throat. "How many pancakes do you want June?"

Anxiety skitters over my skin as I pull away from Seth. That's his *bonded. Why would Bennett want to see Seth hanging all over me? Why would any of them want to smell someone else on my skin?* Not even Seth's brief touch on my arm can curb the panic. Backing up, I ease toward the door, unable to meet Bennett's eyes.

"I'll be right back."

I don't wait for a response, instead I dart out of the room, afraid they'll stop me, afraid of what will come out of my mouth if I let myself stay. I make it to the guest room before I suck in a ragged breath, going straight to the bathroom and turning the shower to scalding. Something about being told I smell like Arin — *an unfamiliar alpha* — my brain unhelp-fully adds — means I can't get out of my clothes quick enough, shedding them just to jump under the burning water.

My skin is pink and red, raw from scrubbing it with the scent-cancelling products, by the time the water turns cold. I want to claw my own skin off as I stumble out of the shower and tug on a sweater and my other pair of leggings. My rounded stomach is bloated, and the leggings cut into it as I push my fists against my eyes.

Don't cry, don't cry, don't cry.

Last night was the most rest I've gotten in a *week.*

This is all too much — too fast — I shouldn't be here — I shouldn't be in this situation. I should be at home in my shitty little apartment writing my silly books and be grateful I've had the small success in my pathetic little life I *have* —

I refuse to look at myself in the mirror as I leave the room again.

The adult thing to do is to thank them for taking me in, but part ways. I can find an omega-only hotel that's willing to let me stay — even if it means taking out some cash from my savings account. If nothing else, I can contact the designation center and ask about the pack with the female alpha. I never should have dropped the card for the heat service.

I take the steps slowly, steeling myself. It will be simple — look at them, say that I'm thankful, and then go back upstairs and pack. I'll leave everything Seth bought for me, I never should have accepted any of it in the first place.

Noises in the kitchen make me slow as I keep my head raised, walking through the archway. My eyes find Seth and Bennett immediately, both seated in the corner breakfast nook.

It's Theo behind the stove, making a pancake, with Arin across from him that makes the words die in my throat.

Their chatter fades. Theo looks up, his bright blue eyes finding mine, pinching at the corners in a glare. Bennett tilts his head, his nostrils flaring as Seth opens his mouth from beside him.

"Had to scrub off last night?" Theo prods at his pancake, his words terse.

I jerk, looking at him sharply, shaken all over again. "What?"

"You heard me." He doesn't bother looking up from the pan. "We'll have to air out the townhouse when you finally leave, everything smells like burnt sugar. I take it from the scent-cancelling soap you didn't like our alpha's scent all over you? Are you about to move on and find someone you can tolerate better?"

"What the *fuck* is your problem?" My entire plan shatters as I stare at him, my hands shaking as I clench them into fists. "All you've done is bully me since I've been here or scurry away with your tail tucked between your legs when I'm in the same room. Go on, run away."

His jaw flexes as he raises his head. "I'm not fucking running in my own home. You must have thought you won the goddamn lottery when Seth came to the designation center —"

"Theo —" Bennett snaps, starting to rise.

"Fuck *you*," I snarl the word, putting my entire chest behind it as I spit from anger, stepping forward. "I'm not some fucking nineteen year old omega you can get off on bullying. I'm a *person* — I have — *had* free will until a *week* ago, something you'd *never* understand." The silence in the kitchen is deafening as I stalk forward, pointing at Theo. "I went to college, I have a life, a *career*. This entire thing has derailed my future, and you don't get to give me shit for taking the *only safe option* I had."

He locks eyes with me, heat and fire burning me as he mutters sarcastically, "So fucking dramatic."

My lip curls. "Shut the fuck up. You don't get to tell me I'm dramatic and overreacting when you've lived your entire life the way *you've* planned it. This is the worst nightmare I've ever had — did you know the center told me that hotels have the right to refuse me? Airports can turn me away?"

At his silence, I barrel forward, too enraged not to keep speaking. "I can't get out of bed without feeling my entire body rebel against me. I feel like I can't even take care of myself anymore. Do you know how *embarrassing* that is? I've spent my entire life taking care of myself. Do you even *know* what it feels like to suddenly feel wrong and like you're missing a part of yourself? I just have this constant fucking *ache* in me, a *want*, a claw in my *chest* —" I choke on the words, the room blurring as my eyes fill with tears.

Theo stares. "You don't have to stay here if it's so bad."

Seth yelps from the table. "What?"

"You heard me." He's talking to Seth, but his eyes never waver from mine. "Clearly this isn't the place for you if you're so miserable." He shoves the pan off the stove, crossing his arms.

The plan I formed falls apart in my hands. "The center told me I would be putting myself in danger."

Theo shrugs, but the motion is jolted, uncomfortable. His words say one thing, but his body language says another. His shoulders are tight, his lips pressed together as he leans away from me. "So?"

"Theo." Arin's voice is barely a whisper, a warning.

"I can't walk around perfuming and drawing every alpha in the city to myself." I stare at Theo — *he can't be this stupid*. Everyone has seen the stories of young omegas out at night at the wrong time, about alphas who think their power means they can do whatever they want.

My blood runs cold. "I'll end up trapped in the center again, stripped of my choice."

His expression doesn't waver, but something in his eyes looks as unstable as I feel. "Take suppressants." He sounds angry, but also, somehow, pleading. "Get on a flight. Go *home*. Go to one of those under the table heat hotels, spend the nights with a hired alpha or toys. Satisfy yourself, because let me make one thing clear." He slams his hands down on the counter, making everyone flinch. "You are *not* welcome in this pack."

"Jesus, Theo —" Seth stands and Theo whips his head to the side.

"No, she should know." Theo snarls, looking back at me. "I don't *want* you. You might be trying to worm your way into everyone else's bed, but I'm a part of this pack too, and I'm *rejecting* you."

Pain — white hot, angry and electric — radiates through my chest, like my body is trying to rip itself apart at the words. I take a step back, putting a hand over my heart, whining at the physical pain the words cause.

"We aren't trapping you here. You want to leave? The door isn't bolted, and I sure as fuck won't stop you." He stalks around the counter and nears me and I stare up at him, my lower lip trembling as he scoffs. "If you're going to be emotional about all of this, do it somewhere else. I'm tired of hearing it."

"You're an asshole." I whisper the words, my voice wobbling.

"Born and raised, princess." He doesn't even look at me. "Go find someone else to —"

"*Quiet.*" The weight of Arin's bark silences Theo mid-sentence. It settles on the kitchen, heavy as the taller alpha stalks toward Theo. I can't move, can't breathe.

Theo doesn't let him reach us. He storms out of the room, shoving past me as Bennett stands up. His shoulders are tight, his jaw tense as he stares angrily at Arin's profile. "*Go.*" He strides forward, and then takes my arm, pulling me away from the doorway, his voice softening. "Come sit, June. I'll make you a plate."

Arin looks over at me, his eyes falling to Bennett's hand

on my arm before he leaves the kitchen. I struggle to swallow, my tongue feeling thick as I mutter, "No, I should go — I need to pack —"

Seth jumps up, moving over to me only to cup my face. "No." He shakes his head, his eyes full of concern as he takes me in. "No leaving. Do you like chocolate chips in your pancakes? Bennett makes them taste so much better than anywhere else. I don't know how he does it."

My heart pounds in my chest, my skin feeling clammy as I glance up at him, then over at Bennett. "I —"

Bennett cleans the charred pancake out of the pan, dumping it into the trash before pouring fresh batter in. "Answer us. Plain or chocolate chip, darling?"

My eyes burn as I lean into Seth's touch, taking a shaking breath. "Chocolate chip."

"Good choice." Seth smiles, hugging me securely, lips pressed against the crown of my head. "I knew you liked chocolate."

CHAPTER FIFTEEN

THEO

"Get in."

Arin's office smells like fresh honey and mint leaves.

He looks rested for once, his eyes cutting me as he leans against his desk.

And then he just... *stares.*

I fucking hate when he does this. The anger helps clear the haze in my brain from the mix of their perfumes, the scents that make me want to charge back out and make her scream at me until I can remember why I hate her so much on principle alone.

"Go ahead, yell at me." I glare at my prime, crossing my arms.

"No." He pushes his hands into his pockets, his gaze narrowing. "You need to explain yourself to me, using complete sentences."

I'm barely in the room, but it doesn't help or abate the overwhelming swirl in my brain, two sides of me fighting tooth and nail with each other. There's the side that *knows* a bad idea when it sees one, and there's the alpha side of me, my hindbrain reacting to biology and scents and fucking *pheromones*. And the alpha is clawing, it's howling, whining, trying to get *out*.

I made her cry. More than that — I reduced her to panicked whines — *twice*.

"I don't like her." I bite out the words, gritting my teeth.

"Don't lie to me."

"I'm *not*," I snap at him, but it's plaintive, and my face screws up as I try to breathe through my mouth, not my nose. The honey coats my tongue, seeping down my throat, sinking into my fucking *blood*.

"You are." Arin glances at me, and I shift, hoping my loose gym shorts aren't giving away my body's confused reaction. "You do like her, you only don't like that you, for once in your life, find yourself wanting something you've insisted you can't have." His eyes flicker down, over my front, lingering on my shorts before he looks back up. "Wanting an *omega*."

I *want* to spit at him. I want to rip his soft, black curly hair from his head. I want to shove him into the desk and *break* it. I want to crash his head into mine. I want my lips on his. I want him to put me on my knees. I want her between us. I — *fuck*.

Arin holds up his hand. "Do *not* speak right now, Theodore. If you know what's good for you, you'll stand there and listen to your alpha."

The snarling inside me dies as quickly as it came on. The weight of his stare makes me want to hang my head and look away, but instead I clench my jaw and refuse to back down.

"You want something you've sworn off of since birth, since becoming an alpha, and that pisses you off, the same way it upsets *her* that the life she knew, the life she was *living* is now gone." Arin says the words plainly. "You're both mourning something lost — freedom. But what you both don't recognize is that you can give each other that freedom back. It's not out of reach, the way it looks has only changed."

My jaw works as I growl, "I don't *want* her."

"*Stop lying to me.*" Arin snaps, the bark rocketing through me, my tongue loosening as he sighs and cards his hands through his hair. "Fuck, Theo." He looks at me, put out and *sad*. "How many years have we known each other?"

I clear my throat, unable to lie. "Twenty years, give or take a few months."

We met when we were both teenagers, I was fifteen, Arin was sixteen. I was there when he emerged as an alpha, more powerful than any other I'd ever been around, on a shared family vacation with his rag-tag siblings. Arin's sisters were always happy, his parents are stupidly in *love*, meanwhile I grew up only knowing the way my fathers constantly barked at my mother, reducing her to tears multiple times a day.

"I would think that those two decades have given me the right to say this." Arin's voice softens and I look up at him. "In all your attempts to get rid of her, you've turned into the very men you were trying to avoid becoming. You've become your fathers — terrorizing a woman who did nothing to you but exist. You might not have bonded her against her will and abused her, but you're making her just as miserable as your fathers do to your own mother. And I'm incredibly disappointed in you."

My stomach drops out of my body, nausea gripping me as Arin pushes away from the desk.

He rests a hand on my shoulder, turning his head. With

the movement, his mint scent fills my senses, scorching the honey from my brain as he mutters, "But there is still time to fix this, if you'll let yourself. Don't fall prey to the same cycle you've spent your entire life outrunning."

Arin walks around me, leaving me in the office alone as my eyes fall to the blankets on the couch. I walk over to them in a daze, picking up the one that normally lays on the back and folding it mechanically, filling my nose with the smell of honey and mint with each wave through the air. The second blanket smells the same as the first, with a hint of fudge, and I bring it to my nose, closing my eyes and inhaling deeply.

It's the second time I've found her scent lingering on fabric — the laundry room has been saturated in it for two days, but I dutifully washed every single piece of clothing Seth brought down. I don't have business this time in London — just Arin — but we all travel here to the town-house when he does. We function as a pack — but now I'm terrified it's going to fracture in my very hands.

Her perfume smells like our pack house in Rochester, like early mornings when the dew covers the grass and I can open the doors from the living room out to the pool deck. It smells like Bennett cooking breakfast for all of us, Seth lingering in the doorway and making fun of me, calling out random numbers instead of actually counting my laps in the pool. It smells like Arin pushing a mug into my hands, telling me to get out before I catch a cold from the crisp air. It's the smell of all of us sitting in the living room, laughing over bad movies.

It's the smell of my mother and I hiding in the back bedroom of my childhood home, watching old British murder mysteries. The only times I could see the true vibrancy of her personality was when my fathers weren't there.

When I emerged as an alpha, Peter and George had looked at her and said, "*As useless to us that you are now, at least you gave us an alpha. We'll make sure he knows his place.*"

And I'd sworn from that point that I'd never bond an omega — because growing up to be like *them* is a fate worse than death.

CHAPTER SIXTEEN

JUNE

I WOKE up this morning in my own bed — well not *mine* — *the guest bed.*

After the disaster in the kitchen yesterday morning, I tried to beg off, to pack, or at least isolate myself, but Seth coaxed me into sitting with him and Bennett to solve a puzzle, then watch TV. It was very reminiscent of the first night here — with absolutely no one else around. When it was appropriately late enough, I dragged myself upstairs and Seth left me with a kiss on my forehead.

It's been quiet this morning.

Bennett offered to make me an omelette and Seth suggested going out again, but I can't fathom it. My stomach keeps twisting into knots, shooting pain radiating through my lower half. Some of the pamphlets the center sent with me said there are small moments of symptom spikes before heats set in.

The worst feeling is how *horny* I am.

I feel like I could grab the nearest person and sink my teeth into them.

As I stare at the bookshelves in the living room, my phone vibrates. Pulling away from a murder mystery, I fish it out, glancing down at Janet's name in shock before answering it immediately.

"I know I said I wouldn't call." Janet clears her throat. "But I got confirmation from the publisher your tour dates are postponed until we can navigate this."

My heart tugs as I stare at the books, wrapping an arm around my torso. "Okay, that's probably for the best."

"I... don't think it's wise for us to make another statement to the press, but I wanted you to be aware that there have been *a lot* of calls. It's kind of out of my wheelhouse, June." Janet sounds a little tired. "I'm only here to represent your books, but a lot of these people have an interest in *you* now. I can put you in contact with one of my friends in LA who's a publicist. I'm not sure what the publishing house wants, but it might be worthwhile for you to speak, or talk about what's happening when you're ready. It would certainly keep your books selling— as it is right now, they're flying off the shelves and they've sold out online. We're rushing another printing so the shelves aren't empty for too long."

"*What?*" I freeze, shock rocketing through me. After a moment, it clicks that people are probably *very* interested in a once-beta author, now suddenly an omega who cancelled her entire tour and was photographed leaving a designation center with two men.

I'd eat that shit up if I was home on the couch with a pint of ice cream.

"A publicist could at least help you navigate the future and coordinate some of the larger scale interviews. You were going to need one before the movie goes forward —"

Janet's words continue, but I'm not listening as the smell

of rich fudge, dense and chocolatey, enters the room. I turn, my mouth watering as Seth walks in, his hands in his pockets. The closer he gets, the more the smells mix, layers of chocolate coated over orange, like Christmas treats and candy. He stops partially behind me, pulling a hand out of his pocket to touch my back.

"June?"

I shake my head, swallowing thickly as I mutter to Janet on the phone, "I'll consider it. Thank you for letting me know."

"Of course." She pauses. "And I hope you're okay. I really do. I can't imagine the stress."

My skin heats as Seth's fingers slide up. I swear I can feel them scorching me through the fabric of my sweatshirt, burning straight through to my skin, making my mind go blank as they dip down. The pads of his fingers snake under the hem of it, skin against skin as they press against the small of my back. I want him to take the phone from my hand and throw it onto the ground. I want him to grab me by the hips and bend me over. I want his hands in my hair and his tongue buried in my cunt —

"We should meet when you're back in the states."

"O-Okay." I get caught on the word, turning my head sharply to look at Seth as my mind goes fuzzy around the edges. I manage to end the call without making an idiot of myself, my hands shaking as he gives me a shit-eating grin.

"Don't hang up on my account."

I swallow, staring at him. His lips look so *soft*, his hair pulled back to expose the silver scar on his throat. My body thrums at the thought of Bennett sinking his *teeth* into Seth, making sure everyone who ever sees him knows he *belongs* to someone else. He's *claimed*.

Seth steps closer, his voice soft. "You okay?"

I blink, shaking my head, trying to clear it.

He lifts his hand from my back, pressing it against my forehead. "You're warm. Is it...?"

"No." My voice is a little rough as I flush, leaning away from him. "I think it's just a flare, or spike, or whatever they call them —" I push my sleeves up, trying to get air as I turn and stare at the bookcase, fighting back the urge to throw *him* against the shelves and give him a matching mark on the other side.

I didn't think omegas had urges to bite — but my teeth *ache* — I want people to look at Seth and know he's *mine* too. He'd look so pretty with my hand on his throat and my teeth marks in his skin.

He's quiet for a moment before he pushes my hair back. I startle, glancing at him as he gives me a soft smile. "You're going to watch the movie with us tonight, right? It's pack movie night."

I frown, my heart stuttering. "Seth..." *I'm not part of this. He* isn't *mine.*

"Don't start." He tilts his head, his smile lingering. "You're invited because *I'm* inviting you, right now." Seth pokes my nose. "So, Junie, what snacks do you like to consume rabidly while mindlessly watching TV?"

My lips twitch. "Junie?"

"June Moon?" He bounces, his hand lingering on my hair, twirling it around a finger. "June bug? Junie Moonie." He snaps his fingers at me, grinning.

I laugh, despite myself, shaking my head, and his smile widens, overtaking his entire face.

THE LIVING ROOM SEEMS SMALLER, more intimate. It didn't feel this way when it was only Bennett, Seth, and I in here, but I feel very *aware* of its square footage now that the TV is on a menu full of movie options and every seat will be full.

The bookcases on the far wall extend the full length. The only furniture is a three seater couch and two oversized armchairs to either side. Seth already has the coffee table piled high with snacks, and he turns, grinning at Arin and Theo as they linger in the doorway.

"I picked a *classic* for this evening's showing."

Arin glances at me, his eyes soft as he chuckles at Seth. "I'm sure you did."

My heart flutters as I make my way around the coffee table, toward the farthest armchair, but just as I reach it and touch the arms, Seth pipes up from the couch.

"Where are you going?"

I hesitate, looking over at him. "Taking a seat?"

Seth shuffles on the couch, leaning back into Bennett and making space between the tangle of their legs. He bends forward, drumming his hands on the sliver of couch cushion visible, smiling. "Come sit with us?"

I look behind him to Bennett, his gaze snaring mine. Bennett dips his chin in a little nod, his voice gentle. "Only if you want to. If you're more comfortable over there, Seth can cuddle Theo."

"No, Seth cannot." Theo's voice startles me as he grabs a handful of popcorn and tosses it into his mouth.

The way Theo says it, the deadpan and the fact his lips turn up into a little grumpy snarl, makes me *lose* it. I giggle, covering my mouth immediately. He stops shoving popcorn into his mouth immediately, his eyes darting down to me, searing. I think I imagine it, but there are creases in the corners, pinched like he's fighting a smile, and I tear my eyes away, scurrying over to the couch.

Seth grins and I don't even get a chance to sit before he wraps his arms around me and tugs me down between his legs, making a pile of the two of us laying on top of Bennett.

"I win." He mutters the words as I watch Arin take the chair closest to the door, leaving Theo to finish his walk around the coffee table to the other armchair. His hand slides over the fabric on the armrest, his body rigid, like he's holding himself back before he turns and shakes his head, folding his massive body and sitting down.

Seth snatches the remote. "Okay, everyone shut the fuck up, it's movie time."

Bennett scoffs, it turning into a light chuckle that transfers through Seth's body into mine with how we're lying together. I smile, turning my head slightly to glance up at Seth as he weaves an arm around my torso and presses play on *The Alpha of the Rings*. It's early enough we might get to its two sequels, but I like the prequel too, *The Omega*.

Seth is warm and smells like the shower and a mixture of his and Bennett's scents. The first ten minutes are barely over before I find myself sinking into him, unconsciously nudging closer and resting my head against his chest. His fingers run up and down my arm, almost absent-mindedly as everyone snacks and grabs whatever they want from the coffee table.

Just as the movie gets into the first act, my phone buzzes.

I jerk up, fumbling to pull it out and freeze when I see the screen, unable to process it.

"Juniper?" Arin says my name, the question hanging in the air.

I blink, making sure I'm not hallucinating, but the screen still says *MOM* across it. Quickly, I answer it, self-conscious of the audience in the room as I mutter, "Mom?"

"There you are." Her voice is chipper, like I've not been trying to contact her for four days straight, or that her last message to me was an outright dismissal. "I wondered if you would pick up, it's quite late here, but I thought, '*Oh, I should call Juniper*.' How is your little signing going? Have you met any nice betas?"

"It's been days." I stare at the coffee table, my voice barely above a whisper. "I've been trying to get you to call me back for *days*."

"I heard you the first time." She scoffs. "It's not ladylike to repeat yourself. Now tell me when you'll be home again? Your father and I think you should come to the club with us, start attending regular meetings like you used to as a kid. Sundays are just *better* when I've been."

My mind spins as I try to figure out what the hell she's talking about.

"I had to cancel my tour." I spit out the words, my throat raw with the admission. "I'm not allowed to fly home until after the first heat passes."

She makes a noise in the back of her throat, soft and admonishing. "Cancel it? I hope you realize how many people you've probably disappointed for that. Don't they plan these things far in advance? Sell tickets? Juniper, I raised you better than —"

"I couldn't go!" I snap at her, at my breaking point, fully

aware of how *quiet* the living room is and the four men around me. "I *had* to cancel. I told you, I'm..."

"Don't you take that tone with me." She interrupts me sharply. "This *omega* play-acting you've done is extremely distressing, Juniper. Rhonda from the club called your father and asked if we'd be taking a trip to London, and I said, '*Now, why would we do that, Rhonda?*' Because, honestly, you know how she is — and then she said that you were telling people that you aren't a beta? And I told your father that this is *exactly* what we tried to prevent you from doing when you started writing those books about..." She pauses, making a distressed noise. "*Packs.*"

"I'm not lying." I clutch my phone. "I was at the designation center, my blood is golden. I'm an omega."

"That's not possible." My mother sounds faraway, and I hear her talk to someone else before she puts the phone back to her ear. "Your father is beside himself, we tried to call the designation center in London and they told us that your records were sealed to us."

Closing my eyes, I press a hand against my head, my voice soft. "Why would you need my records?"

"How am I supposed to believe you're telling me the truth? How am I supposed to know this isn't just you wanting to sell your stories to anyone who will listen to them?" She pauses, then sighs, like I've asked her for the moon and the stars.

"We've had a lot of calls, Juniper. If you..." She trails off. "Well, if you *are* an omega, it's our job to make sure you pair with a *good* alpha, one who can provide for you and ensure the life of you and your future children is built on solid foundation. Of course, there is the issue with your age — there aren't many men who will want an old omega, but that's outside of my control. How much do you weigh right now?"

My eyes flutter open as I stare at the paused TV, my throat burning, unable to think of *anything* to say to that.

"The center at least said you were no longer in their care. Where are you, Juniper? We can have an alpha come pick you up, one has already offered — he's a part of the club and apparently in town."

I blink, looking over at Seth, my heart pounding as he reaches out, his face full of concern. His hand lands on my arm, grounding me.

"No." I clear my throat, my eyes flickering from Seth's face to Bennett as my mother lets out a noise of surprise on the other end of the line.

"Juniper, this is not the time for your wildly liberal ideas about packs. I wish you'd given us time to prepare, but if this is what we need to do, we'll help — it *is* our responsibility. If you're an omega, your father and I will make sure that you go to a suitable alpha. I'm sure they'll be eager to have you pregnant before the end of the year, but we can figure that out after you're home —"

"Absolutely not." I cut her off, my hand tightening on my phone. Arin shifts in his seat, drawing my eyes, as I flounder. My mother has always had *strong* opinions, but I'm having a hard time wrapping my mind around the fact she's so eager to sell me off to the next alpha she speaks to, rather than letting me, her grown daughter, make my own decisions.

She makes a harried noise. "Please don't tell me you let this center place you with multiple alphas. God help us, please tell me you aren't with a *pack* of them. You can be comfortable with someone we've approved, none of this... *shared* omega ideology — it's *disgusting*."

Anger, white hot, and flaming, licks up my spine. It's potent and *wrong* — rising in my chest at the way she splutters. Instead of being happy I'm safe — she's more concerned with the *optics* of me being with a pack. When all Seth has done is make me feel *wanted*, when all Bennett has done is take *care* of me, and all Arin has done is *welcome* me.

My eyes fall on Theo, unbidden, but instead of finding scorn, he's glaring at my phone like he'd like to rip it from my hand and throw it against the wall. He's the outlier — but the fire in his gaze says more about his actual opinion of me than anything that's come out of his mouth since I've gotten here.

"There have been *offers* for you. There is an alpha in London who called us and he could come get you now. He sounded just fine. You need to tell us where you are and you can come home — he'll have to bite you and bond you before you can fly but —"

"Oh my *god*." I recoil, nearly dropping my phone. "I'm not telling you where I am so some strange alpha can come to the door and *bite* me. Are you *insane*?"

A deep snarl cracks through the room and I look up sharply, unable to place which of the alphas it was.

"Well you aren't staying there —"

"Yes, I am." I spit the words out. "I'm staying *here*, because I'm *safe*."

My mother fumbles, like I've actually stumped her. In the next breath, she gathers herself. "I forbid it."

I laugh, bracing a hand on Seth's leg, needing to feel the warmth under my palm as I shake my head. "You have no right to tell me what to do, like you said, I'm old. I'm over twenty-five, the omega guidelines don't apply to me. Legally, you can't make the decision."

"If you let one of those alphas you're with bond you — or *God* — all of them —"

"Maybe I will." My fingers tighten on Seth's leg, my voice sounding cold, even to my ears. "Maybe I'll let them all take a bite just so I'm tarnished and bitten and *used*. Isn't that what you always say about pack-bonded omegas?"

"There might be more alphas than omegas in the world, but that doesn't mean you can spread your legs for *any* one that walks by you, giving it up and bending over for multiple men —"

"And I'm not letting you sell me to the highest bidder." I cut her off. "What have they offered you and Dad so far? What alphas have come knocking? The ones who won't pack up because no one else can tolerate them? Who think they own a female omega because they see a walking womb, willing or unwilling? I'm not letting you hand me over to some alpha who will slap me around when I open my mouth, or — like *you* said — expect me to be barefoot and pregnant by the end of the year."

"Juniper Walden —"

I hang up before she can finish, my entire body shaking as I stare down at my phone.

"June." Seth leans closer, his voice breaking.

"I need a minute." I push up from the couch, walking out of the room without looking back, my feet taking me to the kitchen because it's the closest room and I don't know where else to go.

Blinking rapidly, I try to compartmentalize. This is the same woman who didn't want me to go to college. This is the same woman that told me a degree in English would get me nowhere. This is the same woman who never congratulated me *once* for publishing my first novel, or any of the others thereafter. This is the *same woman* who told me when I was sixteen that I'd be her biggest regret if I was just another beta like she was.

I grab the fridge door and jerk it open, staring blankly as the cool air wafts over my overheated skin, my heart in my throat as I suck in lungfuls of breath, trying not to hyperventilate.

Footsteps from behind me make me jump. I spin, letting the fridge shut as I press my back against it, freezing when I see it's *Theo* — out of all the people in this godforsaken townhouse.

"If you came to yell at me, can you save it? I've had enough today."

He stares at me from the entry to the living room, raising an eyebrow. "Are we bartering now? What do I get if I lay off for the evening?"

I scowl at him, crossing my arms. "You *get* to continue living without my foot up your ass."

His lips twitch, his head tilting slightly. "Is that any way to talk to your host?"

"Host my ass," I spit back at him. "*Seth* is the one who invited me here and *Bennett* is the one who has fed me and *Arin* is the one who's made sure I've gotten sleep. What have *you* done?"

He holds his hands out to me, then takes a step closer. I press back against the fridge, eyeing him warily as he nears me. He doesn't slow until his chest brushes mine, reaching above our heads to the cabinet over the fridge. His shirt pulls and stretches over his muscles, cords of them under the tattooed skin of his arms. My mouth goes a little dry, and my *stupid* body betrays me, cataloging every tiny little twitch of his body as he leans over me, blocking me from leaving the tight space. After a moment of searching, he pulls down a bottle of red wine.

My eyes flicker to the label when he holds it in front of my face.

"What are you doing?"

He reaches back up, and there's more clinking as he grumbles. "There's a bottle of white up here, but I think Bennett normally cooks with it, it's not as good as this one." At that, he sloshes the bottle of red. "Normally we have a bottle of Seth's rum, but I don't think they've been to the headquarters here in the city to pilfer a crate."

I scowl at the bottle as he shuts the cabinet above our heads. This close, he smells like fresh rain on grass, like being dunked underwater and inhaling air after breaching the surface.

"Is it poisoned?" I glance at the label — but it's in French and I can't read it.

Theo makes a noise. "It's not *poisoned*." He flicks the wax seal. "Arin would kill me, and I have a lot to live for —" He shifts. "Apparently."

I snort, snatching the bottle from him to look at it closer, but the seal is untouched. He'd have to be a psychopath to poison it and then put it back in the cabinet. Still, I can't help myself, I look up at him, craning my neck, as I grumble mockingly. "What happened to the whole *'born and raised'* asshole schtick?"

He tilts his chin down, the smallest of smiles tugging at his lips. "Is that what I sound like?"

"Yeah." I scurry around him, putting the bottle on the counter and hunting for a corkscrew. "Grumpy for no reason, completely inhospitable, and mean enough to make my mother look like a goddamn saint."

He makes an amused noise behind me, and I glance over my shoulder as he grabs the *fanciest* wine glass I've ever seen from an upper cabinet.

Recoiling, I raise an eyebrow at him. "Is that *crystal?*"

Theo holds it between two thick fingers, the stem looking positively *fragile* in his grip. He glances from it to me. "It's what we have."

I gawk at him. "I'm not drinking from that. I'll look at it wrong and it'll shatter."

Theo places it on the counter next to the bottle. "Then I'll buy a new one."

I balk. "How expensive are they?"

"I don't *know* — fucking expensive, probably."

"I'm *not* touching that." I glance at the bottle. "Or that. How expensive is *that?*"

"It cost what it *cost.*" Theo stalks closer and boxes me in against the counter, heat in his gaze. "Seth has the movie paused for *you. You* need a drink after that conversation, and I'm going to pour you a glass. Is that understood?"

I raise my chin, narrowing my eyes at him as I open my mouth. "Where do you get off—"

"No." He cuts me off with a little growl, grabbing the bottle and popping it open. "If the next words out of your mouth aren't *thank you,* I don't want to hear them."

I glare at him, setting my jaw. "Why? What's going to happen?"

He pauses. Theo's movements are precise as he slowly lifts the bottle, staring at me as he pours a glass of red wine, then sits the bottle back onto the counter next to me.

"Do you want the answer you expect, or do you want the truth?"

I lean back, my eyes locked on his. "You don't scare me."

Theo shakes his head, and I swear his eye twitches.

I prickle when he leans closer. "What are you—"

He picks up the glass and holds it out to me.

I eye it, and *him*, warily. I almost expect him to do something childish, like pour it over my head, or throw the glass against the wall and tell Arin I started shattering crockery so he'll kick me out. But when we just stare at each other in silence, I finally relent, reaching for the glass.

His other hand comes out in a snap, snaring the back of my neck in an instant, collaring me.

"*Omega.*"

I make a noise, half shock, half whine as my body reacts before my brain, my throat arching as I stare up at him, my mouth dropping open as Theo holds me and the wine, dipping his head lower, his eyes narrowed. My hindbrain scrambles, the basest part of me wanting to go limp in his touch, skin on fire and heart racing.

He could lift me with one hand onto the counter. He could push me down and rip my leggings in half. His thick fingers could gather the sudden slick between my thighs and shove into me while his thumb circled my clit —

"*This* is what happens to brats who talk back to me." His head dips lower, lips caressing the shell of my ear. "I don't need to make you fear me to get your heart rate up, princess. Now take your wine and go back to your beta. No more talking back, you're going to enjoy the rest of your evening."

I flush, head to toe, my fingers catching the glass as he pushes it into my hand. Turning sharply, I dart under his arm, his hand falling away from my neck as I race back into the living room, making a beeline for the couch as Seth sits up.

"Finally." He looks up at me, his eyes slightly wide, but

it's *Bennett* who catches my eye from behind him. The alpha's eyes narrow, lingering on my, no doubt, reddened face, then looking at the glass in my hand as I clear my throat and resettle on the couch between Seth's legs, using him as a buffer as I raise the glass to my lips and take my first sip of the wine.

A hum rises from my chest. It's *so* goddamn tasty.

"It tastes like pomegranate."

"Oh, Theo grabbed you the *good* stuff." Seth grins down at me, picking up the remote as the aforementioned alpha walks back into the room, sliding a glass into Arin's hand before retaking his seat with his own.

My eyes follow him, something in my chest flaring at the practiced look between Arin and Theo. They rotate around each other, but Theo *relents* to Arin — I quickly down another long gulp as Seth starts the movie and drags me back against his chest.

I shouldn't think about Theo's hand on the back of my neck, or Arin's arms around my waist, or Bennett's touch on my bare skin, or Seth's hungry look.

I need to *behave*.

CHAPTER SEVENTEEN

JUNE

THE FIRST MOVIE plays through without a hitch, giving us all something to focus on.

Well, it keeps *their* attention. Mine seems to be divided, and impossible to corral because as Seth switches the movie over to the sequel to continue our marathon, I survey the room, fidgeting between the tangle of his and Bennett's legs. I'm warm, and have already politely declined a blanket, because Seth's chest *radiates* heat.

Or maybe that's just me.

Arin is twisted in his chair, his long legs extended to rest on the coffee table in front of him. Half the snacks are gone, and what's left are picked through. Theo is spread out in his seat, his thighs wide and legs open as his drained glass of wine hangs loosely from his fingers, his head tilted toward the TV.

I down the rest of my glass and lean forward, pushing it onto the coffee table.

"Grab my soda, please, June?"

I make a noise of acknowledgment, reaching for

Bennett's drink as my eyes linger on the movie. Leaning up, I hold it behind me to the alpha, and his fingers snag it. I glance back at Bennet as he takes a drink, flashing me a small smile. "Thank you, darling."

Goosebumps rise on my arms as I put his soda back on the coffee table, my cheeks warming as I readjust on the couch, pulling my legs up underneath me. I'm sitting like an absolute goblin, but the more curled up I am, the better I seem to feel.

Seth's body serves as a buffer between myself and the alpha on the couch, and it feels *safer* this way. He makes a little noise, pulling me closer, one arm hooking around my hip and pulling my body into his chest. It's a comforting kind of weight, a solidness that I turn my head toward, willing myself to behave as he hums and squeezes me. Seth grins down at me, and in the lowlight, my heart flutters.

For just a moment, it feels like it's only us in the room. I can imagine coming home to him after long days of touring, his infectious happiness ready to cheer for each and every new goalpost I pass in my career. The vision shifts, seamlessly adding in Bennett, his cool presence an anchor. I could crawl out of my office after drafting for hours to find him in the kitchen, warm food ready for me.

It feels *right*.

Seth's smile softens as I gaze up at him, my heart in my throat.

As soon as the feeling hits me, Bennett shifts behind us both, his hand moving to reach for the fallen blanket next to me. His hand brushes up my arm, loose near Seth's waist, his nails catching and sending skitters up my body, like striking a match on my overheated skin.

I gasp, arching into the touch, all the careful composure I

tried to keep from the encounter with Theo in the kitchen flies out of the window as my perfume *explodes* in the small living room.

I'm mortified.

Pulling back immediately, Bennett's hand falls off my skin, my heart pounding in my ears as I glance over at him. His face twists in confusion and shock, his eyes locking on mine, his pupils blowing out. I swing my head to the side, suddenly cognizant of the two *other* alphas in the room. Arin grips the fabric of his armchair, while Theo adjusts, his jaw tight as his eyes flicker over to me. Their blue is near-black with want.

Seth untangles himself from Bennett, grabbing my hand and tugging me up from the couch. I feel like I barely blink before I'm in the open foyer, away from the mix of *their* perfumes, their eyes on me. My skin feels tight, my cheeks blazing, as I step away from him, the embarrassment over-riding churning desire as I put my head in my hands.

"I'm sorry, you never should have invited me to stay here. I keep causing *problems* —"

"What problems?"

I jerk my head up to look at him sharply, but Seth just stands almost chest to chest with me, his expression patient, albeit a little confused.

"All I'm doing is driving a wedge between everyone!" I motion to the archway. "I'm making everyone uncomfortable —"

"Not me."

"What?"

"You don't make me uncomfortable." Seth takes a step closer as my mind screeches to a halt. He touches my hands, pulling them away from my face and hair. I didn't even realize I was tugging at my skin, the sweatshirt, heat radiating up out of every pore of my body. Seth smoothes my fingers out, squeezing my hands in his, tilting his chin down, his voice low. "You make me the opposite, in fact."

I scoff at him. "That's only because of my designation."

"No, it isn't." He shakes his head, his voice soft but firm. "You lived as a beta for nearly thirty years, you know your scent doesn't have that intense of a biological effect on me as it does an alpha. You and I both know how it feels to be *outside* of the designation politics, just as much as we know what it's like to suddenly be entrenched in them."

He moves closer and I swallow, my heart in my throat as I stare up at him, my mouth opening. My eyes catch on the bond mark on his throat — he's not wrong. He must have lived exactly like I did, largely ignoring alphas and omegas, until he fell in love with Bennett — until he was *bonded* to someone.

"What it *does* do — what *you* do" — his hands tighten their grip on mine, his confession barely a breath — "is make me want you."

The heat is coming on — that's all this is.

My blood feels like it's boiling, not from anger, but from sheer *want*, scorching me from the inside out. I'm not blind — I've been attracted to him since I stepped into that stupid elevator, with his hair swept back into a bun, and his easy smile. It was an instantaneous spark, igniting the air between us.

I'd risk everything to be close to him.

He drops my hands and then reaches up, pushing my hair back, his palms smooth against the skin of my face.

"But Bennett —" My gasp is soft as he pulls me closer by the chin.

Seth pauses, a hair's breadth from me, our noses almost brushing.

"It would be stupid of me to invite you into our home, our *lives*, when you're about to have your first heat, without my alpha's blessing." His smile is slightly lopsided, juxtaposing the fire in his gaze as his eyes flicker to my lips.

I suck in a breath before I grab onto the front of his shirt and tug him against me.

I don't know which one of us moves first, maybe it's at the exact same moment — the chemical reaction flares, and he's *on me*. Seth sweeps me into his arms in the middle of the foyer, devouring my lips with a kiss that makes my toes curl in my socks. His breath smells like fudge — he tastes like fucking *candy* — his tongue sweeping into my mouth, consuming me from the inside out as he backs me up a few steps. I gasp as I knock into a table, a vase rocking back and forth, the poor flowers inside spinning as their water sloshes over the side and onto the marble tiles.

He presses closer to me, pinning me against the side of the wall as my hands fist his shirt, attacking him with my lips and teeth.

Each touch, each half-panted moan, each brush of his hands on my face, my hair, my neck, holding me to him, tilting me so he can get at me at the exact angle he wants — they're all satisfying, making my blood *sing* — but it's not *enough*. I want to bury myself inside his chest, wrap myself around his heart and sink my teeth into the organ.

It's the best damn kiss of my entire life.

I'm panting by the time he pulls back just enough to suck in a lungful of air for himself. His lips are swollen as he grins down at me like an idiot, voice rough and laced with awe. "*Fuck*, I've been waiting days to do that."

I flush, feeling more right in my body than I have since the night of the signing. Staring up at him, I pull his shirt closer, kissing him again. "That was the kind of first kiss I write about."

He smiles, his eyes lighting up as he cups the back of my head, holding me in place as he wiggles his eyebrows and devours my mouth, muttering, "Oh, I *know* what you write about."

I dissolve into giggles, our noses brushing as he kisses me over and over again. Finally letting go of his shirt, I wrap my arms around his neck, sinking into him as his hands wrap around me, resting on my hips as he kisses my jaw, nuzzling it. His arms transition from holding to hugging, and I screw my eyes shut, breathing in the smell of him, my head finding his neck, fudge entwined with orange.

When I rub my nose against his throat, he groans softly. There's suddenly a long, hard pressure against the front of my thigh, fighting against his sweatpants as he mumbles, "Bennett's going to lose his fucking mind. You're getting that dripping honey smell all over me."

I bite my tongue, shameless as I keep our bodies flush, kissing his jugular as my skin heats at the thought of Seth and Bennett pressed together. They could touch each other, and I could touch them. I could be *between* them, hands and mouths and shared breath —

He inhales sharply, kissing the side of my head, his voice low. "Do you want to sleep in our room tonight?"

The offer is quiet, and my heart tugs as I carefully untangle from him, giving myself space to breathe as I lean back against the wall, shaking my head. "Not tonight." It's not a no, and as I lick my lips, I force myself to be an adult. "We should go finish the movie."

"Yeah." His smile is soft as he takes a half step back, but his eyes drag over me, something rough in his gaze. "We can be done with this for now."

I press my lips together, my cheeks heating at the insinuation.

He grins, grabbing my hand and dragging me back into the living room.

SOMEHOW, we manage to make it through the second movie.

I sit a little further from Seth instead of piling on top of him. He still keeps his hand on my arm the entire length of the movie, and I find it both cute and a little maddening.

There's no way that Bennett, Arin, and Theo don't know what we did in the foyer.

I try to ignore it as we all part ways, Arin heading down the hallway to his office, his shoulders a little tight as I watch him go. Theo jogs up the stairs past Seth and Bennett, like he can't get away fast enough.

I fall into step behind Seth and Bennett, stopping on the second floor as Seth lingers in front of my room.

"Goodnight." He flashes me a little smile, his eyes flickering to his door. "I'll be in there if you need anything."

"Okay." I press my lips together, watching him follow Bennett into the room before turning and slipping into mine.

Even after a shower, I can't stop tossing and turning in the bed. I can't *take* it anymore. My skin is flushed and tight, like my body is trying to rip free from it. I can't get the thought of Seth's lips out of my head, so soft, touching me exactly how my body needed.

Is this it? Is this the heat? It can't be, because I'm *aware* of myself. I'm aware of everything, from the way the sheets brush over my skin, to the sticky feeling between my thighs, my sleep shorts bunched between my legs.

Everything online said I'd be half out of my mind by the time the heat set in — but I can't fathom wanting someone *this* much without there being a greater reason behind it.

I punch my pillow as I turn over again, freezing when I hear something through the wall.

Pausing, I wait the span of a breath, but there's only silence. Sliding out of the bed, I creep toward the door and ease it open, lingering in the threshold as I survey the empty hallway.

There's a groan and my eyes dart to Seth and Bennett's partially open door.

I take a half-step without thinking. The sound of bodies, hips and skin slapping into each other, heavy panting, fills the air, making me flush as I slow to a stop.

I'm transfixed by what I see.

Seth whines, one knee on the bed, his body partially bent forward as Bennett stands behind him. They're both half-clothed. Seth's shirt is rucked up, Bennett's hand running over Seth's chest, holding him upright as his hips jerk forward rhythmically, fucking Seth from behind.

"Please, *please.*" Seth begs.

Bennett grunts something in his ear as his nose drops to Seth's neck, inhaling as his hand on Seth's chest drops down, wrapping around the other man's dick.

I stand, stock-still, my eyes following the curves of their bodies. Seth's sweats are in a pile on the floor, Bennett's pool just under his hips, exposing his bare ass as it flexes. Seth's arms lift, pulling Bennett closer as the alpha moans, *"Fuck."*

It's a mistake the second I inhale — breathing in deep the smells of sex mixed with their perfumes. It's a cloudy haze of orange and chocolate and my mouth waters. Bennett's citrus overpowers Seth's fudge, and it's decadent and dangerous, coating my mouth and throat.

Bennett groans again, and Seth's breath catches.

My eyes open as I shift forward, looking past them and straight at myself. A mirror hangs on the other side of the bed, taking up a chunk of the wall and providing me both a view of the front of Seth's chest and Bennett's hand working him, along with both of *them* a view of me in the open doorway.

Seth's eyes catch mine in the mirror, locked on me as I stop short, my heart in my throat.

He licks his lips and then reaches back, jerking Bennett's head up from his throat and twisting to kiss him. I shiver, pressing my thighs together, stuck in my place, reduced to a voyeur as I watch them devour each other — watch *Seth* devour Bennett with only his mouth as thoroughly as he did earlier to me.

After a moment, Seth pulls back, his voice a low whine. "Use me, alpha. Help me put on a show for her."

Bennett utters a soft curse under his breath, his head snapping up, turning to look at me. I freeze with my hand fisting the side of my shorts, a deer in headlights as his eyes narrow on me. He grabs Seth by the throat, pulling him fully upright as he thrusts faster, pounding into him mercilessly and reducing Seth to a whining mess.

"Touch yourselves, but don't come until I say."

The command makes me shiver, not a hint of a bark to it. I could turn and leave, I could run back to my room and lock the door, but fire flashes under my skin as I slide a hand under the waistband of my shorts, finding my panties soaked through. I whimper at the same time Seth does, watching his hand wrap around his dick in the mirror, jerking himself at the same rhythm that Bennett fucks him.

I muffle myself, shoving my other hand over my mouth as I press against the doorframe for support. My fingers slick through my sodden curls and find my clit. Two rubs has me thrusting against my own hand, writhing a little as I bite down on my tongue, forcing myself to keep my eyes open to watch them. If I'm doing this, I'm not missing a second of it.

Bennett bands Seth's other hand around his back, holding him up by the throat as he snarls and then strikes, biting down on the tanned skin.

Seth lets out a little howl, his hips jolting forward as he groans, his legs shaking. "Oh fuck, I'm going to come. Baby, please let me. *Please*."

Bennett pulls back, staring at me in the mirror as he holds Seth's chin up, his voice low. "Earn it, beta. Show her how well you take me and what she has to look forward to."

Seth groans, his arm moving faster as his hand pumps, the slick sounds of getting himself off mix with the sound of Bennett thrusting into him. I breathe harder, spreading my legs slightly wider, whining around my own hand as I thrust two fingers into myself. It's not enough. I'm so *empty*. I want more — I want them touching me, not steps away. I want to be so overwhelmed I can't think.

My legs shake as I try to stay upright. I abandon keeping quiet to cling to the door, too afraid my knees will buckle the second my orgasm rips through me. With a gasp and a shudder, my eyes flutter, and I clench around my own fingers, lips parting to beg for my own permission to come from the alpha still snarling and thrusting, chasing his own release.

"That's it — *god, fuck* — look at you." I don't know which of us Bennett is talking to, but my skin prickles as he groans. "I'm coming. Come *now*."

Seth's breath hitches, and then I watch as ropes of cum paint the front of his chest and his rucked up shirt, covering himself as Bennett bends forward, his hips jerking as he comes seconds behind him. I shriek, trying to swallow the noise as my muscles spasm, my thighs shaking as I lean against the door for support. My toes curl against the hardwood from the force of the orgasm, my chest heaving while I come down.

A small shiver wracks my body, the aftershocks making me hypersensitive and hyperaware that I just got off watching the two of them fuck each other.

It's quiet for a moment. I pull my hand away from my shorts, taking a half step back as Seth's head rises, catching my eyes again in the mirror. His lips are swollen, his eyes dark as he stares at me. There's cum dripping down his chest. He looks *wrecked*, devastatingly hot with a flush to his already dark cheeks and a rawness in his gaze.

Bennett's voice is low, but soft as he kisses Seth's throat and the bite mark he left. "You both did so well for me." His lips move, pressing kisses to Seth's skin, and I can't breathe as his head rises, his gaze finding mine. "You're so pretty when you come for me."

I flush, head to toe, and then I turn and run. Shoving open the door to the guest room, I slam it shut behind me, adrenaline racing through my now-satiated body. My head feels clearer than it has in days, but the smell coating my skin makes me want to turn back around and crawl between them.

My thighs are sticky as I walk to the adjoined bathroom

and clean myself up. When I crawl back into the bed with a fresh pair of underwear on, I pull a pillow to my chest, closing my eyes as I sink back against another one, willing myself not to pretend they're orange and fudge-scented bodies instead.

CHAPTER EIGHTEEN

JUNE

BENNETT'S HAND *runs over the back of my neck, pushing my head down further, taking Seth deeper into my throat, making my body hum with the movement, the lack of control. I don't have to worry, he has it, they both have* me.

I gasp, shifting against the covers as I stir again. It's been like this for *hours*. I finally fall asleep only to have dreams of Seth, of Bennett, of them together, pressing against me, kissing me, soothing the scorching feeling under my skin, like my body is trying to burn me alive from the inside out.

Whining, I turn, pressing my head into the pillow, letting out the soft, reedy sound as I rub my thighs together. The underwear I changed last night is slick, there's nothing stopping the empty feeling from taking over, the urge to be pressed down, to be *full*.

This is what the articles talked about. This feels like I want nothing touching me but another body, preferably one of the men across the hall — or both of them.

I sit up, dragging fistfuls of the soft comforter closer to

my chest, fighting the internal urge to pull it entirely off the bed. The room isn't right. It needs to be smaller, it needs to be darker and cooler, something more comforting for the flash of heat on my skin. The insistent urge paces in the back of my mind, to be somewhere safe, somewhere quiet, to let someone else touch me and make it better.

In nearly thirty years, I've never felt an instinctual need to *find* something, to find *someone*, but the desire is coiled in my chest, making my eyes dart to the door.

There are three alphas in this house.

Instead of getting up, I reach for my phone, breathing through a wince and cramp at the movement. I unlock the screen, squinting and turning the brightness all the way down as my head aches. The last tab I had up was about heat centers here in London — but the information pages all say the same thing. There are rigid rules, interviews that should be given and forms to be signed before the heat sets in, so the omega can set clear boundaries on what they do and don't want.

Ideally, I'd even have met with the alphas who would help me through my heat, but it's becoming increasingly more obvious that isn't an option anymore.

The cost alone is pricey enough I considered a bank transfer to drain my emergency fund. This *definitely* constitutes an emergency, but I don't even think I can get myself to a taxi and to the nearest location without worrying that every alpha in a fifty mile radius would be chasing the car down.

There's a reason omegas in heat don't leave the safe places allotted for them.

For some reason, my mind goes to college, to the only omega I knew briefly in one of my creative writing courses.

She was sweet and quiet, and always sat at the front — where I did too. I remember the day she walked in, grimacing a little and sat near me, rubbing her back. The *second* the professor walked in — a female alpha — she turned in a jolt toward the omega and quietly stepped back and told her to leave the class.

The omega had given me a teary eyed look, clutching her laptop to her chest and whispered, *"I thought it was far enough away. Will you give me the notes? Please?"*

I'd dutifully taken notes on every single thing the professor said for two weeks straight and emailed them to her after every class — but she never came back. I learned she dropped out from a friend of a friend, and I've never been able to get the look in her eyes out of my mind. It wasn't her *fault*, she just wanted to take a stupid college class without everyone making her biology their business.

Closing my eyes, I sit cross-legged in the bed, breathing in through my nose, and out through my mouth, trying to process the searing pain as repetitive cramps spasm through my abdomen.

I can't even think straight right now. I can't fathom staying here — or trying to handle this alone. I'm so *tired* of making decisions for myself. The room isn't right — it's gorgeous, but it's not what I *want*, what I *need*, and tears prick at my eyes as I press my hands against my head, my pulse rapidly fluttering in my throat.

There's no promise that a heat center could take me in this last minute, and it would *smell*. At least this room smells like *me* and the sheets smell like water and rain and the hallway smells like chocolate oranges and the townhouse itself smells like *mint* and —

A light knock on the door startles me out of my baser thoughts.

After a moment, Seth's voice carries through the wood. "It's just me, June."

Beta.

I blink at the door as a small voice in the back of my mind whines.

Safe.

I don't think, I just lift my head, croaking out a soft, "Come in."

Seth pushes the door open, stopping short, blinking rapidly as his eyes find mine. They soften as he takes me in, and then he pushes the door shut behind him — *good* — and he steps over, reaching for my hands, uncurling my nails from my palms as he pulls me into his chest.

"Oh, it's almost here." One hand moves to rub my back and I shudder as I turn my nose into his shirt, inhaling. It's not the same one as last night, but it smells like *him*, laundry detergent, and the lightest touch of rainwater.

Nice, the voice purrs in the back of my mind.

His hand moves up my back, fingers threading into my hair as he whispers, "What can I do?"

"I don't *know*." My words come out as a whine as I press into him, pulling him practically onto the bed with me, my brain and mouth moving faster than my filter. "Am I supposed to stay here? I don't want to go somewhere else, but if I don't go then I'm going to stay here and cause problems for you and your pack. I don't know what's going on, and I don't know how to deal with it. It's like I *can't* take care of myself and I don't like feeling like this, I —"

"Okay, okay." He shushes me, starting to pull back, but I

grab him and hold him tighter, pressing my head into his chest as I try to climb into his lap.

There's a small part of me horrified at how needy I feel as my hips roll forward, seeking him, but the *omega* part overrides it. He's safe. He's *Seth*.

"You're staying here." He speaks firmly as his hands drop from my hair to grab my hips, lifting me and pulling me into his lap like it's the most normal thing in the world. I straddle him, keeping my head tucked into his chest. I'm probably crushing him, but he doesn't make any noise other than a little groan as he mutters, "We'll make this work even if you just want me to pass you food under the door until the heat breaks."

I whine again, raising my eyes to stare at him. "I don't want you behind a door. I want you in *me*."

He glances down at me, and the angle gives him a slight double chin — but he's so *cute*. I slide my hands up into his long hair, tugging at it as he blinks at me, his brown eyes near black.

"*June*."

"Sorry," I mutter the word half-heartedly, not sorry at all as I tug him against me and press my lips against his jaw, sighing as I shift my hips closer, feeling his sweats between my thighs and *him*, long and the perfect thickness. I shift a little, nipping at his ear as I sigh, "It's all moving so fast — I can move away, give me a second —" *Just let me fucking come first.*

"I know it's fast." He murmurs the words, his hands sliding over my hips as he bends his head and his lips touch my cheek, caressing my heated skin as he talks softly, shifting us on the bed. "I'm going to go out today and I'll get you whatever you need."

I shift against his hips, whining when he turns and pushes me slightly off his lap.

"Blankets." Seth kisses my jaw, grabbing my hands in his, threading our fingers together. "Food. I'll get you some toys too."

I look up at him, suddenly finding myself flat on my back on the bed. His lean body hovers over mine, lithe muscle cording up his arms as he pins my hands loosely. I could move him — hell, my weight alone could probably shove him off me — but as his hips lower between my spread legs, I don't *want* to pull away, I want him on top of me, touching me, *in* me.

Seth's lips twitch as he stares down at me. "I don't have a knot, June, you're going to want that. We can make it work with a vibrator."

Or we could make it work with an alpha.

Biting my lip, my eyes flicker from him to the door, memories of last night licking up my spine like fire. I breathe out, and with it, my perfume flourishes in the space. Seth doesn't waver above me, but he does blink again, a little slower, his eyes dropping to my lips.

He shakes his head, like he's trying to clear it, and I hum softly, smiling to myself.

Join the fucking club.

"Last night..." I swallow, letting clarity wash over me as I stare at him.

He clears his throat, shaking his head. "You and I *both* know that Bennett couldn't and *wouldn't* stay off me last night." He levels me with a look. "The door was open, baby, I didn't think I needed to engrave an invitation too and leave it on your pillow, but I can next time." He leans down, his voice getting lower. "The entire hallway smelled like you before I even saw you in the mirror — which means he probably knew before me. And when you left it hung in the air."

Seth's hips connect with mine, making me gasp as he grinds slowly into me.

"And it lingered long enough Bennett got hard again."

"*Oh.*" I gasp as he grabs my chin with a hand, making me look up at him.

"Do you want to know what I did for *our* alpha, June?"

I suck in a breath as he bends down, his lips barely touching mine.

"I wrapped my hand around him and I crawled down until he could fist my hair and push himself between my lips. And I laid there and took it as he used me like the good beta I am. I let him fuck my face and my throat until I couldn't breathe while he pretended it was you, and I loved every fucking *second of it.*"

I moan, tilting my head up, but Seth moves first, kissing me hungrily as he pushes me down into the bed. My perfume explodes as he grinds against me, holding me in place as he ruts his hips against mine. I feel myself get even slicker as he slides a hand behind my head, holding me in place as he kisses my jaw and whispers, "We're adults. Tell me, baby, doesn't a part of you want at least three of us to fuck you through your first heat?"

Whimpering, I bite my tongue as I drag him closer by his hair, nodding quickly.

He pulls back and gives me a positively *rakish* grin.

"I could probably get Theo on board to hate fuck you through it too." His lips part, his eyes narrowing on me. "Make it all four of us touching you, holding you, telling you how pretty you look when you can't stop squirming and coming."

I moan, sucking in a little breath as I hook a leg around him, pressing against him as I tilt my head back, staring at him. Seth's throat bobs, his pupils expanding. Even though he *said* he didn't have a reaction like an alpha would last night in the foyer, I can see it now. It's the same feeling of *need* burning through me, making me want to claim him and never let him go.

"Let me help you feel better, baby." He kisses me hungrily as he holds my head in place, his fingers tightening in my hair as he breathes out, "Let me take the edge off, please. Just one taste of this sweet honey."

I drag him closer, nodding rapidly as his lips drag against mine, his teeth nipping at my lower lip. He drags the touches to my jaw, then my throat, his hips grinding against my sleep shorts.

"I promise I'll make your needy pussy feel so fucking good."

My mouth drops open as I cling to him, heat scorching my skin as he kisses down my throat and nuzzles my chest through my sweatshirt. He pushes it up around my hips, dropping his head down to kiss my stomach, moaning as he does. Seth's head rests there for a moment, his tongue sliding over my heated skin, leaving a cool patch as he mumbles, "God, I want to suck on every inch of you. I want to make you scream and come all over my tongue."

"*Fuck*," I gasp the word as one of his hands snakes up under the sweatshirt, cupping a breast and squeezing it, kneading the sensitive flesh as he kisses around my belly button. Seth looks up at me, his eyes dark as he mutters, "Is this okay?" His hips slide down as he moves lower, his nose brushing my shorts. "Are you going to let me devour you?" He moans as he pauses, his hand sliding down my chest, over my stomach, and then landing on my hips as he holds me in place, whining, "I just know you're going to taste so fucking good. I wanted to pull away last night and make Bennett wait while I threw you on the bed —" He turns his head, kissing across the top of the waistband.

I gasp, my breath catching as he pauses, his eyes flickering up to me again.

"I wanted you in front of me, baby. I wanted you naked. I wanted to be between these gorgeous thick thighs, drowning with my tongue in your cunt while he fucked me."

"*Yes*," I whine the word, pushing closer as he presses a hand against my stomach, keeping me in place as I reach down to push my shorts off. I need him like I need water to survive, air to breathe — I *need* Seth or I'll die here in this bed, incinerated from the inside out.

He smiles as he drops off the bed, landing on his knees and jerking me to the edge, my hips hanging partially off as he grabs my shorts and tugs them off my thighs. The fabric sticks, and I moan as I spread my legs wider, staring down at him as Seth throws them to the floor, dropping a heated kiss to the inner skin of my right thigh.

He curses, his nose running up and down as he breathes in deeply. "I should be fucking begging for the honor to do this." His words make my skin prickle as he nips at my legs, pulling them open wider. His eyes zero in on the space between my thighs as he sucks in a breath. "*Look* at you, so wet and messy. Is this all for me?"

I pant, writhing closer as I drop a hand to his head, pulling him closer as I gasp, "Yes, but I want to hear you beg for it."

Seth drops a kiss to the top of my pussy, right on the hair above my clit as he moans loud and openly. "You're so wet —

you're fucking dripping. Baby, please let me eat you out." He groans, tilting his head, wetting his lips as he looks up at me through his lashes. "I want to drink you down before I leave the house so I remember what's waiting for me when I get home."

Seth's tan hands slide over my thighs, his fingers digging into my skin as he pulls my hips open even wider. The muscles burn, but it feels so good as he kisses me between my thighs, his tongue sliding down through my arousal.

"June, let me *have* you." He looks up at me, breathing harder. "*Please* let me fuck you with my tongue. I'll make it so good for you, baby. I'll make you scream and clean up every drop."

It's the last plea that makes me push his head between my thighs, shutting him up and getting what I want at the same time.

He relents, his tongue moving over me hungrily as he uses a hand to spread me open, licking a line downward, starting at my clit and ending at my core. I gasp, arching my hips and clamping my thighs around his ears, trapping him in place.

Seth makes obscene noises as I drop back to the bed, biting my tongue as I push against him, rolling my hips into the feeling of his tongue, his nose, his lips covering me, eating me, sucking and moaning the entire time. He forces a hand around one of my thighs, and then pulls me open from one side, wedging his other hand between us just to spear me with a finger.

I shriek, coming off the bed as he curls it, his lips attaching themselves to my clit. He's fucking *magic* — that's the only explanation. One quick stroke of his finger inside me is all it takes for me to come with a shudder, falling apart as he suctions on me, his tongue sucking and licking as I see stars, my orgasm taking my breath away as my thighs shake.

Seth sucks my skin pink, pulling his head back with a satisfied look. He licks his lips, then crawls up onto the bed again, kissing me and holding my chin in place, his voice ragged.

"You're cooler to the touch. Do you feel better? Was I good?"

"*Mmph*," I groan, half-delirious as he leans over me. He could slide a knife into my heart and I'd thank him for the orgasm before I died.

My body feels languid, sinking into the bed as he laughs, kissing my jaw and muttering, "I'll take that as yes." Seth scoops his hands up under my hips, lifting me effortlessly and swinging me back up before tucking the covers around me. He lingers, bending down to kiss my forehead as he whispers, "I'm going to go get you a few things, but I need to find our alpha first."

"*Mm*, okay, you did so good." I pull him closer, kissing him again as I hold onto his shirt tightly, my voice soft. "Are you going to let him taste?"

He grins, and when he pulls back it's wicked. "Yeah, baby, he gets to have a taste." Seth pushes my hair off my forehead, staring down at me, his eyes darting over my face. "I'll be back. If you think of anything you want, let me know."

I smile up at him sleepily, nodding. He makes it to the door before I whisper, "Seth?"

He pauses, one hand on the knob, looking back at me like he doesn't want to go — like it would take one word and he'd be in the bed, wrapped around me.

I turn my head on the pillow, my heart in my throat. "Thank you."

Seth smiles, sucking in a little breath. "Thank *you*. That's the best breakfast I've had in years."

I laugh, choking on the sound and throwing one of my pillows at him as he leaves, pulling the door shut firmly behind him.

CHAPTER NINETEEN
BENNETT

WHEN ARIN BOUGHT the townhouse as our London base, he did it with the intent of every member of the pack having their own space.

However, it quickly became clear there was no point in Seth and I *not* sharing a room.

We didn't start out as roommates in college, but the more classes that overlapped between mine and Seth's schedule, the closer we naturally became. It only made sense to transition to an apartment together, and then our half-cooked ideas of a liquor business grew legs and suddenly became a sprawling brand with rum and mixed drinks. There's always a new avenue to go down — and it's *easy* — like everything else with Seth.

I don't regret biting him, especially not when I can *feel* in my chest how earnest he is about the omega across the hall.

I love him, but it doesn't prevent the worry that I'm holding him back from spending time with June — maybe Seth would be happier if he *wasn't* burdened by my mark on his throat. Maybe our relationship is shifting again.

Or maybe I'm being a complete idiot and refusing to acknowledge how much I want her too.

I shove another one of Seth's shirts into the dresser and sigh, hanging my head for a moment. The pile is all expertly folded — courtesy of Theo, as always — but the methodical task of putting our clothes up can only do so much to keep my mind off the memories of last night. Seth's loud laugh echoes through the hall and I turn, glancing at the door as a burst of excitement and *lust* hits me in the chest.

We normally keep the bond suppressed — it's easier than fighting the urge to constantly rip his clothes off — and I'm rocked as the emotions hit me at the same moment that *my* beta comes barreling into the bedroom.

He doesn't give me time to ask what the fuck is going on before he grabs me by the back of my head and jerks me down, crashing his lips to mine in an attack. The kiss is hot, heady, and heavy, and I groan against his lips, grasping onto him as my tongue darts out, sliding over his lips and into his mouth, tasting the familiar notes of chocolate — but twice as sweet, laced with honey and an herbal tea flavor. He tastes like eating a bar of dark chocolate after drinking a warm mug of green tea.

He tastes like sex. He tastes like *June*.

I jerk back, groaning as I look down at him. "Is that—?"

Seth gives me a shit-eating grin, licking his lips. "She tastes as good as she smells."

"*Fuck.*" I whine and grab him again, kissing him harder. The alpha in the back of my mind is going *feral*, everything in me trying to get more of her, more of him, more of *her* taste *on* him. It's the perfect mix, saccharine sweet, unbearable to let go of. It was bad enough last night, slamming into Seth knowing that she was *behind* us, watching the entire thing. I wanted her *so* badly it took a concerted effort not to come the second I smelled her arousal.

Her perfume lingered for hours after, stuck in my brain until I ended up with Seth's hand wrapped around me, then his lips, trying to take the edge off before I charged across the hall and begged her to at least give me a single kiss.

If I'm not careful, I'll end up in a rut — and that's the last thing any of us needs. She's here for her own safety, not to have an alpha out of his mind chasing her down every corner of the house.

But the back and forth might break me.

"I don't have time." Seth whispers the words against my mouth as I fumble with his jeans, trying to get them off of him. His hands slide over mine as he kisses me softer. "I'm going out to get what she needs to nest, okay?" He moves his lips to my jaw, making me grunt when he stops my hand from snaking into his boxers. "I really need you and Arin to make sure the nest upstairs is alright for her. I know we never go into it, but she's going to need it — she needs *us*, Bennett."

The words bring me back to Earth as I hold onto him a little tighter. My stupid, *impulsive* beta, with the biggest fucking heart known to man, the man that I *love* with everything in me. "*Yes*," I mutter, half hoarse as I kiss his jaw and look down at him, pushing the feeling toward him through our bond.

Seth's lips twitch, and he slides his hands over my chest, slowly bending at his knees and sinking to the floor. "You might as well use me too, alpha, remind me what you do to betas who fuck around."

I groan, deep in my throat as I look down at him. His brown eyes twinkle with mischief as I fist my hand in his hair and smash his cheek against the hard length of me, straining against the fabric of my jeans. "Finish what you started, troublemaker."

His grin is wry as he reaches for the zipper. He has me out in seconds, his tongue sliding over my skin, wrapping his lips around the tip as he braces his hands on my thighs. I growl, throwing my head back as I breathe in and out heavily, trying to keep my wits about me as instinct takes over, thrusting into his throat to the hilt.

He doesn't even wince when I pull his hair, or when I mutter curses and chase the feeling of being on the edge, my brain supplying images of him on his knees for *her*, his mouth on *her* — and I'm done in record time as I snarl, breathing hard as Seth pulls back and wipes a thumb over his lower lip, patting my thighs.

I tug his head back, my nails scraping his scalp as I raise an eyebrow at him. "Good boy."

His grin is unabashed. "I know."

It takes me way too long to get my head back on straight after Seth leaves with a brief kiss that's softer and gentler compared to the fumbling ten minutes ago. I press my thumb against his throat before he goes, touching the bond mark as I murmur, "I love you."

The bond hums happily as Seth throws me a little smile. "I love you too."

It's been almost five years since I bit him — and in those five years, we went from business partners to bonded, to part of a pack with Arin and Theo.

I walk downstairs after gathering myself, passing by

June's door, shut and quiet inside. The smell of her perfume clouds the air just outside, more potent than it's been in days, and something instinctual tells me it won't be long before the heat fully sets in.

I don't have much experience with omegas — my father is the only one I've been around consistently — but I've been out of the house and doing my own thing since college. My mothers and he always spent my childhood reminding me I could do whatever I wanted in life, and I've never really looked back.

Barring Seth, I never really found myself looking twice at anyone, regardless of designation. I know a lot of alphas find solace in other alphas, but my designation has always been the least interesting thing about me. Now though — affection tugs at my chest as I hear a small snore through the wall.

I just want to *help* her.

There's a satisfaction in it, something base, quieting the alpha inside me who only wants to care for someone. But there's more — I *like* her — she's whip-smart, tenacious, and stunning. I would be an idiot not to recognize that I'm probably the last on her list of people in this house to court, but it doesn't make me want her any less.

I could be okay with her and Seth having something without me, I could be okay with anything she wanted, as long as I can still have a genuine friendship with her. Her presence makes life feel brighter.

The foyer is quiet when I step off the final stair. I turn, glancing down the hall where Arin's office door is open, following the lingering scent of Theo's perfume. He's not here, I'd be able to hear them arguing if he was — but that doesn't stop me as I step into Arin's office.

My prime looks up from behind his desk. His glasses are

tilted to one side, off-kilter as he rubs his under-eyes. I don't say anything as I take a seat on the small couch that Seth found Arin and June asleep on yesterday morning — Arin hasn't said anything, but I *know* it affected him.

He might be the pack alpha, but he tends to push off taking care of *himself* in lieu of making sure the rest of us are alright.

"I think we should talk." I broach the subject gently, crossing my legs as I look over at him.

Arin shuffles papers on his desk, dipping his chin at me as he mutters, "I recognize it's probably past time for us to have a pack meeting, but I'm worried that this is the wrong place for her." His voice softens as he glances at the door. "Are we what she needs? Is she going to get the care she deserves here?"

I soften considerably, it hitting me that Arin's never been in a situation where he's seen an alpha, or alphas, take care of an omega properly. The Mohans are betas — and what I know of Theo's family has been against my will. I generally ignore the Clarke alphas unless I absolutely *have* to interact with Theo's shitty fathers.

"It's not the wrong place." I clear my throat, giving him a serious look. "I take full responsibility that I did this *without* your initial input. I know Seth was the one to seek her out and give you the last minute heads up, but Seth and I are fully prepared to help her with whatever she needs. If you don't want to be a part of that, it's fine — if Theo wants to fuck off somewhere for a week, that is more than fine too." I stare at him, making sure he knows how serious I am. "But I am *not* sending her away, Arin."

He freezes, and I see a flash of panic in his eyes at the suggestion. "I wasn't going to *send* her away —"

I hold up my hand, stopping him. "You know as well as I do that calling for a heat service would be more trouble than it's worth. We have no way to validate who would be here in *days'* time and I feel like introducing unfamiliar alphas into the dynamic would be a recipe for disaster."

The heat services are good for unbonded alphas to satisfy their need to care for someone, the need for intimacy, just as it's good for omegas to have a safe place to spend a heat — but in *this* situation? I can't fathom letting another alpha near her, I'm having a hard enough time not ripping Theo's head off when he looks at her.

Besides, half the facilities are as sterile as the center she *just* came from, run by the same people. The others aren't regulated enough for me to ever trust them with Juniper.

The mere thought makes my lip curl as I stare at Arin.

"Whatever your reservations are, get over them now or make your boundaries known to all of us." I clear my throat, my words firm and my decision made. "I am helping her through this, without you or not. Seth won't take no for an answer either, and —" I pause, choking on the words.

Arin's full attention is on me now, catching the pause. "And?"

The prompt is soft, but there's an undercurrent of power in it. There's a *reason* Arin is the prime of this pack. Theo's bark is strong, sure, but it's nothing compared to the calm power that radiates from the alpha in front of me. He just has no need to be flashy about it.

"And I like her." I meet Arin's eyes. "I know it's quick, and I know it's baffling, but I do. And I'm not going to lie to her. She's had enough of that." I swallow, leaning forward. "You didn't see her the day that Seth and I went to the center, Arin." The memory of the purple under her glassy eyes and the smell of stress and chemicals on her sallow and sunken skin haunts me. She looked at Seth like he was a miracle when he suggested she was *safe* and didn't have to keep meeting random packs in the hope one of them would be nice enough to sign a document saying that she, a whole entire *person*, would now be their responsibility.

I can't even wrap my mind around the panic it probably caused her to suddenly wake up and recognize her life was irrevocably changed.

"You're right, I didn't see her that day." Arin's jaw flexes, before his nostrils flare and he relaxes back into his office chair. "But I did see her a few nights after." He glances away from me, his expression shuttering as he clears his throat. "But it's best if we don't overwhelm her anymore. So you and Seth will navigate this and I will remove myself from the situation and handle whatever Theo's decision is."

I stare at the side of his face. "Why don't you just *ask* if she wants you?"

Arin gives me a dry look. "That would be too simple."

"Don't martyr yourself, Arin. It's a bad look when Theo's already a recovering asshole."

Arin's mouth twists. "We should be *courting* her. That's what the situation requires — dating, getting to know each other, making her *comfortable* with the fact she's about to experience something she's never had to deal with before."

I tilt my head at him, staying quiet, letting him talk it out himself.

Arin's eye twitches.

"You're a real asshole, too."

I laugh, grinning at him. "I'm just waiting for my prime to get the words off the tip of his tongue."

Arin's lip curls as he takes his glasses off, scrubbing the

lenses with a cloth, his voice thin. "I've liked her since I saw her stumble in *here*."

"And that's a problem?"

"It is when she never asked for any of this!" He waves his glasses around, gesturing to the townhouse around us. "I don't want to force her hand. I don't want to play the heroic alpha, sweeping in to rescue her. She's a *person*. She has the right to decide what goes on in this new and terrifying development in her life. But I can't deny the heart of me, the part that feels *right* when she's in a room. My feelings were instantaneous — and I can't get that *awful* phone call out of my mind."

I cringe, my jaw tightening at the memory of her squawking mother. "We'll have to cross that bridge if her parents don't take the hint."

Arin sighs. "That's an understatement. It seems like a *when*, not an *if*."

It was inevitable in a society where omegas are such a smaller population that alphas would begin pairing together and then falling for the same omega. Packs are as natural as breathing. But there's always been a subset of people — regardless of designation — who believe that packs are just a constant orgy of twisting bodies and sex. They're also often the same people that assume omegas are stupid, weak, and unable to make decisions for themselves.

Judgement from outliers will always exist, but I know what a healthy relationship looks like. I know that both of my alpha mothers love my father more than anything. That they'd give him the world even if he wasn't an omega, because they *love* him. People seem to forget that personhood comes before designation.

Love looks different for everyone — why would you

waste your energy judging someone else? Why waste your limited time alive on criticizing instead of finding your own happiness?

I glance around the office, my eyes lingering on Arin's bookshelves, thinking of our library back home in Rochester. I do love this townhouse, but it has always seemed impersonal — this is where business happens. This is where Arin sleeps between trips to other countries, where Theo rests between making deals. This is where Seth and I run in and out of the door, taking care of international distributors and offers. It isn't home — and I want to show June what life could be if she *did* find a place of her own with us.

"You don't have to save her, you know." My voice softens. "You could just support her."

He makes a grumbling noise.

I look back at him, my lips twitching. "Why don't you take her out? Or have a night in? You could see what happens."

He sucks in a ragged breath. "Are you suggesting I court her properly, instead of sitting here bitching about it?"

"Well, I wasn't going to use those words." I push up from the couch, grinning. "But I guess I need to look for a few courting presents to give her before the heat sets in." As I step toward the office door, I glance back at him. "I'd suggest you do the same."

Arin shoves his glasses back on, griping something about *unruly and stubborn pack members* under his breath as I ignore him and walk out, heading straight for the kitchen. I need to make a grocery list and decide what the omega upstairs will eat during her heat. Food is the best present I can give her on short notice.

CHAPTER TWENTY

JUNE

I FEEL like a new woman after an orgasm and a nap.

My body is liquid as I stretch in the bed, half-dressed, sliding my legs against the soft sheets and humming, pressing against the pillow next to me. The room smells vaguely of chocolate, and it makes my heart tug at the thought that Seth's back.

I get up, fixing my clothes and electing to put leggings on instead of my rumpled shorts, quickly tucking my phone into my pocket and heading straight for the stairs when I hear voices trickling up from the main floor. I jog down them, walking into the kitchen and stopping short when I realize it's Bennett and Arin.

Bennett glances up from a piece of paper on the island, a pen in his hand. "Morning, darling."

I flush, flashes of last night playing in technicolor in my mind for a moment, looking away only to find Arin leaning against a counter, watching me like a hawk.

It's not uncomfortable, but it's *intense*.

He radiates power. Bennett does too.

There's something easy about the way the two coexist — simply accepting that they're both aware of each others' power, but not fighting. It's fascinating. I've never been around alphas that have an unspoken dynamic, but being *here* makes me recognize the way their strong personalities play off each other. And it almost puts me at ease.

I fidget, clasping my hands together. "Late morning, but hi." I offer them a little smile.

"Are you hungry?" Bennett looks down at the paper, writing something. "I can make you brunch before I go to the grocery store. Is there anything you'd like me to pick up for you?"

"Oh." I skirt around the counter toward the fridge. "It's okay, you don't have to cook for me."

Bennett leans up, his hip pressed against the island as he glances at me and then Arin. "Are you sure?"

"I can make myself something." I jerk the fridge open, sticking my head inside and sucking in a deep breath of the cool air, already feeling flushed again. I can *feel* them both looking at me, and it's making my brain a little cloudy as I try to focus on the random assortment of ingredients instead of the memory of Seth's hands on me, his lips dragging over my stomach, and his tongue circling my clit —

"Would you like pancakes again? Or an omelet?"

I jolt back, letting the fridge door shut as I look over at Bennett. "You really don't—"

"You should let him." Arin interrupts me. My focus snaps to him as he clears his throat. The alpha's body *looks* relaxed, but his hands white-knuckle grip the counter behind him. "We've all tried to stop him, but he loves to cook. It doesn't matter what it is." He pauses. "We want to give you what you need."

My perfume lightly scents the air. *Surely, he didn't* mean *to make that sound so dirty.* I feel my cheeks heat, aware I'm trapped between two alphas. Arin's gaze narrows, something *hungry* in the gesture.

Bennett moves behind me and I glance over at him sharply.

"What do you need, June?" His lips twitch at the edges. "What can I do for you?"

Oh, fuck you. I stare at him, my heart in my throat, praying he can't suddenly hear my thoughts. *Fuck Seth too. Fuck* me *because I'm an idiot.*

Two alphas in one room isn't at all soothing. I'm a warm meal with legs.

My skin feels like it's going to peel from my body as Arin shifts, restrained but singularly focused. "You don't have to tell us, but it would be nice to give you something you'd like."

I'm intimately aware of the two of them glancing at each other, playing the tension in the air like a resonant chord. This is a different Arin from the one I met in his office — the sweet alpha who held me and insisted I rest is gone, replaced with a ravenous predator.

The energy in the kitchen shifts, like Bennett is waiting for Arin's thin grasp to crumble.

I feel heat at my back as Bennett moves, resting a hand on the fridge door. His chest brushes me and the hair stands on my arms as the world spins, temporarily off its axis.

Bennett tilts his head down and I look up at him, my lips parting as he mutters, "You're flushed, you should sit down, June. Let me get you some water."

I stare at him, my mouth dry as I nod dumbly.

Bennett smiles, and I turn slightly, backing up a step,

intending to go around the counter to one of the barstools, but instead, I run right into Arin's chest.

My heart feels like it's going to beat out of my body as I make a little noise, looking back at Arin, my eyes widening at how close he is. He dips his head down, his pupils a void of blown-out darkness against the brown of his eyes as he breathes in. I watch his resolve crumble in real-time as I get a hit of mint, the smell alone making me want to fall to my knees in front of him.

Arin could use me and then Bennett could use Seth and then they could both watch while we used each other —

Bennett touches my arm and then he's pulling me away. The space gives me the clarity to blink rapidly as he fills a glass with ice water and then presses it into my hand. I drink it, my face feeling hot as I try to focus on the water instead of Arin staring at me like he wants to break Bennett's arm.

His eyes track me as I take a step toward a stool, trying to ignore my heating blood.

"Will you go to dinner with me?"

I nearly drop the glass, it hitting the island with a clink as I stare at Arin.

He pushes his glasses up with a finger, clearing his throat. "Tonight. You and I will go out."

I glance at Bennett as he purses his lips, trying and failing to hide the bemused smile on his face. Biting my tongue, I glance back at Arin, who looks as dazed as Bennett, himself, looked in the fitting room a few days ago.

Bennett raises an eyebrow at me, his eyes darting to Arin, as if to say, *Well? Don't torture him.*

I sink down onto one of the barstools, looking over at the prime, nodding with a shy smile. "Okay. Tonight."

"Good." Arin takes a step back, brushing nonexistent dirt

off his pants as he turns one way, then the other. "Right — I have — work — tell Bennett what to feed you, please." He leaves immediately and I stare at the archway, covering my mouth with my hand as I fight laughter.

Bennett returns to the list across from me on the island, jotting something else down and spinning the pen between his fingers.

As my eyes fall on him, I soften as I take him in. His long-sleeve shirt is pushed up on his forearms, his hair is short, but I can see the curl pattern on the top of his head as he tilts it at the piece of paper. He's so *tall*, even half bent over — and the room feels small with him in it. There's an underlying authority in the way he holds himself, and my heart flutters.

As if he can hear it, he glances up at me, shamelessly looking at my lips.

"June..." He clears his throat. "About last night —"

I press my hands against the counter, the cool stone cooling my palms as I suck in a breath. "I'm sorry. I never should have done that without asking."

His brows shift, a line appearing between them as he reaches out and covers one of my hands with his. "That was *not* what I was about to say, at all."

I look up at him, pressing my lips together.

He sighs, then steps around the counter. Bennett reaches out, spinning the barstool and moving to stand between my legs, looking down at me. His fingertips brush my jaw, so gentle, like I'm made of the finest porcelain.

"I want to court you." He whispers the words. "I know this has been all out of order from the normal, and I know that Seth has... meddled." His eyes twinkle at the word, and I smile because he *just* cornered Arin and did the same thing.

My body sings as Bennett gives me a broad smile that makes me want to be his sole focus until the day I die.

"I want you to know that if you... have any kind of passing interest in me, I'd love to reciprocate it." He licks his lips, his eyes searching my face. "I'd love to court you, and be whatever you'd like me to be — for this heat, and any that come after."

My heart cracks at the sincerity in his voice, the honesty and openness with which he speaks. Bennett's hand shakes, the only tell that he's nervous that I might reject him, and I lift my own hand, covering his on my face. "Okay." My voice is hoarse, staring at him. "You promise last night was okay?"

"If I hadn't been otherwise preoccupied with Seth, I would have dragged you into the room between us." His head lowers, his eyes locked on mine. "And I should have fucking done this in the dressing room."

I gasp as he lifts my chin, then bends down, kissing me softly.

I tip into him, wrapping my other arm around his neck and to kiss him just as softly and sweetly in return, savoring the taste of orange on my tongue, so bright and vibrant. It's almost chaste, how he touches me, letting me hum into the movement of his lips on mine. Bennett brushes his lips over my cheeks, then kisses the tip of my nose.

"You really are warm." His hand leaves my face, and he rubs his thumb across my jaw one last time, his brow pinching. "Tell me what you like to eat, darling. I'll make sure we have it."

I stare up at him, utterly and completely *fucked* because I was a fool if I ever thought I wouldn't fall for this kind alpha who's done nothing but make sure I'm alright since the moment we met in that stupid elevator.

Of course, it only takes me about twenty minutes to make him disgruntled again.

"You're too amenable." He mutters the words as he kisses my cheek, grabbing the grocery list in his other hand as he pulls back. All I did was tell him whatever he normally cooks is fine — which is apparently unacceptable.

I sigh. "I like risotto."

Bennett glances at me as he lingers in the foyer. "I can do something with that, thank you." He casts me a little look before he steps out the front door.

I watch him go, chewing on my lower lip as he disappears outside, just as my phone starts to ring in my pocket.

When I fish it out and glance down at the screen, the lightness in my chest suddenly weighs a thousand pounds.

Three notifications stare back at me. The screen flashes before an incoming call overtakes the display, giving me two options: to answer or to ignore my mother.

CHAPTER TWENTY-ONE

THEO

My phone won't shut the *fuck* up.

When I check it again, I read only one of the litany of messages he's sent, between the pack group chat and his private stream of consciousness that my phone is unwillingly subjected to.

He's already sent a barrage of photos from nesting stores, of items and various fabrics — all with input about how he's spent the morning shopping for the omega currently taking up all the real estate in my mind. She's living rent-free in *two* places now.

After being reamed out by Arin *and* the events of the movie night, I'm just fucking confused.

I don't *want* to want her — that's the entire problem.

I've spent my entire life actively avoiding finding an

omega that calls to the alpha part of me. My fathers, at every opportunity, have told me repeatedly it's what's expected — to find an omega to *serve* me. I've tried for a decade to get my mother to talk to one of the omega rights groups that I support, to walk away from the men I'm embarrassed to share DNA with.

But she won't do it.

I spent a good portion of time last night in the laundry room, folding clothes because it at least got my mind off the woman above my head. But then I'd had the misfortune of walking up the stairs at the wrong moment.

She'd been standing in the hallway, partially inside Bennett and Seth's open doorway, her hand down her shorts as she gasped and played with herself.

And I'd bolted.

I, at least, made it to my room and my shower before I wrapped a hand around my own cock and stroked myself to release, painting the walls with it. It didn't do a damn thing to help take the dripping honey and sex smell out of my brain. *Fucking alpha senses.* There's no reason for them to be heightened other than to make my life a living hell.

I'm not going to survive this. And all it's doing to me right now is leaving me confused, horny, and a little angry.

I've been hiding in my room like a coward all morning, trying to convince myself to venture downstairs. I'm trying not to pass their floor again. If I have to smell her scent mixed with Bennett and Seth's, I might actually lose my tenuous grip on reality.

Some packs don't intermingle with each other. My fathers certainly don't touch each other with anything resembling love or kindness — though I'm not entirely sure they're capable of it to start. My intent when I packed up with Arin was that we would continue our childhood friendship, but somewhere between Arin seeing me at my worst and me recognizing he prioritizes everyone else over himself — it shifted.

I don't know how. I wouldn't want to fuck *myself*, I'm a goddamn wreck.

One day Arin came home after touring homes with a new pack, driving all over upstate New York for them — and he'd been distraught. After spending an entire day with a brand new pack, in a true honeymoon phase, where all the alphas couldn't keep their hands off their male omega — it'd wrecked him. He came in distraught, feeling utterly unwanted.

And I'd felt this deep-seated urge to show him just how wanted he really was.

I'd dropped to my knees in the living room and made Arin come with my mouth before fumbling partially onto the couch with him, where he'd fisted us both in one hand and jerked himself off a second time while my dick was pressed against his.

It's never been as frantic as that first time, but we *do* take the edge off for each other.

But I've seen how Arin looks at June when she's in the room. It's the same haunted look — the same bone-deep need. It isn't the man looking at her, it's the alpha, with the primal urge to care, protect, *love*.

I blow out a breath and run my hands over my hair, dressed for the gym. I can't stay in my room all day like a sulking teenager. Going to run off excess energy like I have been for the past week is a far better use of my time. And then when I feel exhausted, I'll push myself even further with some weight training. It's better to be totally spent than pathetically waiting in my room for someone to give me an ounce of attention I don't deserve.

"Mom —"

I slow to a stop on the stairs when I hear her voice carrying up from the foyer.

"No." The woman on the other end of the line is so shrill it makes me wince. "You need to *stop* ignoring my calls, Juniper. I've said what I've said, and I mean it. You're a disappointment, I never should have let you out of my sight for *one* second because it's clear you can't be trusted to make your own decisions. If you intend to stay with this pack, you are *no* daughter of mine, you're just a brainless omega whore. I'm disgusted you're even considering it, let alone what you've probably already let these alphas do to you. You deserve whatever repercussions you get."

I see *red.*

I'm moving before I can think it through, stomping down the stairs to see June — sweet, honey-scented June — leaning back against a wall, shrinking into herself, thick, fat tears dripping down her face. She looks up at me, and I don't think — I snatch her phone from her hand and slam my finger down on the end call button, hanging up on her harpy of a mother before throwing the offending device onto a table.

I hope it fucking shatters.

She stares up at me, her big hazel eyes watery.

Fuck, where's Bennett or Arin when you need them?

I can tell from her body language I'm her last pick in this damn house, but I don't care. I step forward and then wrap my arms around her, pulling her to my chest tightly and tucking her into my arms.

She's so soft, every inch of her yielding as I stand there, letting her sniffle and hiccup as I stare up at the ceiling. I don't purr — I'm not even sure I'm capable of it, I've never had a reason to try — but I cling to her tightly, hoping my scent does *something* to fix this.

Seth once said that my perfume is better than drugs, inherently calming. I've always liked that it's fresh; the smell of the world after a nice, long rain, washing away anything else. It's not overwhelming, or overpowering, it just *is*. And it's biological luck that I got a dice roll that made me smell like rainwater over sweaty gym socks.

Slowly, her hiccuping sobs quieten.

As I stand there, stock-still with my arms around her, I wait. The moment she starts to pull back, I let go immediately, looking around the foyer, my voice sharp. "Where's Bennett?"

"U-uh." She sniffles, her nose bright pink as she stares up at me, tear tracks on her cheeks. "The grocery store?"

Fuck. And Seth's gone too.

"Arin?"

She glances at the hallway. "He said he had work."

No pulling him away from that then — he's a fucking dog with a bone. He'd work twenty-four hours without eating, sleeping, or going to the bathroom if he could.

"I'm okay." Her voice is so soft, so sweet, that it breaks a part of me, leaving jagged edges in my chest — tearing at my cold, dead heart. I tip my head down, staring at her as she blinks her glassy eyes at me, determined to *be* okay. *Strong little omega.*

"I'm just going to..." She pauses, her lip trembling as she frowns. "Rest today?"

I nod at her. "Yeah." That sounds... right. Omegas need lots of sleep, right? And probably blankets and soft things and alphas who aren't so hot and cold they give you whiplash. Clearing my throat, I take a step back, nodding toward the stairs. "You should do that. Go on."

She gives me a confused look, then cautiously reaches out, picking up her phone. Easing past me, June glances back one last time before she starts up the stairs.

I grunt, "Don't answer any more calls from her."

She freezes on the stairs, looking over her shoulder with wide eyes.

Clenching my hands into fists, I breathe out slowly, realizing what a colossal fucking idiot I've been. But I can't *say* that, so instead I stare at her, hoping it looks genuine. "Please do not answer any more calls from your mother. They just upset you and nothing she said is true. You're allowed to make your own decisions."

Her cheeks flush and I watch as she reaches a hand up, scrubbing at her eyes like she's trying to stop a fresh wave of tears. *Already fucking this up, awesome.*

She takes a moment, then bites her lip, her shoulders tight. "Thank you, Theo."

And that's it.

Those are the words that shatter my heart to fucking pieces, so tiny, so fractured, that there's no amount of glue that could put me back together.

I would pay to have a bond with her at this very moment, to *know* how she feels. It's confusing enough for me, but I can't imagine what it feels like for her — and as quick as the thought comes, so does the realization that I need to fix my shit *now* because I'm about to watch my future be destroyed by my own ham-fisted inability to confront my own baggage.

I don't even bother going down the hall to tell Arin that I'm leaving. I just turn on my heel and stalk out the front door, my mind clouded as I shut and lock the townhouse behind me. If anyone asked me, I wouldn't be able to articulate the *why*, but I need to leave, and I need to do it for *her*.

Climbing into my car, I choose not to unpack that as I back out of the drive, having to navigate around an unfamiliar car parked directly across from the townhouse in an awkward spot. I growl at it in the rearview, pushing it out of my mind as I focus on my task at hand.

Seth might be out shopping for her — but none of them will be *right*. *I* need to be the one who gets her shit too.

I jerk my car into a parking spot and find myself outside a row of stores, staring down at my phone in my hand as I search *"what do omegas like"* and *"omega nest essentials."* There are *lists* of options, most of them boiling down to the same non-answer, *"A good alpha will know what their omega prefers for nesting materials, but be sure to let omegas make their own decisions in organization and nest arrangement because all omegas are different."*

All good in theory, but realistically, I *know* this heat is going to come on far faster than any of us are prepared for. If nothing happens — if I have to leave the townhouse and go to a hotel for a week — I'll do it, just so I don't lose my sanity *or* make her uncomfortable. But that doesn't mean I'm going to keep ignoring the soul-burning need to provide and care for her.

I'm so fucked.

As I walk into the first store, I'm painfully aware that the nest at the townhouse is practically fucking empty. I should know — it's on the top floor with my room, on the opposite end of the house. We've never had any reason to use it, I'm not even sure we have *sheets* for the mattress.

And there's no way I'm letting her sleep on a bare mattress on the floor.

She could refuse every single thing I buy today, but it doesn't stop me as I walk toward a display of blankets, staring at the litany of options. There's some kind of... book, hanging off the display, with the different fabrics available, and I reach for it, rubbing my hand over the samples of thickness, fabric quality, and colors. A sign next to the display says not to touch the packaged blankets so scents don't transfer to them.

It's all... mind-boggling — an entirely different world that I'm supposed to know about, but I'm oblivious. I tilt my head at the blankets, trying to puzzle out the best one for her, when one of the workers pops up out of nowhere.

"You can't go wrong with these!" He shoots me a wide smile. "As long as you take it out of the package and rub your scent all over it, your omega will *love* it. These are our highest rated blankets, with varying levels of scent-retention and softness."

I shoot him a look and he swallows, paling slightly.

"What is your price range for your visit today? I'm happy to show you options that —"

"Money doesn't matter." The words come out as a growl as I glance at the most expensive blanket and pick it up, shoving it at the worker. "Put that behind the counter, I have more to buy." *Expensive equals good. More money, better materials.*

The man scurries off as I stalk around the store, grabbing things as I see them. There's a pillow meant to support her head and neck in the big, round nest, a set of flickering flameless candles meant to cast soft, ambient lighting, a white noise machine — fuck knows why I pick that one up, but it feels right.

I act on pure instinct, piling it onto the counter before

reaching the section of loungewear in all shapes, sizes, and types. There's some pants and sweats, and then... night... dresses? I stare at the rack, squinting as I try to think of a single time I've seen her in anything but leggings and a sweatshirt, the same clothes that she's worn all week.

Of course she isn't wearing anything else. She doesn't own *anything else.*

The thought chokes me. I know Seth and Bennett went out with her last week and shopped, but I don't think they bought her anything soft or to wear at night. And from the state of her, I don't think she has the energy to go *back* out and pick out items for herself. I suddenly want to buy her an entire separate wardrobe of only the softest things she can wear. No one wants fancy shit to sleep in — just something comfortable.

I stare at the clothing, my mind spinning at all the options. Just as I start to question if I should walk away and cut my losses, I see an older alpha — at least thirty years my senior — with an omega woman, her silver hair pulled back into a bun as she laughs up at him.

The older alpha is doting on her, telling her to pick whatever she wants, and she giggles, hanging on him like a lovestruck teenager.

My heart clenches as I force myself to look back at the clothing rack.

"Those are better."

I flinch, looking up to see the omega smiling at me, her voice softly accented.

There's a lilt to her words as she motions to one of the racks. "You looked lost. Is this your omega's first heat..." Her eyes flicker over me, and I know what she's seeing — a colossal idiot, *way* too old to be lingering near nighties and having an existential crisis.

Her alpha comes up behind her, resting a hand on her shoulder. His presence shakes my mind clear as he stares at me warily. I also know what *he's* seeing — a grown ass alpha who should know better, and a potential threat to his omega.

I clear my throat, trying to soften the scowl that's no doubt marring my features. "Yeah, it's her first one."

The omega brightens, careful not to touch the display, but motioning to a specific pair of silky looking shorts and a thin top. "Go with something like this, she'll want to crawl out of her skin with the heat." Her alpha rubs her shoulder as she smiles at me, lines near her eyes. "Whatever you get will be okay."

I look at the set and then reach for a size that looks right. June's all curves — *not that I don't want to see her in something skin tight* — *but that probably wouldn't be the best option for when you want to claw your own skin off.* The omega peels away from us, going to look at something else in the store as her alpha lingers.

He clears his throat, his voice gruff, but kind as he meets my eyes. "Trust your instincts, you have them for a reason."

I nod at the other man, standing with the set in my hand as I suck in a deep breath. After a second, I turn, stalking over to the register and throwing the clothes onto the pile I already have, pulling my credit card out.

The total doesn't even register as I pay and turn on my heel to go to the next store. Whatever the best is — I'm buying it for her.

CHAPTER TWENTY-TWO

JUNE

THE TOWNHOUSE IS VERY quiet when it's only Arin and I.

After Theo stalks out, I wipe my eyes and stand on the steps, wrapping my head around both the call from my mother, and the way the alpha charged down the stairs like he was going to personally reach through the phone and throttle her.

Honestly, I might let him.

She left me a string of nasty text messages about hanging up on her, and I mute the thread, pushing it out of my mind as I try to find something to do with myself. I only see Arin once when he walks past the living room while I browse the shelves of books.

I miss *home* — I miss my book collection, my shitty secondhand desk with a wobbly leg, and the urge to be productive. This tour wasn't supposed to be long, which is the entire reason I left my laptop at home, but now I itch to do *something* with myself and to distract from the miserable feeling simmering under my skin.

My original flight home was scheduled for three days from today.

The thought is sobering as I stare at the book in my hand. *Is this my life now?* Is my new life just isolation and emotional outbursts, untrusted to be alone, or be able to go where I'd like because of danger? The thought is *crushing*, and I push the book back onto the shelf, turning when I hear a noise down the hall.

I wander out of the living room and into the kitchen, finding Bennett unloading brown paper bags of groceries. Soundlessly, I join him, unpacking various ingredients and putting them onto the counter for him, careful to watch where he stashes everything.

He flashes me a little smile, then pauses, a line splitting his brow. "What's wrong?"

I snort, picking up a block of cheese. "Is it really that obvious?"

Add no poker face to my fun new *omega* life.

He takes the cheese from me and throws it into the fridge without looking. Then he steps closer, his hands sliding over my forearms as he looks down at me, softly cataloguing my features before he whispers, "It probably isn't to someone on the street, but to me? Yes, it's obvious something is bothering you."

The words make my lip tremble as I stare at his chest, unable to meet his eyes. "My mom called."

"Ah." He leans in and kisses my forehead, bringing with it his orange scent, enveloping me in it as he rubs his cheek against my hair, squeezing my arms. "I bought the ingredients for risotto." He pulls back, finishing unpacking the groceries. "I think Seth will be home soon."

Home.

The way he says it so casually, including me in it, in this *place* makes my heart clench.

But my mother's words echo quietly in the back of my mind — *disgusting, a disappointment.*

"June!" I jump as Seth's voice echoes through the house, the front door banging open. "Where are you? Come see what I bought!"

I blush, glancing at Bennett who rolls his eyes. "Go out there before he wakes the dead, please."

Wrapping my arms around myself, I step back out into the foyer, stopping short at the sheer amount of *bags* covering the marble flooring. There are so many labels and packages that I can barely take it all in.

After a moment, I gasp his name, scandalized. "*Seth,* what have you done?"

He whirls, looking up at me with a wide grin, then dances over, avoiding stepping on bags as he wraps his arms around me and picks me *up,* spinning us in a little circle. "Do you want to unwrap it all down here? Or we could get Bennett and Arin to take it all upstairs and show you the nest." He bounces a little, his joy infectious as he looks down at me. "You *have* to see the nest." I feel the warmth of Bennett's presence behind us just before Seth jerks his head up and shouts. "*Arin!*" I jump, but the beta keeps his arms around me, chattering my ear off. "You're going to love it. It's all the way upstairs, but we can make them carry all the shit up, you don't have to lift a finger."

"Oh?" I tilt my chin up at him. "That doesn't seem fair."

"It's biology, June bug, it's what they're *made* for." Seth pecks my nose, kissing the tip before he leans to the side and makes a face at Bennett. "Come here."

The alpha laughs, but relents. And in only a second, I'm squashed between the two of them, Bennett's warmth at my back as he leans into Seth and kisses him once, gently, pulling back before Seth can get carried away.

I flush when a throat clears.

"You rang?"

Seth pulls himself away, leaving one arm draped across me as he looks over at Arin, motioning to the bags. "Grab as much as you can carry, we need to show our omega her nest."

I open my mouth to correct him, but Arin's eyes snag mine. With one look, I acquiesce, pressing my lips back together as the four of us move upstairs, past the second floor with my room and Seth and Bennett's, all the way to the third. In the light of day, I can see the couch where I sat the first night, confused and overwhelmed. To the left of it is the short hall that leads to Theo's room, the door firmly shut.

I wonder where he went. Seth motions to the other side of the hallway. "Theo's up here, but you knew that. He took the room furthest from everyone because he's a grumpy dick." He tugs me over to the opposite end, where a narrow hallway ends on a single door.

Arin casts Seth a look and Seth slows to a stop, holding my hand as Arin brushes past us. There's an unspoken shift of power as Arin steps to the door and twists the handle, letting it swing open, not stepping inside, and instead giving me space to walk past him.

"Consider this room yours, you dictate who's allowed in."

My throat closes as I let Seth's hand go, slipping past Arin into the room.

It's *plush*. The carpet and decor is starkly different to the rest of the house. Instead of the wooden parquet throughout the other areas, there's a thick carpet that I sink down into, my bare feet being swallowed by it. A mattress is set into the floor in the center of the room, cushioned walls around it.

I stop as I near the huge mattress, big enough for multiple people to sleep on it. It's bare, and there are no pillows either, but the low ceiling and the soft, dark heather gray walls make the space feel cozy. Can lights line the ceiling, recessed and on a dimmer, not a window in sight.

I turn in a slow circle, spotting another door on the far wall.

"That's the nest's private bathroom."

I jump, turning to look at Arin, remembering that I'm not alone. Seth crowds the doorway, looking at me eagerly as Bennett hangs back behind them both.

I glance at them, confused. "Why aren't you coming in?"

Arin opens his mouth, then closes it.

"It's generally up to the omega to decide who's allowed into their nest." Bennett's smile is soft as he speaks from behind them. "Invite only. We're respecting that."

"But it's *your* house." I stare at them, my eyes wide.

Arin's smile is gentle. "And this is your space, for as long as you'd like to be."

It's the tiniest shred of control, and I grasp at it, my chest feeling tight as I look at the three men, my eyes snagging on Seth first. "Come here."

He nearly knocks Arin through the wall in his haste to jump into the room. Seth throws his arms around me in an instant, humming as he presses his lips against the side of my face, peppering me with kisses as he mutters, "I *knew* I was the favorite."

I laugh, shaking my head at him even as I lean into the

feeling of his lips against my skin. It takes me a second, surrounded by the chocolate smell of him, before I turn and look at Bennett and Arin hovering in the doorway.

"Will you come into my nest, alphas?"

Arin looks like I kicked his knees out from under him. His eyes go wide and his face flickers between shock and awe before he strides directly into the room, heading to the door to the bathroom and opening it for me.

My eyes dart to Bennett, my heart flipping when I realize his sole focus is on *me*. He doesn't waver on the carpet, instead he reaches me, slides a hand across the back of my neck, holding me in place before bending down and giving my forehead a scorching kiss that I feel down in my toes. He turns his head, capturing Seth's lips again, and butterflies explode in my stomach as he pulls back and glances down at me, something darker in his gaze.

I lick my lips, biting my tongue as I whisper, "Which part did you like more, being invited in, or called alpha?"

"Behave." He leans closer, staring at me like he can see right through me. "Go to our prime before I completely lose the last bit of my sanity, Juniper."

I grin, unable to help myself as I scamper away, going straight to the bathroom where Arin is lingering. The tile is warm under my feet as I look down at it in awe. Arin motions to the huge space — a tub fit for multiple people sunken into the floor — and a large glass shower that's more like a room than a bathroom fixture.

"It's a little brighter than the nest, to help when you're in the middle of the heat and" — he clears his throat — "keeping clean."

I watch him adjust his glasses, biting my tongue as he so

clearly fidgets. "It's very nice, thank you for letting me use it."

Arin tilts his head, eyeing me. "You're welcome. We should have let you use this space from the beginning. Let me know if there's anything else you need, I'll get it, no question." He clears his throat, hesitating for a breath before leaning closer. Arin's warm voice glides over my skin. "I'm looking forward to our dinner tonight."

I stare at him as he brushes past, leaving the room.

I lose track of the sheer amount of trips it takes for Bennett and Arin to bring all the bags up both flights of stairs and to the nest. Seth provides input and commentary as I pull each item out, touching blankets, pillows, sheets, and all manner of other soft, cushy things. We manage to get the sheets on with Bennett's help and only a little laughter when the corners keep snapping off.

"We knew that there was a nest when we bought this place, but obviously we've never used it or needed it." Bennett shakes a pillow into a case, handing it to me so I can put it exactly where I want it on the bed. They keep doing that — helping up to a point, but deferring to me to make the final decision.

"And Theo wanted the room on this level for himself, but other than his moping and crying himself to sleep, it's *very* quiet up here."

I give Seth a look, my lips twitching. "Stop making fun of him."

Seth holds his hands up, grinning back at me. "It's not making fun of him when it's true."

Bennett pauses as he holds a pillow. "Theo doesn't have to be a part of the heat — whatever you decide is *perfect*."

I ease them both with a little smile, wringing my hands together as I look around the room. "It's nice in here." I whisper the words, feeling an uncomfortable itch under my skin as my fingers twitch, eyeing a few of the blankets. It smells like... nothing, just stale air from being shut for so long.

All the fabric is very nice. The pillows are plush and were clearly expensive and meant for nesting. The blankets and sheets were pre-washed and completely ready for setting it all up. But it's all neutral, there isn't a hint of *me* on any of it.

And I think I'd really like it to smell like chocolate and oranges and mint... and rain.

My eyes land on Bennett as I chew on my cheek. "Are you sure it's okay if I add a few things?"

"Yes," Seth answers first. "Like Arin said, this space is yours. Tell us what you need and we'll get it." He motions at me. "And none of us will darken the doorstep unless we're invited, like well-behaved vampires."

I laugh, looking over at him with a wry smile. "I find that hard to believe."

He grins at me, but Bennett speaks softly. "Is there something missing, Juniper?"

I glance at the bedding again. Seth did well, its neutral colors, soft browns and earthy greens, nothing shocking or vibrant. And it all feels luxuriously soft.

"I would really like something that smells like each of you."

Bennett smiles slowly, and it devastates me. "We can do that, can't we, Seth?"

"Absolutely." He answers quickly, moving with Bennett toward the door. Before he can leave, he spins and kisses me, stunning me as he whispers, "I'm going to steal Bennett's best sweatshirts for you."

I laugh as Bennett tries and fails to grab him. "No, you aren't. You're not going to clear out my entire closet."

Seth darts around him and down the hall, shouting over his shoulder. "Says you!"

Bennett curses and runs after him.

Their laughter echoes up the stairs and a smile tugs at my lips as I linger in the hallway. I glance over my shoulder at the nest again, taking it in, letting myself get used to the idea of coming in here and not leaving for a week. I want it to feel safe, and it... does.

The thought shocks me as I hear rustling. Turning back around, I peek down the hallway and find Theo manhandling bags into his room at the opposite end of the house.

I watch, silent as my brain reconciles this side of him — the alpha who comforted me in the foyer, demanded I not answer my phone — with the other — the alpha who barked at me, who refused to welcome me into their house. Which one is the real Theo? Which one should I trust? I know what my heart says, but I also know it's a fickle thing and too easily swayed by the sparks I feel every time I look at him.

You can be attracted to someone and know they're still a bad idea.

The omega part of me, new and unfamiliar, is quiet for once. There's no input from my hindbrain — and I can either take that to mean there's nothing to see here, or that there's no reason to fear him.

Or maybe we've all lost our goddamn minds.

Seth comes barreling back up the stairs, shouting with an armful of fabric. "Take it before he kills me! Grant me the safety of your nest, omega!" He falls into me as I stumble to hold onto the *armload* of sweatshirts and bundles of shirts. They all smell like they were doused in orange juice, and I burst into giggles as Seth grabs onto my hips, stabilizing us both as we fall backwards into the nest.

Bennett's footsteps pound up the stairs as he shouts, "Seth, god damnit, get *back* here! You can't leave me with only underwear!"

CHAPTER TWENTY-THREE

JUNE

I PACKED EXACTLY *one* skirt for my tour, and I'm lucky it still fits.

I was fully expecting it *not* to, but my options are limited for tonight's dinner with Arin. It doesn't feel right to wear the brown dress that Bennett bought for me, so instead, I wiggle myself into a tan suede skirt that's a little tight on my bloated belly. I pair it with the cashmere sweater Seth got for me, and a plaid trench coat that Seth also slipped into the bag under the guise of London being *chilly*.

The air outside clings to winter, and with it, I wonder where I'll be by this time next year.

I push away the strange feeling as I make myself presentable, brushing my fingers through my hair and trying to make it lay correctly instead of frizzing at the ends. All my other clothes are clean again, smelling of laundry detergent and fresh rainwater.

Swiping a light wash of makeup over my cheeks, I forgo blush, the redness in them already more than I'd like. I glance at myself in the bathroom mirror, pausing for a moment as I stare, unsure if it's a trick of the light or if I do truly look different.

My hips are fuller, the skirt pulling over my rounded stomach, and I tug at it, trying to adjust the sweater so it covers it a bit more. It took a lot of years to be content with my appearance, and the rapid changes have made me feel uncomfortable again in my own skin, my mother's voice echoing in the back of my mind, reminding me not to order too much and to skip dessert.

But there's another voice too, deeper, softer — *Seth's* voice, whispering that I'm beautiful, paired with memories of him kissing the very stomach I'm trying to hide.

I give up, grunting at myself and turning away from the mirror as I slip on my boots, teetering on one foot, then the other to get them on. All I have to do is get through the dinner tonight with an *alpha* who is the prime of the *pack* that I've somehow found myself hopelessly intertwined with.

No worries.

I snatch my new coat, swinging it over my shoulders as I suck in a breath, trying to calm my pounding heart as I shove my phone into one of the pockets. Something crunches, and I pause, glancing down as I tug a crumpled piece of paper from the pocket.

Be yourself. If he upsets you at all, I'll make Bennett fight him for prime. — Seth

My heart tugs painfully as I stare at the words, pressing my lips together as I hold the note to my chest. Closing my eyes tightly, I fight the burning in them before I tuck the note carefully back into my pocket. The townhouse is deceptively quiet as I descend the stairs.

I don't know if Theo has even left his room since I saw his weird behavior earlier, and Seth and Bennett's door is closed when I walk past it. I try to ignore the thoughts as my boots click on the stairs, reaching the foyer and hesitating as I stand in the center.

Footsteps echo in the hall behind the stairs and I whirl, freezing when I see Arin coming from the back. He adjusts the cuffs of his dress shirt as his eyes flicker up, taking me in from my toes all the way to my head, his eyes lingering on mine as he smiles.

"We match."

It's ironic — his dress shirt is a light taupe, complementing his skin tone and matching my skirt. His slacks are black, like my sweater. Arin reaches into a closet and pulls out a coat similar to mine, shrugging it on.

"I'd offer to change, but I don't think you want me at dinner in leggings and a sweatshirt." I shrug, pressing my lips together with a small smile. "This is what I have."

He steps toward me, holding out his hand. When I take it, he pulls me into his side, his voice soft. "I wouldn't blink. You look beautiful in anything you wear, Juniper." I don't try to fight the blush rising on my cheeks as he leads us outside and ushers me into the same black town car that Bennett put me in when we left the designation center.

Smoothing my skirt, I glance out the car window, taking in the other townhouses and the few cars parked on the road. My eye catches on a dingy white one parked directly across from the townhouse, but I push the question over it out of my mind. My eyes find Arin again, sucking in a breath as he sits across from me, staring.

"I'm not used to having a driver." I press my palms against my skirt.

"It's easier." Arin answers softly. "We only stay in London for brief periods of time. It was... a stroke of luck, really, that we're even in town." He licks his lips. "I had business in Paris — still have it — I need to go back and facilitate a contract at the end of the week." Arin lets out a soft laugh, running a hand over his mussed curls. "But you probably don't care about that."

"I do!" I lean forward. "Seth said that you were in real estate. Or maybe it was Bennett."

Arin's lips twitch as he looks at me. "I am. I do contract law, but I occasionally help others tour homes or locations. That's how I met Bennett and Seth, actually."

I smile at him, the car stopping and starting in the evening traffic. "And let me guess, Seth just never left."

"That's accurate," Arin chuckles, a fond expression crossing his face.

I feel a *pull* in my chest, like a string connecting me back to the townhouse and the beta inside it. I'm glad to have a moment of peace alone with Arin, even if it's only to get to know him in this odd situation we've all found ourselves in. Still, it wouldn't bother me at all to have Bennett and Seth with us at dinner... and maybe Theo too.

"They were purchasing commercial property." Arin speaks softly as the car pulls to a stop. He steps out first and then offers me a hand. I take it as he keeps talking. "Bennett and I hit it off immediately — we have very similar personalities, I've found. And I'd met him prior at a networking event in..." He squints as he walks us toward the door of a tall building. "God, I don't even remember where it was."

My eyes flicker up and up, taking in the high rise as Arin guides us inside where a man behind a desk greets us.

"Mr. Mohan." The man smiles at Arin. "Thank you so much for your call earlier. We're happy to have you this evening. Please, follow me."

I take in the fancy decor as the man leads us away from the main area, which resembles a regular office building, to a private elevator off to the side. He glances at Arin first as we step into the elevator, and I shift closer to the alpha holding my hand as the elevator itself sways, beginning to rise. I don't have a great track record with elevators, but at least I'm not alone.

Arin bends down, his voice soft. "I'd have you close your eyes, but I'd like to see your face when the doors open."

I turn toward him, about to ask what he means, just as the doors click, the elevator dinging as they slide open. The host motions for us to step off, but instead, I *stare*.

The floor is entirely made of glass, looking down at some kind of club on the level below us in the building. Arin chuckles softly as he guides me off the elevator, walking across the lit up surface into an empty room. When I finally drag my eyes away from the floor, I'm met with a view of windows, the entire wall looking out onto central London in the evening, the sounds of traffic trickling up from the street below, at the peak of the city's hustle and bustle of evening traffic.

I stop near a single table in the center of the room, two chairs across from each other. Arin pulls one of them out, smiling at me as I take a seat.

He takes his place across from me, folding a napkin

across his lap. "I think it was Berlin, now that I've thought about it." His lips lift. "Bennett wanted to expand to a European market, then a year later — the next time I met him, while showing the property — I also met his partner, both in business and in life."

I stare at him, sucking in a little breath. "And you just let them into the pack?"

"I had to speak to Theo, of course." Arin glances at his napkin. For all the activity underneath us and the lights flashing, the room we're in is quiet, only street noise filtering through the open windows.

I stare at Arin, realizing I know *nothing* about any of them.

"He tried Seth's rum and was pretty keen to have them in our little pack." He laughs lightly, looking up at me. "I'm sorry he's not been on his best behavior. I can't make excuses for him, but I do hope that one of these days he can find it in himself to explain to you the reasons behind his actions, as misguided and rude they've been."

I almost say that it's okay — but it's really not. Instead, I swallow and thank a waitress as she appears to fill each of our glasses with cold, still water. Arin orders a bottle of some kind of wine, and then the waitress is gone again.

I lick my lips, glancing around. "I"m sorry, I'm having... I..." I pause, trying to gather my thoughts. This place could easily hold a hundred to two hundred people, and it's just... empty. Because apparently the alpha in front of me *made a call.*

He takes a sip of his water, and then lays his hand on the table, palm up. "I wanted to be able to talk to you one on one." I eye his hand, then place mine in his, my throat tightening as his fingers wrap around mine. "And we couldn't do that with other patrons around... potentially watching. I didn't want you to be uncomfortable, but now I'm realizing I unintentionally did that anyway. This wasn't meant to be flashy, I'm sorry."

I stare at him, chewing on my lip. "People wouldn't be looking at me."

Arin's lips twist as he stares at me. "Oh, Juniper." His voice softens. "They *would*. Not only you, but me as well. You've heard the saying, *money talks, but wealth whispers*, well —" He glances away at the open windows. "I've done well for myself in the last fifteen years of my work. The people who need to know who I am, do." He looks back at me. "I've found something I enjoy doing, and I have found I enjoy the connections I make as much as the deals I seal."

My heart beats in my ears as I whisper, "I don't know how to do any of this." The admission is soft. "I never wanted to be... known for anything." My mind flickers back to my books. "I know that's now how most people operate, or what they dream of, but now I find myself not only having a career exploding, but a world interested in my personal life. One would be overwhelming, both is..."

Arin gazes at me, his lips dipping into a frown. "I can't imagine."

I nod, my throat feeling dry. "I feel like I woke up one day and I suddenly wasn't just Juniper Walden, the beta daughter to two beta parents who wished I was more."

Arin tilts his head at me. "I'm sorry. That sounds like a lot of change in a very short amount of time, possibly the biggest change you could go through."

The server reappears, pouring us both a glass from a bottle of red wine before leaving it in a chilled bucket on the table. Arin looks up, his hand tightening on mine, a reminder that the conversation is only paused, not over.

"Tell the chef the menu he sent over is perfect."

The server nods her head before she leaves the table again. I look over at the windows, sucking in a deep breath as I tighten my fingers around his, clinging to him as much as he seems to be holding onto me. There's something so... solid about him — for as awkward as he is, there's a sense of serenity when I glance back at him and find him quietly watching me.

He's really beautiful. His dark brown eyes are framed with thick brows, a softness in his expression that speaks of kindness. Messy curls are pushed back on his head, resembling slight order, but one piece keeps flopping forward on his forehead. He must have trimmed his stubble, because his beard is a little cleaner around the edges.

I glance down at our hands, my pale fingers wrapped around his bronze ones.

"I think I understand now why Theo thought I was just trying to worm my way into a rich pack."

Arin *snarls*, and I nearly pull my hand back at the noise. His nostrils flare, his eyes narrowing. "I didn't know he said *that*."

A shocked laugh barks out of me. "You look like you're considering ways to kill him."

"A lot of options are currently crossing my mind," he mutters the words under his breath as the server returns with two salads. I finally let his hand go and pick up my fork, spearing fresh spinach, nuts, prosciutto, and dried berries all in one bite.

Arin clears his throat after he takes his first bite. "We grew up extremely close." I tilt my head, eager to *understand* what the reasoning is behind the two of them being the baseline of the pack. "Theo is complicated and it's not my place to say why, but for all his faults, he has a heart that's begging to be unthawed."

Balsamic vinegar bursts on my tongue as I look up at him. "He's kind of prickly."

"He's a fucking asshole." Arin takes a drink of his wine, leveling me with a look. "I apologize for his behavior. I'm very pleased with Bennett and Seth, though, and I hope you are too."

I blush, spluttering around a bite of the salad. "They've been very nice to me."

"Good." He puts his glass back down, and then sighs, laying his fork on his plate too. "If I had more time, I think I'd have more tact." Arin wipes his mouth, his full focus lighting me up from the inside out. "Do *you* want to stay in our home for your heat? Is that what would make you the most comfortable? Because I will do whatever you want, Juniper. I will hire someone for you, I will take Theo by the ear and drag him across the world so he doesn't bother you, and I will leave you in the careful and capable hands of Bennett and Seth — but I want it to, ultimately, be *your* choice."

My hands shake as I place my wine glass down.

How is this the *first* time someone has truly and earnestly asked me what I've wanted during all this? Seth is well-intentioned, but leaving the center with him and Bennett wasn't so much of a choice as my only option.

I stare at Arin. "I don't want to make anyone uncomfortable."

"That is *not* what I asked." He stares at me, his eyes dark. "Was it, Juniper?"

"No." I whisper the word, embarrassment mixing with

something else as my perfume blooms under his attention. I'm not going to be able to bullshit this man — and it's equal parts terrifying and electrifying.

Arin's hands flex as they rest on the table. "Answer me." His nostrils flare. "Please."

I suck in a breath, my chest tugging as I admit what I've known since the beginning. "Yes, I want to stay."

He nods. "Then you're staying."

CHAPTER TWENTY-FOUR

ARIN

She's ethereal.

I thought she was stunning the night she cautiously walked into my office, but this version of her is something to behold. Her cheeks are lightly flushed, the smell of honey permeating the air as we clean our plates, each course more decadent than the last. And with each bite, she becomes a little softer, her smiles growing easier to coax out.

I can't think, because every time I try, I inhale her perfume and feel like I'm reduced to a slobbering idiot, a starved man ready to beg at the feast laden altar between her thighs.

She laughs at something I manage to bumble out, and I'm rewarded with the vision of her head tilting back, her eyes sparkling with *delight*.

The servers return for the final time, bringing with them the chef's signature vanilla bean mousse, which is whipped to a light and airy perfection. June takes a swoop of it onto her spoon, and I watch, transfixed, as her pink tongue darts out. She moans at the taste, her eyelashes fluttering.

I wonder if I'll make it back home to the comfort of my bedroom before I completely lose all my sanity and self control.

"This is *incredible*." Her eyes dart up and she beams at me. "Everything has been delicious. Thank you so much, Arin."

I shiver in pleasure at the sound of my name on her lips. I need to get a grip, because she's a person and I don't want to reduce her to the object of my affections and desires — but *god* do I desire her. I would cut off my own arm and gift it to her if she asked for it.

"I hoped you would like the chef, he's a favorite of mine."

She smiles as she glances down at the floor again, her tongue sliding over the spoon. I clutch at my own cutlery, watching her cheeks darken, her eyes swiping over the view below of the private club, licking the spoon clean.

The sun set maybe twenty minutes ago, casting the room in a golden light that perfectly matches her honey scent. She's seemed curious about the room below us since we walked in, and more so now that it's busier. It's an exclusive club, for members and shareholders of the building — there are offices above us that manage the public relations of well known alphas and omegas.

I have a black card that could get us into any private room we desired.

June stands, abandoning her spoon as she stares at the floor below her boots, tilting her head. "Is it... a business club?"

"Something like that." I let my own spoon fall, standing quickly to move over to her. Her eyes dart up as I gently take her by the shoulders and point her in the direction of the corner rooms below us. "The entrance is just there." I don't *need* to talk in her ear, but I find myself bending closer, whispering the words. "There are private rooms, it's very discreet — and a lot of well-known public and private figures frequent it because the club is known for its discretion in all manners."

She flushes, and I'm hit with a new wave of her perfume, my head spinning as I resist the urge to drag my tongue over her jaw. I want to bury myself inside her skin and live there.

Her eyes flitter back and forth, taking in shadowed figures as they chat, dance, and drink. The other activities are hidden behind closed doors, not matters for regular dinner guests to experience.

"Can they see us?" Her voice is breathy as she turns her head, looking up at me.

"No." I straighten, clearing my throat. "The ceiling is mirrored below. We can see them, but they can't see up. Normally this space is used for dinner meetings, patrons of the club aren't the only guests allowed on this floor."

"Normally." Her lips quirk as she looks at me. Whatever lipstick she put on before we left is gone, worn away from eating, but I don't mind. Her lips are a deep pink, a rosy mauve that's entirely too biteable. I want to sip from them and find out if she tastes as good as she smells.

I give her a coy smile. "The private rooms have one way mirrors."

"Oh." She blinks, then looks down, her eyes widening as she whispers softer. "*Oh.*"

I take perverse pleasure in the way her cheeks heat. Her coat is gone, and in only the soft sweater and her tight little skirt, she's driving me up the wall. The open windows to the London night air ruffle her dark red hair as she looks up at me, running her tongue over her lips.

"Have you had first hand experience in these rooms?" The question knocks me on my ass. She sounds so innocent, like she's asking about the weather, but the smell drifting up from her throat, from between her *thighs* tells another story.

I step closer, groaning softly. "No, Juniper, I have not."

She shivers, glancing away from me and chewing on her lip. "I always hated that."

I pause, confusion sweeping the haze of arousal from my head as I reach for her. Sliding a hand over her arm, I reach down and hold her hand. "What?"

She shrugs. "My name." Her eyes roll, laughing, but there's no mirth behind it. "I never introduce myself with it — *Juniper* — so earthy and free. I shortened it for my pen name because it fit better on book covers. And I always wondered, does anyone even know me? Or do they just know the parts I've parceled out into books, the little bits I've written of myself into my characters?"

I stare, seeing her in an entirely new light.

"I would be happy to introduce you to the club when you aren't about to have a heat."

Her eyes find mine, something darker in them — something that makes me think her mind is too clouded. I want to clear her thoughts for her, give her only sensations to focus on. My brain spins with the sheer amount of ideas, of the *things* I could show her, or experience with her.

"I had to become familiar with kink for a book I wrote." She tilts her chin, nodding toward the floor below us. And *god* this woman, I want to sweep her into my arms as her eyes twinkle. "I interviewed a few experienced persons back in the states, polished the manuscript, loved it, and never could bring myself to publish it." She shrugs, something sad overtaking her expression. "I couldn't do it. My agent *loved* it, but I knew the second it was public, my mother would call."

My tongue feels thick as I squeeze her hand. "You don't belong to them. You're allowed to make the decisions that lead to your happiness."

She raises her eyes, staring straight into my soul. "I think I'm beginning to realize that."

We're both quiet, and I take the chance to move closer, holding her hand in mine as my other one raises, pinching her chin between two fingers. She sucks in a little breath, her head tilting.

"I love to play, Juniper." My voice is soft, thick with promise. "Will you let me play with you one day?"

Her eyes flicker to my lips as she licks her own, her voice breathy. "Yes, alpha."

Fuck.

I dip my head down, barely managing to get the words out. "Consider this me courting you, omega." And then I tug her to me, kissing her with every ounce of my body, pushing every unhinged feeling into the movement.

Her soft form presses against my chest as my lips move over hers. My brain isn't even in the *room* anymore, I'm so overcome by her. She's sweet, honeyed with a touch of vanilla from the dessert, and it makes me *hungry*. I want to eat her, I want to press her down to the lit up floor and truly test if we're hidden from the people below us.

My chest feels tight, something settling in it that I didn't even realize was missing until I touched her.

I drop her hand, grabbing onto her hip instead as she moans, moving into me. She breathes out harshly as she lifts her hands up and slides them into my hair. She's not slight, by any stretch of the imagination, and I relish the handfuls of her hips, her ass, her plushness, as I kiss her harder.

My control slips through my fingers like water as I touch her little skirt, meeting the bare skin of her thighs. She whimpers, and I'm *gone*, pressing us backwards until I knock against the table. It takes one swipe of my arm across it for the plates and extra tat to hit the floor, shattering and clanking.

She gasps, but I ignore her shock as I push her up against the table, using it to pin her back as my hand drops from her hip to the hem of her skirt, toying with brushing my fingers under it, teasing the soft skin of her thighs.

Her whine makes my head spin. "Oh, *yes*."

I stare down at her, the arch of her throat, bare from teeth marks, her hair cascading back as my hands slide up the front of her thighs. I stop just before moving between them, parting her legs slightly, but not very far because of the structure of the skirt. It's okay — it's enough room to do what I need to.

"My love," I breathe the words, kissing her jaw, her pristine throat, "I don't have time to fuck you properly here." Her eyes find mine, lust-drunk and pupils wide. "I"m so sorry," I apologize as I pet her thighs, "but I can make it better. Would you like me to?"

She nods, her voice reedy. "Yes."

I smile, then slide a hand between her legs. My knuckles glide with ease over her panties, the entire seat of them wet with slick, her skin sticky as I rub back and forth, leaning her further back against the table. I crowd her, holding her up as I kiss her jaw, her skin, running my nose over her, drenching her in my scent as her body soaks my hand between her thighs.

"Such a waste of sweet honey." I move my fingers over her underwear until her hips are canting up against my touch, her breathing labored. I smile as I kiss her again, rucking the seat of her underwear to the side, letting my fingers graze over her, parting her folds under her skirt. I bet the view is fucking *incredible*. My fingers explore, making her keen out as I whisper, "I bet you taste better than our dessert, do you think so?"

She whines, grabbing onto my forearms as I brush her clit. I slide it lower, teasingly pushing it into her entrance, feeling the soft flesh relent as I pump a finger shallowly into her. There's a delightful give to her body, but I still feel her muscles fluttering at the intrusion.

"I —" She twitches, crying out softly. "Oh god, *please*, Arin."

I click my tongue, enjoying myself far too much. "Please what? I can't taste you how I'd like to, Juniper. But I'd love to know if you've tasted yourself." I whisper into her ear as I nip at the lobe. "Have you sucked yourself off your fingers after making yourself come? Have you tasted your new, sweet omega slick?"

She jerks in my arms when I flick her clit again, whining. "No, I haven't."

"Well," I hum sadly, then I thrust my finger back into her, making her body jolt as she cries out and presses her hips against me, seeking friction. I can feel her cunt fluttering before I start to thrust my hand, fucking her slowly but surely, getting her needy enough that I can easily slip in another finger. My thumb circles her clit. "Let me solve that for you, my love."

I attack her lips hungrily, pressing her against the table and pinning her hips in place with my own, the table shaking as her cries grow louder and louder against my lips.

"It's a shame the people below us can't see how well you're taking me."

The words have her spasming around me, and I know I'm going to have to leave a *substantial* tip for the waitstaff to keep this discreet, but it's worth it as her nails dig into my arms, her body tightening around my fingers.

"I — Arin — *uh* —" Nonsense comes out of her mouth as her lips part, her head dropping back, her throat aching.

"That's right, say my name as much as you'd like. It's yours. Take my fingers and your orgasm." I don't change a fucking thing about the way I'm fingering her, letting her ride my hand as I smile. "Drench me in your honey, sweet omega."

Her cheeks go scarlet, a little shriek clawing its way out of her throat as her body bows under my ministrations. She comes in my hand mewling like a kitten, slick releasing onto my skin, making everything wet and messy between her thighs and under her skirt as I murmur against her jaw, helping her ride it out. "So good for me. You're so pretty, love. Do you feel better now?"

She nods, moaning as her lashes flutter. I pull my hand out from between her thighs and lift it between us, offering my glistening, sticky fingers to her.

"Open."

June stares at me, her eyes hazy as she opens her lips, sticking her tongue partially out. I place my fingers on it and her tongue swirls around me, cleaning herself off my fingers, tasting herself on my skin.

I groan, pulling my hand back before she can get it all and lick the side of my hand, my nostrils flaring at the scent of her. Scooping her up, I support her weight and bend my head down, kissing her hungrily, seeking more of the taste as I whisper, "Let me take us home, Juniper."

Her head lolls, dropping against my shirt as she gives me a tiny smile, satisfied and flushed. "Okay."

Bile rises in my throat as I stare down at her — because I don't need a bond to feel the band snapping around my heart, tying me to her irrevocably. I'll be inconsolable if this is only temporary for her — I'll never recover if she doesn't end up a member of the pack and a permanent part of my life.

CHAPTER TWENTY-FIVE

JUNE

Arin is a perfect gentleman.

He helps me into the car, then sits beside me as I tuck my head against his shoulder, saturated in the heady mint scent rolling off him. It's late — nearly midnight, and something about the way he made me unravel has given me a giggly, drunk feeling.

I lean into him, trying and failing to stop myself from gazing up at him as we walk back into the townhouse. I wonder if we're going to go to his room or if he's going to come up the stairs with me.

"Go to bed, Juniper." He presses a kiss to my forehead, and in one gentle motion, it feels like he dumped a bucket of ice water on me.

I swallow down bile, turning sharply to the stairs and muttering, "Goodnight, Arin." I throw the words behind me before I run up the stairs, painfully aware of the stickiness between my thighs, my skirt feeling too tight and my skin flushed. He got what he wanted from me.

I don't know why I expected anything else.

Tears prick in my eyes as I reach into my pocket, fisting my phone and the note, realizing I didn't think about either during the dinner. But now I am — I'm thinking of my mother warning me of the way I've just *let* myself be *used* —

"June."

I freeze in front of my door, glancing to the side to see Bennett lingering in the doorway of his and Seth's room. The light highlights the smooth, dark skin of his chest. It plays off the movement of muscles under his skin, not rippled and cut, but instead softer, speaking of a well-maintained diet more than anything.

My mouth goes dry as I fumble to pull my hand out of my pocket, unsure what to say.

"I thought you'd be wearing the dress."

I stare at him, my voice soft as I admit. "It didn't feel right." I turn slightly away from my door, licking my lips. "I... I wanted to wait and wear it for you."

The hallway is silent, the air hanging with tension until Bennett whispers, "Did you have a good time?"

I glance away, my throat closing. "Yes." Despite Arin cutting it short — I *did* enjoy myself. He's an incredible conversationalist, and I felt like I was on a *true* date for the first time in years, where someone across from me was as interested in what I do as I am in what they do. It's been a long few years, multiple dates with men, women, and nonbinary people — but there was never a *click* like I felt tonight.

The floor creaks, and I glance up as Bennett steps closer. He pauses for the barest of moments, his eyes closing as he inhales deeply.

"You smell like mint and honey."

I exhale harshly, fighting the urge to go on the defense, my body prickling, *screaming* to move closer to him. Ever since this morning — since Seth's lips on me — I've felt like I'm on a hairpin trigger. I've mediated it as best as I can, but the closer he gets, the closer I want to grab the man in front of me and *let* myself fall into him.

But the shame fights the feeling that this is how it should be. My mother's voice rings in the back of my mind, harsh and shrill — *whore*. A date with one alpha, a night with another? Who the fuck do I think I am?

I turn, reaching for the door.

"Juniper."

I close my eyes when Bennett says my name, my shoulders tensing.

His soft footsteps echo across the floor, and then he's *touching* me. His fingers slide over my shoulder, the soft fabric of the sweater, touching the side of my neck as he bends down and nearly brushes his lips against the side of my head. He doesn't *quite* touch me, but my skin burns all the same.

"I'm happy that Arin made sure tonight was something you enjoyed." His soft voice has a hint of a smile in it, before it turns earnest. "Did you know that's called —"

"Compersion," I whisper the word, turning my head, my temple nearly knocking into his lips as he looks down at me.

The definition filters into my mind, snippets of a conversation I had years ago with a nice, older beta when I researched packs for my first book. It made more sense to meet someone my same designation — to figure out how he fit into a dynamic that my parents had convinced me that wasn't *for* betas.

"But don't you get jealous?"

He'd smiled at me, tilting his head like my question was something he'd not thought about in a very long time. "It makes me happy to know the people I love are also loved ten times over. Them being happy with each other, makes me happy."

Bennett and I stare at each other for a soundless moment. I lick my lips, and then I close my eyes. I can't think when he's this close — he's overwhelming, like handing a starved person the ripest fruit in the middle of the desert.

It's easier to speak without seeing him, even though he's surrounding me — his presence, his perfume, his *touch* —

"I don't know how to do any of this." I swallow the lump in the back of my throat, fighting back a whine. "I'm scared. I keep thinking I'm coming between you and Seth... that Arin doesn't want something with me because there's something between you and I, and then Theo..." My head spins.

His hand suddenly grips my chin and I look up at him, dripping orange juice awakening my senses, chasing away the flare of anxiety.

"Let me be very clear." His voice is stern as he stares at me, his lips parting. "I am *very* happy that you and Seth like each other. I am *very* pleased that he makes you feel good." I shiver, feeling the burn under my skin as he continues. "And I'm *very* glad that you and Arin shared this evening. I meant what I said in the kitchen earlier, June, I want to court you."

I fight the urge to fidget, letting his hand on my chin ground me. "So it's okay that I like all of you?"

"It is *more* than okay," he relents, stepping closer. "Arin might not know how to express to you that you have a place here, Seth might just embrace what happens, but *I* will make it very clear to you now."

I stumble back a step, my hip hitting the wall, caught in his eyes as Bennett's head tilts down.

"I am not going to walk away if you develop feelings for

every single one of us. I will not shun you for exploring what you want, what you like, and what desires each of us can fulfill for you." Bennett's lips near mine, barely brushing. "In fact, I welcome you to *use* me in whatever way you'd like."

I stare up at him, sucking in a breath before I surge up and kiss him, wrapping my arms around his neck. *This* I can do.

Bennett grabs onto me, holding me tightly as he kisses me. His fingers slide under my jacket, pushing it off my shoulders and throwing it across a table in the hallway before he drags me against his bare chest, his voice rough.

"Your room, or mine?" He pulls back, staring at me. "With Seth."

Sparks ricochet up my skin. "Yours. With Seth."

Bennett wastes no time. He drags me toward the door, kissing me as we go. I lean into him, my hands slightly shaking as I stumble into the bedroom with him. There's a rustle, and then Seth gasps, "*June.*"

I turn, Bennett's hands landing on my hips as he pulls me back against his chest, his lips falling to kiss my jaw, then my neck. My eyes find Seth in the bed already, half rumpled and ready to sleep. He sits up, his eyes widening as he takes in Bennett behind me and my outfit.

"I got your note," I whisper the words as Bennett's hands dig into my hips, fingers seeking my skin under the waist-band of my skirt.

A smile creeps over Seth's face. He's slow as he leans up, kneeling on the bed. "We can talk about that later, baby."

Bennett kisses the back of my head, murmuring in my ear, "Go to your beta, darling."

I shiver, stumbling away from the alpha and toward the bed. A little laugh bubbles up and escapes my throat when

Seth reaches for me, grabbing onto my arms and tugging me against him, making me fall to the bed. I brace myself on my knees as he kisses me deeply. He drags a giggle from my lips as I try and fail to multitask, one hand in his hair and the other reaching down to tug on my boots so I don't get my dirty shoes on the bed.

Bennett's hands encircle my ankles, and then he tugs my shoes off, letting them fall to the hardwood with soft thumps. I hum against Seth's lips as Bennett's hands slide up, over my hips, touching my stomach and pushing my sweater up so he can hold me from behind.

My hair flies everywhere as I pull back long enough for Bennett to tug my sweater over my head, staring at Seth as I kneel on the bed in only my tight skirt and bra, my cheeks flushing.

I don't care what I actually look like, because the moment Seth's eyes track over my skin, I feel like a goddess. He scrambles up the bed, getting himself untangled from the sheets before he surges forward and kisses me again, groaning against my lips. "God, you're so pretty."

I flush, pressing against him, trying to clamber into his lap and grunting when the skirt stops me. "This thing has been the *bane* of my existence tonight."

Bennett laughs behind us, his thumbs rubbing small circles into my back before he grabs the zipper and helps me tug it down.

My socks are half falling off as I kneel on the bed, looking up at Seth again as Bennett's hand skims across the backs of my shoulders. I turn into his touch, putting my back to Seth as I stare at Bennett.

His dark eyes take me in, dancing down my exposed skin. "Just as stunning as I imagined."

I smile up at him, the bed shifting behind me as Seth reaches forward, his hands on the hook of my bra. I glance up at Bennett, locking eyes with him as Seth unclasps it from behind. Shifting my arms, I let Seth ease it off me as Bennett's throat bobs, his eyes darting down to stare at my chest, breathing a little harder.

"Seth," I whine his name as his hands move, cupping my breasts. With one in each hand, he kisses the side of my neck, kneading them slowly as I lean back into him. I swallow another moan, sinking into the feeling of his hands on me, exploring the expanse of my body.

"Why don't you take a seat, June?" He whispers the words into my ear, nipping at me. "Bennett can enjoy the show while you ride my face."

Bennett steps back, and the smell of him leaves my senses, quickly replaced with Seth as he drops heated kisses along my shoulders, kneeling behind me. I watch as Bennett drops into a chair parallel to the bed, against the wall. I didn't notice it the other night, but it's positioned under the huge mirror where I watched them, and my heart flutters at the implication.

Seth nips at my collarbone and I watch his reflection, his hands sliding over my bare form. My body is larger than his, but it doesn't change the revenant way he touches me, his body pressing into mine, me in nothing but my ruined underwear and him in a pair of pajama pants.

"Come here." Seth pulls my attention to him, guiding me back. I turn as he drops onto the bed, adjusting himself as he stares up at me with a little grin.

I chew on my bottom lip, sliding my leg over his chest. Pausing, my eyes flicker to the side, catching on Bennett, uncertainty mixing with anxiety that this is okay with him.

The alpha looks at me, rubbing a thumb over his lower lip. "Sit on his face, darling."

His silken words drape over me and I knee-walk up, Seth's olive-skinned hands grabbing onto my pale thighs and pulling me up, the seat of my panties in line with his nose and mouth. The beta groans under me as he leans up and kisses my inner thigh, his voice hoarse. "Jesus, I want to worship you. You smell like Arin. What did he do to you tonight, baby?"

I shudder, lifting up enough so Seth's hands can hook on my underwear, tugging them down and ripping a seam so the fabric exposes me to him faster. My eyes find Bennett as Seth jolts me down on top of his mouth, leaving wet kisses on my thighs.

"He made me come with his fingers."

Seth moans between my legs. "Yeah, he did." His tongue runs from my clit all the way to my ass, rolling over me. Hands hold me in place by my thighs as he settles himself on a pillow and jerks me down, flush overtop his mouth.

I gasp, dropping forward to hold onto the headboard as my back arches, sitting on his face as my thighs widen. I drop a hand to hold onto Seth by the hair, whimpering as I look to the side and meet Bennett's eyes, breathing harder with the way he's watching the two of us.

Seth attacks me, single-minded, his tongue dragging over me as Bennett presses a hand against himself, rubbing over the front of his sweatpants. His chest moves up and down as he adjusts in the seat, watching us, his eyes scorching over my skin as he mutters, "Suck, Seth."

The beta between my legs complies, suctioning his lips around my clit and *sucking*. I squeak, bending forward, gasping and clawing at his head as the humming vibration from his moans travels through me, clenching on nothing as I rock forward.

"I want your mouth." Bennett's words are rough, his hand pushing his sweats down as he doesn't move from the chair, wrapping a hand around himself and jerking it once. I watch, my mouth dropping open as I squirm against Seth. Bennett's breath saws in and out. "But you're going to come all over his face first, darling."

The words set Seth off, and my body coils, electrified as I press down against his tongue. He thrusts it into me, pumping it as he moves a hand, brushing my clit with his thumb as he alternates between eating me out and sucking. I can't tear my eyes from Bennett as my thighs begin to shake, watching his arm pump up and down as he tugs on himself, stroking to the same rhythm of Seth messily eating me out. Occasionally his hand dips, grasping himself at the base just to squeeze, his lips parting as he does it.

I come unexpectedly with a gasp, clenching around Seth's tongue as I fist his hair and hold onto the headboard with my other. His name falls from my lips as the orgasm hits me out of nowhere. Slick gushes out of me as I shiver, riding the wave with my hips rolling onto his tongue, using him until I feel boneless.

Seth's hands move from my legs, grabbing onto the dips in my hips before he lifts me and slams me back onto the bed. I grunt, half-laughing as he crawls over me and kisses me, sloppy and tasting like *me*.

It's fucking addictive, something obscenely hot about tasting both him and I at once. I fist his hair again, holding him against me as I press up against him, sighing softly and pressing my hips up against his pajama pants. He'd taste so good as Bennett's sloppy seconds too.

A hand strokes my hair and I pull back, looking up as the alpha in question lingers on the other side of the bed, standing over me, his sweats abandoned. I lick my lips as Seth leans up, pushing his pants off as he eyes the two of us.

"Be a good girl, June." Seth's hand skims over my calf. "Turn over and kneel, chest to the bed. Present for your alpha and your beta. Let us decide which holes we want tonight."

I flush, but I sit up, crawling up and turning. Dropping my torso down to the bed, I arch my back, closing my eyes as my heart pounds in my ears. A hand touches my back, following the curve of my body, before another spreads my thighs wider.

"What do you think of her, Seth?" Bennett's voice is sinful. "You did such a good job making her pretty pink pussy wet and ready. I think I'd like to watch you fuck her, if that's what you'd like, Juniper."

I moan, turning my head so I can speak without the covers muffling my voice. "Yes." I nod, swallowing back my whine as I whisper, "Fuck me, Seth."

"That sounds like a phenomenal idea." Seth's groan isn't even contained as his hands slide over my thighs. I jerk when his lips are suddenly on me from behind, sucking and licking up the mess still dripping out of me as I press back against him.

I lift my head, staring up at Bennett as he moves to stand in front of me, my mouth dry. I've never felt more ready to be *used*. Caught between these two feels like an indulgence I should be paying for, a reward for good behavior that I haven't earned.

"Fuck, she tastes like honey straight from the hive, Bennett." Seth pulls back, pressing his lips against the swell of my ass. As he does, his fingers spread my pussy, and then slide in. I gasp, wiggling back against his hand as he pumps them in and out, then he pulls them free.

"Come taste her, baby."

My mouth drops open as I stare up at Bennett in front of me. His eyes spark, and then he leans over me and I hear the sound of his lips wrapping around Seth's fingers, sucking messily as he groans, "Delicious."

I wiggle back, gasping, "Oh my god, someone *fuck* me."

Seth grabs me by the hips, pulling me into the exact position he wants as I look over my shoulder. My heart stops at the view of him moving into place behind me, wrapping a hand around himself and rubbing the head of his cock through the slick dripping out of me. "You want me to fuck you bare, baby? In front of Bennett while he listens to you beg?"

I moan, nodding as I push back against the head of him. Bennett touches my chin, turning my head toward him as he stares down at me. "You're sure? No condoms?"

"I'm sure." I nod again, eye-level with his beautiful erection. Pre-cum drips down from the weeping tip, slicking the head of his cock. My mouth waters as I focus on it, the smell a mixture of chocolate and sweet orange. I lean forward, wrapping a hand around him, my lips twitching as he grunts. I flash him a coy smile. "I'm going to be too busy to beg, I want this down my throat."

Just last week I was an unaware beta happily on birth control. Now I'm a single-minded omega on a mission. I *will* fit the length of him down my throat, even if I choke in the process.

Bennett curses as I wrap my lips around him, sinking my head down and hollowing my cheeks at the same time Seth thrusts into me, my body giving into him like this is our thousandth time together, not the first.

I gasp around Bennett as Seth toys with my clit, setting a steady, deep pace that has my toes curling. I roll my hips back into him with each thrust, finding a rhythm as I focus on Bennett's cock. Bobbing my head up and down, I slide my hand down his shaft until I feel the tight skin, pulled around the ring of muscle near his base.

The knot.

I pull back, licking my lips as he grunts. His hand lands on the back of my head, guiding me to take him again as my fingers explore the warm, throbbing skin. I squeeze his knot, sucking on him as his hips punch forward, pushing him deeper into my mouth. The motion makes me gag, but being trapped between him and Seth makes me even wetter. I couldn't escape even if I tried — and the omega inside me is fucking *preening* because both of their attentions are only on me.

As it should be.

Seth sets a dizzying pace that makes me feel like my body is torn between both of them, trying my best to focus on the feeling of him filling me, the tightness in my body as my muscles flutter around him, and the way Bennett presses my head forward each time he thrusts. It's overstimulating, a perfect fit. I'm *made* for them to hold me like this, to use me. Seth's cock strokes in and out, hitting every spot as I gasp, breathing out as my lips leave Bennett.

From behind, Seth snakes a hand under us, flicking my clit rapidly as my body shutters, unable to take it, dipping lower on the bed as I grasp at Bennett's thigh, trying to hold myself upright as I pant.

Bennett's hand fists my hair, pulling my head back up as

his eyes flash, pressing himself against my lips. "*Suck,* omega."

I gasp, wrapping my lips back around him, letting him guide the pace, guide *me* as I moan and press back against Seth, desperate for the friction I need. I clench down on him, crying out. The overstimulation is too much to handle, and Bennett's other hand wraps around mine at the base of his cock, squeezing himself and my hand as he moans, "Seth, make her fucking explode all over you. Cover him, Juniper."

Seth rubs my clit faster, his chest bending over me from behind as his hips punch forward, bottoming out with each thrust, pounding into me. I gasp at the same moment that I come, screaming around Bennett as he thrusts forward, filling my mouth with a loud groan. The knot pulses under our hands with each twitch of him and Seth moves faster, shouting behind me as he angles his hips and comes deep inside me.

I see stars as he keeps rubbing my clit, feeling him fill me as my body shakes. My toes curl and I pull back from Bennett in time to drop down to the bed, burying my face in the sheets as I shake.

Seth's hips stagger, but he doesn't stop moving, his fingers pinching and toying with me. "One more, give me one more, baby." His voice is rough, scratching over my body as he plays me like a goddamn violin, making me scream as I spasm around him.

A second orgasm rips through me, ten times more powerful than the first. My muscles clench so hard I feel him leave my body, and I shriek into the bedsheets as slick gushes between my thighs.

The room fades as my brain tries to recover. Distantly, I'm aware of a mess dripping down the backs of my thighs as the room fills with the sounds of heavy breathing. The bed shifts and Bennett's hand strokes through my hair, his voice raw. "God, you did so well for us. You made the perfect mess. Don't move, darling." He stumbles away and I shake my head, unable to fathom doing anything more than sawing in breath after breath.

Seth kisses the back of my shoulders, his hands rubbing over my hips. As he moves, he bends over me, getting near enough that I can turn my head. I kiss him slowly as Bennett returns, a warm cloth running over my thighs and between my legs. I'm so sensitive that I jerk a little, letting out a breath as Seth chuckles into our kiss.

He leans up and I watch, enraptured, as Bennett bends down, taking Seth's dick deep into his mouth with a little groan before pulling up with a pop. Bennett licks his lips, his eyes finding mine as he wipes off Seth's cock.

"Time to get you both under the covers." His eyes soften as he rises, getting rid of the washcloths. I start to move, but my thighs shake a little and Bennett's lips twitch. "Let Seth and I help you."

I nod, too tired to argue as, between the two of them, I move from being on my hands and knees to being flopped onto a pillow. Seth pulls the blankets up as he crawls in beside me, his arms automatically wrapping around my body. Bennett disappears into the bathroom before he returns and climbs into bed on the other side of me.

The warmth of his body lays partially over my back, one arm slinging over me and stroking up Seth's shoulder. I watch with heavy lids as Bennett's thumb circles the scar on Seth's shoulder, but instead of jealousy or anxiety, I *yearn* to see a matching one on him — given by me.

Squashed between the two of them, I sink into the

mattress, my body liquid as I press a kiss against Seth's chest, my eyelids drooping lower. He reaches up and touches my jaw, his voice rough. "God, how did I get so lucky?"

My lips twitch as I turn and find Bennett's nose near my shoulder, brushing my lips against his cheek. My voice is raw when I whisper, "I was just thinking the same thing." The smell of them makes my head spin as I murmur, "It feels so..."

"Perfect." Bennett finishes.

I look back and forth at them. Seth's long hair mussed, Bennett's mouth lifted in a tiny smile, and I can't believe it. Reaching up, I brush Seth's hair back from his face as Bennett's lips move over my jaw, settling in beside me.

Between the heat of their bodies and the way we all fit together, my eyes drift shut. I tangle my fingers with Seth's, palm to palm as my forehead rests on his shoulder while the weight of Bennett's head rests against mine.

CHAPTER TWENTY-SIX

JUNE

My skin is on *FIRE*.

I sit up with a little gasp, my stomach jolting with the movement. My hand lands on a bare chest and Seth grunts as I scramble out of the center of the bed. Bennett's arm snaps out, wrapping around my waist and stopping me in my tracks as his eyes snap open, alert in a moment.

"What's wrong?"

"I'm going to throw up." I shove him away, clambering over Seth as he groans. My feet hit the floor as I swallow bile, running into the bathroom and dropping to my knees in front of the toilet, heaving before I throw up the remnants of last night's fancy dinner.

It's nice in here. The marble is pretty.

The sound of movement in the room behind me makes me lift my head, weakly watching as Seth stumbles into the bathroom, half asleep and stark naked. He bends down, pulling my hair back from my face and whispering, "Bennett's grabbing the thermometer. Is it the heat?"

I groan, turning my head back toward the toilet, shivering and hot all at the same time. My stomach roils, threatening to purge itself again, but I'm not sure anything will come up.

"I don't know." His hands feel good as they move over my neck, pressing against my skin, soothing the clammy feeling. "I just felt so *sick*."

He murmurs, rubbing my back. "What can I do?"

"I don't *know*," I whine as I repeat the words, pulling away from the toilet. He flushes it for me — and it's the most romantic thing anyone has ever done for me as I fight back the feeling of throwing up all over again.

"Here." Bennett comes into the bathroom, half-dressed. He hands the thermometer to Seth, then turns the faucet on and wets a washcloth. Bending down in front of me, he wipes my face off with the cool fabric, his eyes searching mine as Seth presses the thermometer against my forehead.

It beeps and Bennett leans back, glancing at the read-out. "You're higher than normal, but not high enough to call it a fever."

I groan, turning into his touch, wrapping an arm around his bare torso as he adjusts, dropping the washcloth onto the tile and winding both arms around me. Bennett rubs my back as Seth shuffles around. He leaves the room and then comes back with a pair of pants on and a can of soda.

Bending down, he pops the top and offers it to me. "Ginger ale, for your stomach." I reach for it, but Seth shakes his head and tips it slightly, holding it to my lips. I sip from it slowly, letting him take care of holding it as I press my shaking hands against Bennett's chest.

Bennett strokes my hair, kissing the side of my head as he sits with me on the floor. After Seth pulls back and puts the can on the countertop, he glances down at the two of us, frowning. "What can we do? Do you want to get back to bed, baby?"

I suck in a deep breath, the adrenaline of waking up with the urgent need to vomit fading to exhaustion as I nod. Bennett helps me up, pushing me into Seth's arms before he turns and opens one of the drawers under the sink.

"I don't know if these will be *helpful*, but I have them." The alpha pulls out a stack of very familiar looking pamphlets and drops them onto the counter.

I stare at them before I bark out a laugh.

WHAT TO DO WHEN YOUR OMEGA IS IN HEAT stares up at me, almost judgmental with its offensive neon color palette and italicized font. Reaching out, I shuffle them, unable to stop laughing at the other titles like *HOW TO BE A GOOD ALPHA* and *AN OMEGA'S HEAT: HOW AND WHEN TO KNOT.*

"Jesus." Seth chokes out a laugh behind me, peering down at them.

Bennett looks mortified when I raise my head. "Listen, the lady at the center shoved them in my face when we left. I didn't know what to *do*. I didn't want to throw them away, just in case."

I lean back against Seth, shaking my head as I put it in my hands, mumbling as my stomach cramps again. "My god, I don't know what I'm doing."

"Why, June," Seth laughs, rubbing my hip. "We can read you *AN OMEGA'S FIRST HEAT: 101* and you should be right as rain."

"Oh shut up." I turn in his arms, pressing my head against his shoulder as he rocks us both back and forth.

"I can make breakfast!" Bennett blurts the words behind us and I glance back at him as his eyes dart down to my bare ass, then back up. He doesn't even look ashamed, his eyes just flicker again, cataloging my body in the light of the day.

I bite my tongue, reaching for the ginger ale to take another sip. "I'm sorry I rushed our morning after."

"Don't be." Bennett's eyes soften, rubbing my shoulder as he shifts closer. "Why don't you both stay in the bedroom and I'll make something and bring it up."

Seth presses his lips against the side of my head. "I think we should have pancakes, because chocolate helps everything, and it'll definitely help this."

I roll my eyes at the beta, then glance back at Bennett. "Okay, breakfast and then... maybe I should talk to Arin?" If my body is any indication, the simmering heat under my skin will only get worse. It's not quite been two weeks since I was at the center, but the doctor did warn me that it could come early, as it's the first. Something about latent hormones and my age.

Bennett smiles, bending down to kiss my head first, then Seth's cheek. "I think that might be wise. There are things we should know while you're out of it, and it'll give us time to get our schedules and food in order." He pulls back, moving toward the door. "I think most packs take the week off, but we'll do whatever you're comfortable with."

My heart flips as I watch him linger in the doorway. "Thank you."

Bennett nods toward the bed. "Get back into bed, both of you."

As he leaves, Seth wraps his arms arm me tighter, crab-walking us back to the bed and dragging me down to the sheets with him. I laugh, turning into him as his hands wander, grabbing handfuls of my hips, my ass, my arms, kissing me again and chasing away the flushed feeling on my skin.

Everything feels better when he's touching me.

I LINGER in Seth and Bennett's bedroom until sometime mid-afternoon.

Bennett brings pancakes up, with a spread of different toppings. Them feeding me turns into lingering kisses that dip lower and lower. Even both of their focus on me can't ease the flushed, tight feeling in my skin. It's like a bad flu, symptoms layering on top of each other, making me feel feverish, hazy and out of it. I don't like feeling out of control, and this makes me feel like a walking zombie.

I finally beg off to go take a shower, loathe to wash off their combined smells but feeling the urge to be clean. My muscles relax under the warm water, and I avoid the scent-cancelling products and instead use the other, lightly scented ones Seth grabbed for me among the nesting supplies. They're made to retain the scents my biology needs in the middle of a heat.

My mind wanders as I scrub my hair — I could get used to this. Last night wasn't what I expected, but I feel an undeniable safety when I'm between them.

I get out, rifling through my clothes and tugging on a pair of leggings and an oversized t-shirt I find on my bed. When I tug it over my head, I turn my nose into the collar, inhaling Seth's light scent on the fabric, undercut with the smell of laundry detergent and a mixture of orange and rain. It's almost comically big on me, flowing over my chest, which means it probably swallows the beta whole.

Still, I love it. It's the best present I've ever been given.

I should move things upstairs.

Taking another hit of the scent on the shirt, I stare at my few possessions, but there's nothing that I really care to have upstairs in the nest with me. It's all already up there — between the items Seth bought me and the clothing I stole from Seth and Bennett, I'm sure I'll be fine.

I squint at the windows, turning away from them. Anxiety sits heavy on my chest as I think about all the symptoms and information I've read about in the last week and a half. Omegas have up to four heats a year, coinciding with ovulation in females. It all comes down to individual biology, and there's no telling what kind of reaction I'll have — it's all up to chance, the same chance that makes omega blood golden-hued, or alphas' silver-hued.

Grabbing my phone, I glance down at it, seeing multiple missed text messages from my mother again, ranging in the severity of insults, from pleas for me to respond, to nasty insinuations. My stomach roils and I drop the device back to the bed, leaving it as I turn away from the room and head downstairs, chewing on my lower lip.

Will I be begging? Will I even know what I'm asking for?

I walk down the hall, hesitating in front of Arin's shut office door, steeling myself to tell him that it's near — that the conversation has to be had *now*. It would be best to be open about it, let him know that Bennett and Seth will be helping me. It's easier that way.

Opening my mouth, I shove the door, and then stop short, staring at the empty room.

For once, the prime isn't in his office.

I blink, looking back and forth down the hallway before backing up to the foyer. I turn down the hall behind the stairs — where he emerged last night — and push open the first door I see. A garage greets me, two sleek cars side by side in it, with a key hook on the wall. Pulling the door shut, I turn to the other side, finding the laundry room.

The smell of rainwater hits me the second the door swings open, making me feel dizzy all over again as I step back and tug it shut. Of course — all my clothes have had that same smell — *Theo* has been doing my laundry since I got here. It's why he's on a little bit of everything, from the blankets in the living room down to Seth's clothes.

I focus on the end of the hallway, heading toward the last door. As I linger outside, I hear running water and push it open, stepping into a bedroom bigger than Seth and Bennett's — almost the same size as the nest two stories above.

The bed is huge. Windows encompass the far wall, looking out to a backyard I didn't even know the townhouse had. It's pretty, and private, with lush grasses and multi-colored flowers. There are even pavers and a small table, though the drizzle of London rain has everything dripping in a fine mist.

Eyeing the bed, I inhale the deep-seated smell of mint saturating the room.

The water stops.

I take a step back just as a door on the far wall opens. Arin walks out, a towel slung around his hips, another ruffling his wet hair.

He stops short, his eyes widening as he mutters, "June?"

My own perfume turns fragrant as I open my mouth, then close it immediately. It's embarrassing how quickly the sight of Arin's half-naked body fills me with incomprehensible *need* again. I fumble for a moment, before finally turning around, just to stop myself from standing like an idiot staring at him. "I should go. I'll find you later."

"June —"

I grab the door handle.

"Juniper, *stop*."

Freezing, I cringe and glance back at him. Arin tosses the towel he was using on his hair to the side, then levels me with a look.

"You clearly came to find me for a reason."

I turn, pressing back against the door. "I — well."

He takes a deep breath, like he's prepping himself for what I'm about to say, only his shoulders tighten with the movement, his eyes narrowing as his nostrils flare, his eyes locking on me as he growls. "You didn't go straight to bed last night."

Oh God. I'm mortified as I press back against his door, feeling like a rabbit cornered by a fox. I'm in Seth's shirt, I probably smell like both him and Bennett, and Arin *knows*. *Fucking alphas and their stupid strength and their stupid noses and their stupid biology that makes* me *want to please him.*

I suck in a breath as I stare at him, my eyes narrowing slightly. Why should *he* care? He's the one who sent me upstairs to go to bed without a second glance. He started it, and when he couldn't finish it, I went to two people who could.

"I spent the night with Seth and Bennett." I blurt the words out, a confusion of emotions rearing up in me — anger, indignation — Arin didn't satisfy me fully, why should I hide the fact I spent the rest of my night with them? Bennett's words echo in my mind — he encouraged me to find my footing with all of them individually — if Arin isn't okay with that, I don't need the stupid, hot alpha in front of me.

I take a step forward. "What, does that bother you?"

He stares at me cooly. "It only bothers me if you feel like it wasn't your choice."

"It *was* my choice." I spit at him. "At least they care. At least they *helped*."

"And you believe I don't care." He stays firmly on the other side of the room, volleying the words at me like a javelin.

"I don't know! Do you?"

"I just don't want your decisions to be based on the proximity of your heat—"

"So you regret last night?"

"Not at all, but we have to think before we do things." Arin's voice softens, near pleading. "I never should have crossed a physical line with you without *talking* first. I can't take *advantage* of the power imbalance here —"

"Oh my god!" I stomp my foot, glaring at him. "You were not taking advantage of me! I begged you!"

"Still —"

"No!" I jab a finger in his direction, fury overtaking rationality. "Because that makes me think that you believe I don't know what I want, and that makes me feel like a total fucking idiot. If I stand here and ask you to fuck me, will you? Will you say no because it's too close to the heat and I can't properly consent to it? Because I sure as shit did when Seth was in me last night and Bennett was down my throat."

He snarls, stepping forward. His voice is a sharp warning. "Juniper."

I glare at him, my lips pulling back in my own little

growl. "No. Don't you *dare* 'Juniper' me. I came in here because I came to tell you the heat is imminent. At least I think it is. But if you want me to leave —"

"No." He barks the word at me. "Do *not* leave."

"Is that an *order*?"

He scowls back at me, something breaking in his expression as his hands fist at his sides. "Do not seek me out just to pick silly fights with me."

"Maybe I want to pick one." I step closer to him, emboldened now.

He doesn't want me to leave? Fine.

"Maybe I'd like you to act like you *want* me here, instead of taking everything slow one moment and fingering me in a fucking restaurant the next, promising me you'll *play* with me." I stride closer. "We don't have *time* for slow — I'm not some barely legal omega who's suddenly hot for the nearest alpha. I'm a grown-ass woman who knows in a few days time I won't have any sense and I want to make sure I'm *safe* and that —" My voice breaks, my emotions swinging a hard left as reality crashes down on me. "— that I won't feel hurt or used."

My eyes burn as I turn my chin away from him, trying to swallow the lump in my throat.

Arin steps closer, his voice softer. "June…"

I close my eyes, pressing my thumbs against them to ward off burning tears. Admitting the same thing to him that I did to Bennett last night feels like I'm carving my heart out with a rusty knife. "I'm scared."

He sighs as I look back at him, watching his shoulders fall.

"I think I'm supposed to anticipate your needs, and I won't lie to you, I don't know how to do this. I feel like I'm failing you, failing my biology, failing this pack — I need to go back to Paris. I have work I should be finishing and a deal to complete."

Something in my chest snaps and I take a step back, my voice barely audible. "Oh."

"But" — Arin stops me with a single word — "I will remain here for your heat, if that is something you want from me."

My eyes burn as I suck in a ragged breath. It's a no brainer. "Yes, I want that."

He reaches up, rubbing the light dusting of hair over his jaw and chin, staring at me — seeing right *through* me and the flimsy defenses I keep hiding behind.

"I don't know that I can do this without something more, Juniper." Arin shakes his head. "I can't stop thinking about how much it will hurt me if you walk away from this pack after the heat's over. I want to give you a *choice*, I want you to feel like you have the control in this chaotic situation, but what happens when it's over?"

I stare up at the ceiling, exhaling a shaking laugh as I try not to lose it. Here I am just trying to make it the next day, the next hour, the next *second* — and he's already thinking about the aftermath.

"I'm afraid if I stop and think about any of it for more than five minutes, I'll fall apart again." Tilting my head down, I whisper, "And we don't have time for me to be a mess."

"I'm not taking you to my bed if you're having any kind of doubts."

I choke. "The heat isn't going to *wait*. That's the whole point! That's why I'm here!"

He takes a step forward, his eyes firm. "I need you to trust me, June. I will find suppressants. I will buy you whatever you need. I will stay up night and day to see you to the end, in whatever capacity you're comfortable with — but what I won't do is reduce this to some biological transaction between the two of us. You deserve more than that, and my heart can't survive fucking you if loving you won't be a part of it. So do not question if I care." He takes another step, almost close enough to touch me. "If anything, I care *too* much."

"*Arin.*"

"Don't tell me you didn't feel it last night. Don't tell me you didn't feel it the *second* you walked into my office." He reaches out, his hand cupping my cheek, wiping a tear away from under my eyes. "Don't make me sequester part of myself away, because what I do with you will never, ever be casual. I can't do this without strings attached, and I don't think *you* can either."

His other hand rises, and then he holds my face in the palms of his hands.

"I know you're scared." He gazes down at me. "I'm not asking for a bond today, but I am telling you that being involved with *me* will not be temporary. That's my condition — if you want me to be a part of your heat, you cannot run the moment it's over. You're *safe* with me, with this pack, but I will not allow it to be fleeting or temporary."

It feels like someone carved a hole into my chest as I stare up at him, silent tears rolling down my cheeks. Arin wipes away each and every one of them.

"I need you to talk to me, love." His voice is gentle as he strokes my cheeks. "I need you to let go and let yourself accept my help."

"Did you mean it?" My voice breaks. "Last night when you said you wanted to court me?"

"Yes." He answers without hesitating, voice low. "I have meant every single word I've said to you. But I won't go forward with any of it if *you* don't understand there's no backing out for me. There is no future in my eyes where you walk away without taking my affections with you. They say when you know, you know."

He gives me a tight smile, like he's expecting me to bolt as he whispers, "And I know."

It feels like I'm standing on a cliff's edge, staring down at an abyss. Seth's insistence that I would be safe here — Bennett's admission that he won't walk away — and now Arin telling me there is no leaving if I stay —

But there are other issues. He doesn't know my family. We've never had a conversation about what I'll do *after* the heat, when I can go home. None of us have spoken about my work, my writing, or my apartment back in Virginia. There are so many logistics to what he's saying. Reality won't stay pushed to the side for very long — I have an entire *life* to get back to.

My eyes rise, meeting Arin's.

But he could be yours.

My hindbrain supplies the thought, almost quiet amongst my anxiety. The deep part of my heart, untouched and lonely, calls out to him even while he's standing in front of me, clutching my face, offering me the world if I just say yes.

My breath catches in my throat. Running my tongue over my lips, I lift my chin slightly, taking in every inch of his expression, down to the slight bump in his nose and the way his eyebrows furrow, making a little line that points directly to his lips.

"I accept."

He sucks in a breath, his eyes flittering over my features one final time, before he tugs me to him. One hand slides around, cupping the back of my damp hair, making my heart burst as he kisses me, sinking every ounce of passion he can into it. It's soul-ending — it's an unspoken vow — not a bite, but the closest damn thing to one.

"Let me show you all that I should have done last night. Let me prove that you, your body, and your soul are safe in my capable hands."

My lips mold against his as I reach up and run my fingers through his damp hair. He groans into the kiss as our noses graze. The fabric of the towel around his waist bunches near my stomach as Seth's shirt rides up on me. I sigh into the kisses, reaching down with my free hand to pull the towel completely off his hips.

Arin grunts, tilting his head down as his eyes spark with something playful. "You've got me naked, now what do you want, omega?"

I shiver, taking him in. His body is a work of fucking art — where Bennett is lean and solid, and Seth is lithe like a dancer, Arin is tall, natural muscle cording through him. There's an undeniable strength, but softer, and I step closer, running my hand over his shoulder and then down his chest, following my hand with my eyes as my fingers brush over the hair on his stomach leading to his Adonis' belt.

"I want you." I glance up at him as my fingertips briefly graze his erection. "You..." I pause, biting my tongue. "You make everything quieter."

His brows relax as he reaches for me, tugging the shirt up over my hips and head, throwing it to the floor with his towel.

His eyes dart down, catching on my chest, and then moving lower to look at my hips. He makes a strangled sound, running a thumb over one of my nipples. "Fuck, *look* at you."

I flush, shivering as I back up toward his bed. He follows me as I crawl up onto it, stopping when he grabs my leggings and mutters, "Lift your hips for me, love."

I arch, letting him tug the leggings off, barely getting on my back before Arin crawls overtop of me, caging me in with his arms as he leans down to kiss me again. One hand caresses down my body, his voice low against my lips. "You're so soft — so fucking pretty. I've wanted to sink my teeth into you since the moment I first saw you — do *filthy* things to you." His lips touch my jaw, my neck, lingering as he breathes out, "I thought maybe I could make you come over and over again until you can't do anything but fall asleep. Or putting you on a display at the club, making others watch while I fuck you until you shake. I'd love to make you so sensitive you can't imagine having another orgasm, and then give you one more while I bury my knot deep in your sweet cunt."

I flush, flummoxed for a moment as I stare up at him. "God, Arin."

His fingers glide over my skin, his lips following as he lavishes my breasts with kisses. Moaning, I grab onto his hair as he kneads my chest, alternating with lips and fingers. "Smell so delectable too," Arin laughs, licking and sucking on one of my nipples. "You're like a marble sculpture, all softly carved curves, a goddess' body better than any of the art I've ever seen."

I gasp his name again as he sucks on my other nipple, his teeth dragging over it, sending a bolt of desire straight to my core.

His eyes flash as he moves to the valley between my breasts. "I love hearing you say my name. I loved hearing you call me alpha too." His hands slide down to my sides, then he grabs two handfuls of my thighs and pulls me open as he kisses down over my stomach, nuzzling my skin. He pauses as he kisses the top of my underwear, breathing in. "I'm going to learn every inch of your body and make you sing."

The sound of fabric shredding startles me as he rips through the sides of my underwear, discarding it only to part me with his long fingers. Arin wastes no time, diving in to lick. I tangle my fingers in his hair, crying out at the feeling of his nose nudging my clit as he sucks on my feverish skin. Seth's energetic eating out last night doesn't compare to the feeling of Arin paying careful attention to each inch of me, toying and winding me up at the same time.

He wedges a hand between my thighs and then thrusts two fingers into me without preamble. I jerk into them, seeing stars as his long fingers find and stroke a spot on my inner walls that has me clenching down on him immediately, shrieking as I writhe against his bed.

"That's it, fucking drown me, love." He pulls back enough to look up at me, his hair a tangle on his head as he smiles. "Have you ever squirted before? Let's see if you can."

He crooks his fingers, his expression dark and wicked as his eyes dart to my pussy. Arin leans in and suctions his lips over my clit, humming as he drags his fingers back and forth.

The same type of orgasm as last night hits me, only this time, my entire body *rocks* with it, my very soul coming undone.

A fire-laced shiver tears up my spine as I arch off the bed, slick gushing out of me, making wet, obscene noises as he rocks his hand back and forth, cooing the entire time. "Yes, oh *fuck*, look at you. That's my good, sweet omega."

He wastes no time, bending down and burying his head between my thighs to gather it up, groaning as he eats me through the orgasm and right on the cusp of another one. My entire body resets as I squirm, gasping and shoving at his head. His fingers keep stroking, thrusting steadily, gathering the slick dripping between my thighs before he pulls his hand away and wraps it around himself, pumping his cock with my arousal.

I stare down at him, my mouth dropping open as he kisses up my body. Arin smirks as he kisses my jaw. "Good girl. That got me nice and wet so I can slip right into you. You feel so fucking good on my cock and I'm not even inside yet."

Oh my god, he's going to kill me.

My eyes rise to meet his, seeing myself reflected in their darkness as Arin smiles. "I'm going to make you come so many times, you'll be begging me to stop."

I cling onto him as he hitches one of my legs up onto his hip, and then he thrusts into me *deep*. His knot kisses my cunt, not pushing in as he grinds down, making my toes curl as I roll my hips against his on instinct, needing the friction, the *pressure* of him all over me.

"*Fuck*." I whine, breathing hard against his jaw as he *laughs*.

"I bet no one else has fucked you this good, hm?"

I gasp as he pulls back and then slams home again. Arching into him, my nails slide down his back as my mouth drops open, my body bowing and giving into his.

"Say it, Juniper." Arin bends closer, his voice dark. "Say, '*No one fucks me as good as you do, Alpha.*'"

It's not a bark, but it might as well be as I cry out, my head spinning as he sets a brutal pace. I tangle my fingers in his hair, pulling his mouth to mine as I bite at his lip, barely holding off from breaking the skin as I squeal out, "No one fucks me as good as you do!"

His hand comes down on the side of my hip, a *crack* echoing through his room as he smacks the side of my ass, making my skin sting and my pussy clench. "Finish your sentence, omega."

My eyes roll back as I whine, "*Alpha*."

Arin crashes his lips against mine again, his voice ragged. "That's right — only yours."

We move together, chasing the pleasure igniting between the two of us as Arin cups the back of my neck, pulling me close as he mutters, "Can I make you come?" He kisses the edge of my mouth, his request quiet. "Can I bark?"

I shiver, my eyes opening as I stare up at him. My body feels like it's going to spontaneously combust already, and I feel my lips part, wondering if he really *can* do it with only his voice.

"You can try."

His eyes snap to mine, then he smirks.

"Come for me, Juniper." He whispers against my lips, kindly, sweetly, the power of a full bark behind it. "Right *now*."

All my muscles clench on command, and I gasp as the forced rush of the orgasm hits me in the chest. I arch into him, cursing as I flood him with my slick, trembling as he grins down at me, kissing me softly again. I'm a boneless disaster, only a body that he continues to thrust into as I tremble under him, tears pricking in my eyes from the overwhelming sensations.

"Never, *ever* question how much I care for you." Arin holds me as I ride out the shaking high. "How much I want to hear, see, *feel* your happiness and pleasure." I slump in his arms, breathing hard as he keeps thrusting, his knot kissing my clit with each movement of his hips. Every other thrust he pauses long enough to grind into me, sending sparks over my skin and making me clench all over again.

"I'm not going to knot you tonight because it's our first time, but you are going to come for me again, omega. And I'm going to let you milk me dry until I'm dripping out of you."

Bliss overtakes my brain, floating away all sense of self as he takes care of everything, keeping me upright, keeping us moving as he kisses all over my face. I'm both with him and not, floating in a haze of pleasure that keeps building and building until I can barely breathe from it. There's a rightness to his touch, his focus being only on me.

The third orgasm is like a weight on my chest, all my muscles tight as my body shakes from holding it back. I don't want to come yet, I don't want it to be over. I don't want him to not be with me anymore — I claw at him again, screwing my eyes shut as I clench around him, gasping.

"It's okay." He murmurs soothing words, kissing my jaw, rubbing my hip as he thrusts faster. I'm crying and I don't exactly know why, just that it's all too much, that it's not enough, that it's him and everything and —

"It's okay, Juniper. Let go for me."

I bury my face against his chest, screaming his name as I come again, completely and utterly spent as he growls, his hips jerking into mine as he comes seconds after me. Arin cradles my head, stroking my hair as he sinks down to the bed, kissing my forehead and slipping out of me.

I turn into his touch blindly, burrowing against him as my heart jerks, the tears flooding down my face as I try to get ahold of myself, stuttering, "D-do you need to go?"

He stiffens slightly. "No, love." The blankets lay heavy on my satiated, sticky skin as he tucks us in, kissing my jaw. "We're going to lay here, and you're going to rest." Arin touches my chin and I raise my eyes, only to see him gaze down at me like I'm the only other person on the planet. His thumbs carefully wipe over my cheeks, his lips chasing the touch, his voice gentle. "You're going to tell me every minuscule thing you need for your heat."

I shift, biting my tongue as anxiety creeps in. "Why?"

Arin pulls me closer, grazing his lips against mine again and again. "Because I want to. Because I'm going to take care of you. Because you're not leaving this bed or my arms until you let me solve every problem that's bothering you, and provide every single thing you still need. Because that's what alphas do."

I squint up at him, one of my hands snaking around to touch his side, breathing in raggedly. "I don't —"

His lips twitch. "Juniper, I *want* to. Please let me?"

The words stop my protests before I can even start. I scoff, burying my face in the crook of his neck, muttering softly, "Okay."

CHAPTER TWENTY-SEVEN

THEO

THERE IS no amount of exercise that will solve this.

This being the fact my dick enters a room before I do.

I grumble as I readjust myself in my gym shorts. I squeeze my hand once, trying to release some of the aching tension as I stare in the mirror. They could kick me out of the private gym for being indecent at this rate, it looks like I'm smuggling a fucking two-liter in my shorts.

I've already jerked off *twice* this morning in the shower, because I'm a goddamn wreck.

Last night, I headed downstairs to grab a late night snack when I heard noises. I thought everyone was already asleep, but as I slowed on the second floor, I found myself moving toward Bennett and Seth's open door.

I *shouldn't* have — but sometimes they like to leave it open as an... invitation of sorts.

Their open-door policy has benefited me. When I'm in their room, Bennett and I dominate Seth — together. It's a release to be in control, but I'm always aware that Bennett has the final word.

I only looked in because I thought it was just the two of them — but then June's smell hit me and I felt like I was drowning. Her back arched, her thighs spread as she sat on top of Seth's face, riding her way to a gasping, mewling orgasm that left me stumbling back in shock.

The alpha in me didn't know what to do. Part of me wanted to barge in — but stopping them didn't feel right — and joining them *wasn't* an option. Instead I'd gone the rest of the way downstairs and mindlessly grabbed my keys, leaving for the gym in the middle of the night to go sweat off the fact I can't even be in my own fucking house anymore without losing my mind.

She's all I've wanted for the last week, and she probably won't even let me touch her at this point. All I've done is yell, make her feel like shit, and keep a random assortment of bags piled in the corner of my room because I'm too embarrassed to give her what I bought for the nest.

Stalking downstairs, I shake out my hands, all my muscles screaming and my body aching from the rigorous gym routines I've been putting myself through. I turn, heading down the hallway toward Arin's room, sucking in a breath that I swear tastes of honey.

Now I'm hallucinating her perfume. Great.

I make a pitstop in the laundry room, switching out two loads of clothes and dropping some clean towels into a basket to fold later. I can at least *do* something with the mindless housework to keep myself from thinking of her. I haven't seen Bennett or Seth this morning, though I did scrub a pan earlier and put some leftover pancake batter in the fridge.

It's probably best not to breathe in the house anymore — they're probably going to fuck all over it. I'm going to have to open all the windows and invest in a mask so I don't go insane.

I stop as I stare at the basket of towels.

Or I could just *leave.*

If her heat is truly this close — she doesn't want me anyway — I could go to a hotel early. I can tell Arin and maybe he'll come with me — fuck the townhouse — she, Bennett, and Seth can defile every surface for all I care. Then we hire professional cleaners, she goes on her merry way back to America, and I lobotomize myself so this never happens again with any other omegas.

I stride out of the laundry room, my mind made up. My hand is on the doorknob to Arin's room before the sounds coming from inside register in my brain.

"No one fucks me as good as you do!"

My mind short-circuits as I stare at the door, willing myself not to lean forward to look through the small open sliver, but my body does what it wants.

Arin's soft accent spews filthy things, the sound of their bodies colliding, skin against skin slapping, matching the tempo of their movements as I glance through the door and see Arin's corded back, lean, bent over her on his bed, slamming home between her legs. From this angle, I can see June's face, flushed, pink lips open as she cries out, gasping and moaning.

Where Bennett lets me join in and Seth eagerly accepts whatever we do to him — Arin is different.

When I end up in Arin's room — he's in control. It looks like he's in control of her too.

What the fuck am I doing?

I jerk away and turn around, the floor creaking for a heart-stopping moment, but the sounds behind me don't falter. I can smell it now, the mix of mint, burning down my throat, soothed only by the herbal honey — it's like it's dripping from the fucking *walls*.

How didn't I notice that? How didn't I hear that?

I barge out of the hallway, nearly barreling into Seth in the foyer.

The beta takes a startled step back, looking up at me. "*Whoa*, Theo —"

"Gotta leave —" I cut myself off, my eyes finding Bennett immediately.

Fuck, fuck, they both know. Everyone knows I'm a disaster.

"Where's June, Theo?" Bennett's calm, even voice is like nails on a chalkboard.

I make a strangled noise, stepping toward the front door even as I look back at the hallway to Arin's room. Giving it away, giving *them* away.

Seth snorts, his eyes darting down to the front of my shorts. "What's wrong, buddy? Got a *hard* problem you can't solve?"

I growl at him, shooting him a look as anger flares through me. "*None* of this would be happening if *you* hadn't brought her into this *house*, into our *space* —"

"Theo," Bennett barks my name, "go take a walk."

Fuck him.

He's right.

But also *fuck* him.

I stalk away, ripping open the front door and inhaling lungfuls of fresh air as I run down the steps and out the front gate, fleeing from the only place that's ever truly felt like *home* to me.

CHAPTER TWENTY-EIGHT
JUNE

It's the next morning before Arin lets me leave his bed. I gave him a list of three foods that sounded nice for my heat — and, in exchange, he gifted me one of his shirts for my nest. He even managed to coax me into considering the fact that I *might* just feel better if I spend the next few nights in the nest.

I *am* considering it, even as I get redressed with him, ending up in Seth's shirt and my leggings again. Arin slides an arm around me as we step into the kitchen together. The nest is just so far from the rest of the house and I don't relish the thought of sleeping up there all alone.

Opening the fridge, I rummage around for a moment before pulling out the extra pancake batter and holding it up to Arin. "It's really handy to have a chef in the pack."

He glances over at me, his smile softening as he stares at me. "Yes, it is."

It takes me a second to process my own words, freezing in the middle of making the first pancake. Arin moves around, slicing up fruit, the clock ticking closer to lunch than is really socially acceptable to still be eating our first meal of the day, but my heart aches as I realize how easy the sentence escaped.

No running, that was Arin's caveat.

He glances up as he slices an apple, looking over at the pan. "You're burning it."

"Oh *shit*." I look down sharply, jerking the pan away from the heat and grabbing a spatula, prodding at the charred pancake burnt to the pan. "Oh *no*."

Arin laughs as he comes up behind me. "Be careful, don't burn yourself — *how* did you manage to scald it to the surface? It's *ash*, Juniper."

"I don't know!" I start to laugh, leaning back against him as I look down at the destroyed pancake, the ruined pan, and the sheer *ridiculousness* of the entire situation.

He wraps an arm around me, pushing my hand down to drop the pan back onto the stove. It clanks before I turn in his arms, lifting up on my toes to kiss him softly. My body sinks against his chest with the touch of our lips, like nothing else matters except his hands eagerly moving to wrap around me.

There's a quiet voice in the back of my mind, purring happily. My hindbrain preens, whispering the words, *Prime — home.*

Arin cups my face, kissing my slower, unknowingly making my heart sing.

When I pull back, his eyes flicker over my face, his expression gentle as he tucks my hair behind my ears. I smile at him, wrapping my arms around his neck and hugging him tightly, mumbling sheepishly, "I'm sorry about the pan."

"I can afford another one."

I laugh, shaking my head at him. Pulling away, I turn and

reach for the pan again to figure out if I can clean it up — but I stop short when I see Seth leaning in the archway to the kitchen. There's a *giant* shit-eating grin on his face. Bennett lingers behind him, his eyes landing on me as his lips lift at the edges.

The small smile quickly fades, though, when he sees the stove.

"*My pan!*" Bennett exclaims as he strides into the kitchen.

I back up closer to Arin, grimacing. "I'm sorry."

The other alpha makes a mournful sound as he prods at the ruined bottom of the cookware, the pancake so stuck it makes a squeaking, crunchy sound.

Seth rubs Bennett's back. "We can buy another one."

Bennett sighs heavily, looking up at me. "What in the *world* did you have the stove set to?"

I glance down at the knobs, frowning. "High?"

"For a *pancake?*"

I press back against Arin unconsciously, turning my head slightly. "Protect me?"

He wraps an arm around me firmly, without question. Arin's hand splays across my stomach as his eyes narrow. "This just means you should teach her how to cook a few things, right Bennett?"

Bennett looks up from the ruined pan, then takes us in. "Yes, and the first lesson is that pancakes don't need to be charred into *hockey pucks.*"

Seth rounds the island as I try to hide my snicker. He reaches for me, the grin still on his face, but Arin growls *just* slightly, pulling me out of reach of Seth's hands.

I flush, glancing up at him. "Are you territorial?"

Arin pauses, then has the good graces to look mildly

embarrassed. "Potentially, I don't think I've ever had a reason to be before now."

I lean up, unable to help myself, pressing a kiss to his jaw. Seth groans from beside us and I turn to look at him.

He pouts. "I saw you *first*." I let out a bark of laughter as he steals me from Arin's arms, eliciting another growl from the alpha as Seth whisks me to the other side of the counter, past Bennett poking at the ruined pan. Seth bends down, kissing me sweetly, his voice barely audible. "You good?"

I nod, kissing him back as I smile against his lips. "Mhm, all okay."

"You smell like minty green tea." He laughs as his hands squeeze my sides. "Don't let any of them kill me when I inevitably have to kidnap you from their territorial asses."

"I promise. I'd never let them hurt you." I kiss Seth's nose, pleased that our faces are almost equal, our heights evenly matched compared to mine and Arin's, or even mine and Bennett's. The warmth in my chest blooms, but there's a small feeling that something is missing as I sink into Seth's arms.

Arin picks up an apple slice, holding it out to me. I reach for it, but he pulls it back and shakes his head, pressing it against my lips.

I scoff at him. "I think I can feed myself."

Arin steps closer, his fingers brushing my lips. "You won't *want* to when your heat sets in, we might as well start trying now before you bite my hand off later."

I scowl at him, but open my mouth.

Arin puts the apple slice on my tongue, tilting his head down as he whispers, "I can't wait to make you take Bennett or Seth like this. Maybe both of them. The last to come gets your cunt."

I nearly choke as my eyes widen, jerking back into Seth as the smell of my perfume floods the kitchen. "*Arin.*" I cover my mouth, trying to chew the apple at the same time Seth wraps an arm around me, groaning and burying his head in my neck.

"If you fuck in this kitchen, you better not break any more of my cookware." Bennett drops the pan into the trash can, sighing heavily. "It's ruined. I can't salvage that."

I pull away from Seth, feeling genuinely bad as I move over to Bennett. Sliding my hand over his back, I rub it, my heart tugging. "I'm so sorry, I'll get you a new one. I should have been paying more attention but I got distracted."

Bennett tilts his head down, kissing my forehead. "If anything, Arin is right. I'm giving you cooking lessons. How have you kept yourself alive for nearly thirty years?"

"Take out?"

"Oh."

The kitchen goes quiet and I startle. Turning sharply, I freeze at the sight of Theo filling the doorway to the kitchen. He's in gym clothes, his eyes darting around the room in a panic.

"You're all in here." Theo fidgets, and then his eyes find me. He stares for a moment, pressing his lips together, almost like he's *nervous*, before he nods once and hooks a thumb over his shoulder. "I got you stuff for your nest." He blurts the words. "Or... whatever you might use it for. I brought it all downstairs. But now I think I should have just left it up there. It doesn't make any sense for it to be down here. Sorry about that."

I stare at him, opening and closing my mouth.

"I'll just return it —"

"No." I leap forward and Theo *flinches*. Closer, I can see

the sheer panic on his face. His eyes dart behind me and someone's warmth heats my back. Getting a hit of mint, I stand up straight. "Theo is going to show me what he bought." I announce it to the room, my eyes staying on the big alpha, thinking of all the bags he was stuffing into his room days ago. "Lead the way."

His eyes widen as he steps back out into the foyer. I follow him and have to suppress my shocked gasp. Random piles fall over, triple the amount of bags that Seth bought me all scattered across the floor. Theo looks ready to bolt as he points at random piles.

"Those are blankets. Those are pillows. That's a white noise machine. There's clothes in that one, because I know you don't have a lot here and I thought pajamas would be nice."

I nod slowly, taking it all in as I bend down to the first bag. I pull the softest blanket out, getting a hit of rain off of it. The fabric is a deep blue color, reminiscent of the eyes of the alpha hovering above me.

"Why?" I whisper the word, my heart lurching.

His voice breaks as he steps closer. "You need it." Theo fidgets, then his expression shuts itself off from me. "Keep what you want, anything else can be donated to an omega help shelter —" He takes a step toward the front door. "I'm going to the gym."

I kneel in the foyer, utterly baffled as he runs away from me, yet again. As the front door slams behind him, I reach into one of the bags to find a well-worn sweatshirt, absolutely drenched in his petrichor perfume.

CHAPTER TWENTY-NINE

JUNE

"We'll be back soon."

Bennett kisses my forehead before he pulls away. I fight back a complaint as I look at him and Seth. Arin left for Paris this morning to finalize the deal he left on the table last week. I know they all have things to do, *jobs* to actually show up for, but everything feels *wrong* today.

Seth steps back into the foyer, rubbing his hands together. "Bags are in the car." He moves closer to us and wraps his arms around Bennett and I. "We're ready to go."

I turn and a small, pathetic whine actually slips out as I tuck myself between the two of them.

Bennett sighs, stroking my hair. "I'm *so* sorry, darling. Arin said Theo would keep an eye on you and the house — we'll be back as soon as we can."

The last twenty four hours have been accompanied by a weird, floaty feeling in my body that I can only assume is because of the upcoming heat. According to the ridiculous pamphlets Bennett had — it's close, but close could mean imminent or take another four to five days for it to set in.

Basically, it made more sense for them to go ahead and take care of what they needed to, and be present for whatever happens in the next few days. And even though this pack isn't *mine* in the bonded sense, my omega is screaming at the idea of both Arin and Bennett being gone, *and* Seth not being by my side.

It leaves me with only Theo — the same Theo who gave me enough stuff that it took Seth and I two hours to sort through it and carry it up to the nest. I still couldn't bear the thought of sleeping alone in there, so I ended up between Bennett and Seth in their bed last night.

"I'll be okay." I suck in a breath, staring up at them. "I'm an adult."

Seth kisses my cheek. "I'll keep you updated the entire time. We'll be back in twenty-four hours, max. I promise, baby."

"And I left food." Bennett gives me a sad look. "It's all in the fridge, please eat it. You'll need your energy and I want to make sure you're getting something nutritious."

I nod, licking my lips before I throw myself at them again, one last time, choking back tears. When I finally pull away, I wrap my arms around myself, hating how needy and clingy I feel as they walk down the steps to the car. I linger in the doorway, watching until they pull away.

Slamming the front door shut behind me, I lock it and press a hand against my burning eyes.

I already feel like I'm being *cleaved* in half just by the simple act of saying goodbye to them. It was even worse with Arin this morning. I shed more than a couple tears when he held my face and vowed he'd be back before the ink dried.

Hanging my head, I inhale and pull away from the door. I haven't seen Theo since yesterday. He's been lurking somewhere in the house, hiding from me, and the thought makes my chest ache as I bite my tongue and head upstairs. I completely bypass the guest room and slink into Seth and Bennett's room, lying down on the bed and turning my head to press it into Bennett's pillow.

His scent is stuck to the fabric, and it envelops me as I lay there.

The orange circles my senses. I wish there was a way to bottle the smell of him. Or, better yet, glue him to my side like a little barnacle on my hip or something. I wouldn't even care if Seth came with him. And I'd have a whole other hip free for Arin.

I might be slightly losing it.

I don't know how long I linger, losing time as I drift in and out of feeling flushed and nauseous. My skin is tight and sticky with sweat when I finally stir, my stomach cramping. I curl up on the bed, wincing and pressing a hand to my stomach. I want them back. I want them all back right now — but I can't have them.

Squeezing my eyes shut, tears well as I sit on the bed. *Fuck this. Fuck being an omega.*

I want someone to hold me and tell me it's going to be okay.

Forcing myself to move, I crawl off the bed, moving to their closet and ripping open the drawers inside of it. I grab handfuls of shirts, the softest fabrics they own that are left. Bringing them up to my nose, I inhale, then turn, charging out of the room and back downstairs. I repeat the process in Arin's room, leaving it an absolute wreck as I take my stolen items all the way up to the third floor. Shoving the door to the nest open, I storm into it, letting it swing mostly shut behind me as I stare at the mattress.

CHAPTER TWENTY-NINE

The room is missing *so* much.

There are still bags of unopened blankets and supplies, but as I drop the clothes onto the bed, I turn and rifle through the ones Theo left for me. My hands find two prizes — the soft, blue blanket that smells like rainwater and the worn sweatshirt he tucked in with it. There's lingering smells in the room, but they're faded, and nothing has the level of intensity I want to it.

I should have listened to the pamphlets. I should have made them all sleep in here with me instead of trying to fight it.

I flop down to the mattress, pulling the sweatshirt over my already tangled hair, and shoving my face into the blanket, my shoulders shaking as I succumb to the ache in my chest, letting the tears fall where they may.

I MUST FALL ASLEEP, because the next thing I know, a voice is rousing me from a hazy dream. *Hands and kisses on my bare shoulders. A soft accent talking me through it. The smells of fudge, orange, and mint mixing — overpowered by pouring rain drenching me head to toe.*

"June?"

Stirring, I glance around at the nest, disoriented by how dark it is, nothing cluing me into what time it could even be.

"June!"

I sit up, wincing as my abdomen cramps again, my throat dry and raspy. "Theo?"

The door to the nest nearly hits the wall as he throws it open. Theo stops short of walking fully in and I can see his muscles straining as he holds onto the door frame, breathing hard.

"Jesus — I didn't know where you *were* —" He pauses, his eyes zeroing in on me in the center of the nest.

Pulling in on myself, I drag the blanket closer, aware of how tiny the bed makes me feel. Alone in the center of the mattress, I fist the blanket against my chest, huddled in his sweatshirt.

"Are you feeling okay?"

There couldn't be a *worse* time for him to finally show his face.

I shake my head at him, glancing down at the blanket and picking at the soft fabric. This stupid alpha, who flits between hot and cold, who poured me wine, bought me gifts, and is the reason I've not responded to any of my mother's angry text messages in the last week.

He's also the same alpha who made me feel like fucking *garbage.*

I glance up at him as a flash of anger goes through me. "Why do you ask? Do you suddenly give a shit? Or are you going to feel bad if you kick me out of the house when no one else is here and I don't feel well?"

Theo leans back, his fingers turning white on the door-frame. "I told Arin I'd make sure you were alright, and I fucking meant it. I'm not kicking you out."

"Don't bother trying to smooth things over now," I spit the words at him, kneeling up. "You and I both know you probably just told Arin that so he'd get off your back."

He laughs, his eyes narrowing to sharp points. "Arin hasn't been on my back, but from what I know, he's had you on *yours.*"

"You're a *dick.*" I stand up, stalking closer to the door,

but not near enough to touch him, or him to reach me — especially since he's still respecting the rules of the nest, dutifully outside of it because I've not extended an invite.

Tension hangs in the air, crackling like it's waiting for a reason to ignite.

His lips twitch as he looks down at me. The dark blue of his eyes glimmers as he takes me in, his eyes darting down my body, stopping on my bare legs. I know what he's seeing. I know he's seeing me in this sweatshirt and thinking that he already won.

And maybe he did. Because for how *angry* my heart is, my body is reacting to his presence like it always has. That undeniable allure that I would have acted on already if he knew how to *shut the fuck up.*

"Stop it," I snap at him, heat warming the back of my neck. "You don't get to look at me like that when you can't stand me."

Theo raises his eyes from my legs, burning my face. "Seems like I'm standing fine, princess, and so are you *in my sweatshirt.*"

I'm so *tired* of the cheeky jokes, the back and forth — I glare at him.

"So what? You're the one who *gave it to me.* What happened to hating me? You practically shouted it from the rooftops the first night I was here."

Theo winces. "I didn't —" His jaw clenches, then he snarls, leaning closer. "I couldn't fucking *stand* you, is that what you want to hear? I thought Seth was the stupidest son of a bitch in the entire world to run to the center and bring you home. All that was missing was the cardboard box and the new toys to play with."

"I'm not a fucking stray cat!"

He shakes his head, sucking in a deep breath. "No, you aren't." His eyes trail over me again, "And the more I got to see you, the more I *saw* the way they all gravitated toward you, the angrier I got. Do you want to know why, June?"

He's the only one who shortens my name and makes it sound like a curse. Arin always says '*Juniper*' like he's one second away from donning a Mr. Darcy cosplay and strolling across a foggy field to reach me. Bennett's '*Juniper*' is the one who embraces him, who's allowed to just *be*. Seth's '*June*' is the total goddamn disaster that brought me here in the first place.

I swallow, my throat tight.

"Because they had you," Theo whispers the words. "And I *didn't*."

I suck in a breath, staring at him as he lowers his arms from the door, just standing there.

"And god, do I *want* you."

I can't think. My heart pounds in my chest. The whole time he's *wanted* me? Like some twisted playground game of a boy pushing a girl into the dirt because he didn't know how to handle his own feelings?

Fuck *that*.

"I can't do this." I bristle, stepping forward. "Let me go. I'm leaving — I don't know — I can't *be* here."

Theo blocks the door.

"Call me a fucking asshole, scream at me until you can't speak, but don't you *dare* walk out, June. Not when you were crying, not in *my* goddamn sweatshirt, under *my* care."

"So you get to run from me, but I can't?" I snap at him. "You get to berate me and yell at me? You get to tell me I'm just looking for a rich pack, that I'm not welcome here? But I'm supposed to *accept* it? Boo fucking hoo, Theo, so Arin will yell at you if I leave — guess what? He *left me*. And I was too stubborn to admit that I needed him — that I needed all *three* of them. Instead, they just left me with *you* and I don't know what's worse — that they didn't stay or that I *still* want you, despite everything."

His face breaks, and my chest smarts at his expression. "I shouldn't have said those things to you."

"No, you shouldn't have." I whisper the words, my voice shaking. "And that's not an apology. You *hurt* me, Theo. Maybe I wouldn't be trying to bolt from you if I didn't feel like you hated my very existence."

The normally calming, soft scent of him reaches me and it's tinged with stress, like muddy water. It makes me want to go to him, to comfort him, and I fight it with every ounce of my being. He doesn't get that from me.

"You're right." His eyes lock on mine. "I'm sorry for the things I said." His foot moves, and he stops short, looking distressed at the door frame, like it's what is keeping him from entering the nest. "You deserve an apology, a *true* one. It's not an excuse, but I think I need to realize that my... *want* to be around you wasn't something that was wrong or that I needed to avoid." His voice softens, and I watch his jaw clench. "In pushing you away, I became exactly what I was trying to avoid. And I'm sorry for that. I'm sorry for my words and my actions."

I stare at him, my heart raising in my throat. "How am I supposed to believe you?"

"*How am I supposed to believe you're telling me the truth?*" My mother's voice echoes in my head, making bile rise in the back of my throat. "*How am I supposed to know this isn't just you wanting to sell your stories to anyone who will listen to them?*"

Regardless of how hard I've tried. I'm just like her at the end of the day.

Theo's expression crumbles as my body *begs* me to embrace him, to let him into this space that's supposed to be mine. It's missing his scent — it's missing *him*.

"Fuck" — his voice breaks — "the second I smelled you, I *needed* you, June. Every goddamn day I thought I was different from every other alpha out there, better than them. Then you walk in and make it impossible to ignore. I heard you that night — in the hallway outside of Seth and Bennett's door — touching yourself."

I gasp as he licks his lips, barreling forward without hesitation now that the words are pouring out.

"I could hear your wet fingers slipping as you tried to rub your desperate little clit, and I thought, '*Good, let her her be on the fucking edge like I've been this entire time. Let her feel the same thing she's made me feel. I hope she doesn't come. I hope her legs shake so much she can't go back to her room.*'"

I balk at his words.

"And I heard them *fucking* you, too." Theo leans closer, his eyes darkening. "I saw Seth under your thighs as you rode his face and whined. Then I went downstairs and heard Arin making you beg, making you say he fucked you better than they did. And I was *ready* to tell him that I couldn't stay here because you've driven me to insanity." He laughs, pushing a hand through his hair. "And then I got hit in the face with your sweet honey slick, dripping out while he fucked you, invading my *brain*. And I *ran* because I wanted to burst in there, but I also knew I couldn't. I couldn't after all the shitty things I've said and done, and isn't that *just* like me, to ruin something good before I've even gotten it? I can't get you out of my head, June, and I think I've finally decided I don't want to."

My heart races as I stare at him. This man, this *alpha*, who unlike Bennett with his quiet assurance, or Arin with his uncanny ability to get me to let go — Theo is my option to be *me*.

I want to be a fucking *nightmare* with him. I want to feel too much. I want to scream. I want to tear my hair out. He makes me want to spiral and unravel in every terrible way.

"I can't do this clean." I stare at him, my heart in my throat. "Not like I do with the others."

Theo stares me down. "So be messy for me." He goes quiet for a moment and his next words eviscerate me. "Be bad. Act out. Fight me. I'm not going to run away when I see your ugly side. I showed you mine, now you show me yours."

And just like that, my decision is made.

I take a step back, breathing out. "You can't come into this nest until I invite you, right?"

His eyes narrow. "Arin would kill me if I did."

I nod, then I tug on the sweatshirt, padding backwards as I stare at him. I slipped on the little satin set that Theo bought me last night before bed with Bennett and Seth. It was the only thing that felt good on my heated skin, the fabric soft and the straps falling off my shoulders. The little shorts are barely long enough to cover half my ass and I know he can see it as I turn around and bend over, crawling on my hands and knees to the center of the nest.

"Good." Turning, I flop back, staring up at him in the doorway. "Because I'm about to make you watch me come while I wear your sweatshirt, in the pajamas you bought me, surrounded by the blankets you gave me for my nest."

His fingers clench on the doorframe, making it creak as I

slip my fingers into the shorts and slide them down my legs, kicking them away just to spread my thighs for him.

"And I didn't want to wear underwear today."

"*June.*"

"Maybe I won't even invite you in, and your punishment will be watching me get off until Seth or Bennett or Arin get home." I feel a flare of heat crawl through me as he gives me a tortured look. "I mean if you've already watched them fuck me, it won't be new for you."

He groans, his eyes wild as he drinks me in.

I drop back to a pillow, already warm with his sweatshirt still on my upper half. Sliding a hand over my chest, I ruck it up, pushing the silky top with it and flashing him my breasts.

"Oops."

Theo snarls as I press a hand over one, then the other.

"Arin likes my thighs. Seth likes my pussy. Bennett likes my mouth..." I glance up at him, grinning wickedly. "What do you like, alpha?"

His resolve snaps, his eyes going black as he growls, "Let me in."

"Is that an order?" I look up at him as I move to cup my dripping pussy. When my fingers slip, they make a messy, wet sound between my legs as I sigh, "Ask nicely."

I watch him struggle, greatly enjoying seeing him shatter as he whispers a broken, "*Please.*"

I preen as I lean back, pulling my hand away from myself. "Come in, Theo."

He strides in without another word, ripping his shirt off. I get a glimpse of the patchwork of tattoos on his pale skin before he jumps down into the nest with me, covering my body with his. His hand slides into my hair, jerking my head up as he kisses me roughly.

I gasp as his jeans rub against me, feeling him sink every single unspoken word into the kiss. Arching into him, I moan as he cups a breast, his voice rough. "Fuck every single one of them. You're *mine*, and when I'm done with you, you won't be able to fucking crawl out of this nest."

I moan as he ruts his hips against mine, my head spinning as I gasp his name. *"Theo."*

He groans, kissing me again before he drags his tongue over my throat. "I was an idiot. I was a fucking idiot, June, please forgive me." Theo's head drops to my chest, staying there as he breathes in and out like he's barely holding himself together, his voice breaking. "I like every inch of you. I couldn't pick a favorite part. Your mind, your stubbornness, your ability to drive me to insanity — *all* of you."

His hands drop down, grabbing onto my hips, and suddenly I'm in the *air*. I shriek as he sits up, bringing me down onto his lap, one hand on the back of my head to keep me stable as he grins and rolls his hips up into mine. The pressure is even better, and swallowed in his sweatshirt, with him *right* against me, all I can smell is his scent, all I know is *him*.

"I like the sounds you make too, *especially* when you say my name."

I straddle him, shifting so my legs fall open. Glancing up, I run my fingers through his hair, twisting the locks between my fingers. "Any way I say it?"

"Oh, I plan on making you sigh it." Theo leans in and nips my lip, kissing me as he tugs at the sweatshirt. He manages to pull it over my head and the cool air sends a shiver up my spine.

Theo's eyes dart down to the sham of a silk top, cataloguing my breasts as it does nothing to hide my hardened nipples. His hands grab it and in seconds it's gone too, into the piles of clothes around us.

"You're going to whine it." He lifts me with one hand, not even grunting as he shoves his jeans down. I bend, helping him get them off his legs as the smell of his fresh perfume hits me, making me dizzy as he presses a hand against the small of my back, both of us finally naked.

"You're going to scream it for me, princess."

I tug him against me by his hair, kissing him hungrily as he pulls my hips down on top of his, grinding up against me. The feeling is indescribable. He's shorter than the rest of them, but he makes up for it in thickness and girth. I rut forward, canting my hips into his, chasing the feeling of working myself on him, slicking him up without meaning too.

"I want to fuck you." He mutters the words through a pained groan. "But I want to make sure this isn't only your heat making you want me because I'm the closest alpha."

I lift my head, grabbing onto his chin and forcing him to look at me. "Theo."

He raises his eyes, his hair mussed, his pupils blown out as he breathes heavily.

"You're going to fuck me." I bite the words out, my eyes narrowing so I can make sure he understands me. "I don't care if it's selfish, but you don't get to push me away after this. Don't tell me it was nothing. Don't *hurt* me. I know what it's like to be scared and I'm a fucking hypocrite after everything but —"

He grabs my chin, kissing me deeply as his other hand rests on my ass, guiding my hips against his. "Are you sure?"

"Stop talking." I hold onto him as I breathe out against his lips, about to plunge myself down on top of him if he doesn't shut up. "I'm lucid. I invited you into my nest. You're the *only* one who will have fucked me in here. I *want* you to be the first."

He moans as I grind down. "I'm the first?"

"You're the first, so you better atone for your sins, Theo. No one else will do it for you."

He kisses me again, desperation behind it as he grabs onto my hips and lifts me. I feel him brush against my thighs, and I don't even *see* him before he lines us up and drops me down on top of himself. I gasp, my body locking up for a moment at the sudden intrusion. He's so thick, a too-full burn lingers before my body suddenly gives and it's *euphoria*.

My back bows from the pleasure, holding onto his shoulder with one hand and the edge of the nest with the other as he works himself into me with slow, deep thrusts. I don't think anyone else could *take* him except an omega, and I must be fucking made for it because the second our hips collide and he's fully seated, save for his knot kissing my entrance, I want to sob from how *good* it all feels.

Theo grunts, holding himself still for a moment before he lifts me with a hand, pumping his thighs up and bouncing me. Our skin ripples together, and the stretch marks on my stomach brush the echoes of the ones on his.

"You're right, I should be groveling." He leans forward. "But the thing about me is" — he drops me down to the mattress as he pounds into me — "being on my knees wouldn't let me have you like *this*." He kisses me heatedly, moving his lips to my chest, sucking on each of my nipples. "But maybe I can do that later."

My nails claw up his shoulders as he pushes me back into the pile of pillows. His lips suck on my skin as he growls,

"I'm not going to bite or knot you either, but I'm going to leave every inch of this pretty skin red and make you wish I did."

He grabs my hips, pumping into me rapidly. He's fucking me so hard we shift up the nest, inch by inch. Theo's lips leave bright red hickeys all over me, making his way up to my throat until he can suck on my pulse point, moaning, "You smell *so* good, princess. You feel like goddamn heaven around me, so wet and *tight*."

I shiver at the nickname, fluttering around him, because unlike every other time he's said it with derision, this time, in my nest, with him buried inside me — it sounds *reverent*.

"I feel you clenching around me. You just can't help yourself, can you?" He drops a hand between us, rubbing my clit quickly. "That's okay. I can finish you off. I can make you scream louder than any of them, and it's a damn shame they're not here to hear it. Are you going to come for me? Are you going to make this nest smell like we've been fucking in it every single second they've been gone? Where do you want it, June? In you? On you?"

I cry out as he moves faster. "On me!"

His eyes flash, almost black, his lips pulling back in a snarl. "Done."

I spiral out, unable to hold back as I turn my head, biting down on his forearm to muffle my scream as I climax around him. All my muscles tense, but he pulls out in a rush, reaching down and stroking himself, wrapping a hand around his knot and strangling it as he leans up, coming with a broken groan all over my chest and stomach.

He gives me every last fucking drop before he sinks down, his head dropping as his arm shakes beside my head.

I breathe hard, staring down at the mess, my eyelids

drooping as he slides a hand through his cum, humming softly. One thumb rubs it in a little circle over my nipple, and his smile is slightly deranged as he mutters, "I should probably have fed you dinner. We're not going to leave this nest anytime soon, are we?"

My lips twitch as I sink back, spreading my legs wide, splaying out for him. "No, we're not."

Theo pauses, his eyes roving over me like he's taking a thousand mental pictures. His thumb strokes over my other nipple, and then he lifts his hand and sucks his own cum off, smirking slowly.

"That's what I like to hear, princess."

I grin, laughing as he kisses me again, his weight settling on top of me as I wrap my legs around him, tilting my hips up to rub against his already semi-hard cock. It slips back into me and we both make little noises of surprise as he begins to pump his hips slowly again, his breath heating up the side of my face as he clings to me.

"You feel so *fucking* good. You're so warm around me."

I score my nails through his hair, jerking his head back to mine so I can kiss him hungrily, devouring his mouth as he ruins me for anyone else.

We can stop when we get too hungry to keep going.

But that's going to take a while.

CHAPTER THIRTY

THEO

WAKING up next to her half-naked body, breathing deeply and heaving little sighs every time she adjusts, is all I want for the rest of my life.

I could die right now and be satisfied. The thin straps of her top slid down at some point during the night, dangerously close to letting the scraps of fabric over her chest droop. She only put it back on because we ate leftovers like rabid animals and then went straight back to fucking.

I shouldn't be looking, but my eyes trace the round swell of each breast, and I want to reach over and slide my hands over each one, to grip them and let my fingers sink into her soft flesh as I bury my head into her neck. The entire bed smells like her perfume, light, herbal, and warm. I've fucked her so much the other smells are dimmer, undercurrents of fudge, orange, and mint.

June shifts, and her hair falls to one side, exposing her neck to me. I bite my tongue, trying in vain not to give in. I fail — arching my head so I can press my lips to the curve of her throat. Her scent is concentrated here, and nearly knocks me back on my ass when she makes a little sound, a half-moan that turns into a sleepy sigh.

Fuck it, I'm a goner anyway.

I slide my hands up, my chest pressed against her back as I skim them under her sham of a top, fingers finding the soft skin of her tits as I cup them and squeeze once. June whines and drops back against me, and I don't know if she's fully awake, or coherent, but I run my tongue over her pulse point anyway, leaving filthy, wet kisses as she arches her back and yawns.

"Mm," she sighs, sinking back against me. "Shouldn't you take me to dinner before you fondle me?"

"Where do you want to go, princess?" I nip at her earlobe, watching goosebumps race down her skin with a little smirk. "Paris? Luxembourg? Monaco? I'll have a jet chartered before you're done with your first orgasm, then I'll give you another one on the plane for fun."

She laughs, and the sound echoes off the walls, high and delighted. June turns her head and stares up at me, her eyes bright, but half-lidded from sleep.

"Theo..."

I don't let her finish, I dip down and crash my lips to hers, holding her body to mine possessively as I devour her. She may be allowed to overthink with every other asshole in this house, but not me. Her anxiety is going to come to heel even if I have to force it every damn time with a handful of mind-blanking orgasms. She can't think if she's dumbstruck by pleasure.

I don't even know what fucking time it is. I just kiss her, and every single other mark I left on her in the past however long it's been.

Before I lost our phones, I sent Arin a text that we'd

eaten some of the dinner that Bennett left, but that was hours ago, before another two rounds and however long the last nap was. I couldn't bring myself to admit to him that we've been in the nest the entire time. He'll figure it out when he gets home.

June wriggles under me and I grab her by the hips, grunting as I kiss down her thighs. "Stop moving."

She laughs, trying to get away. "You can't eat me out again, I have to *pee*."

"Good, me too." I slide my arms under her and pick her up. June laughs even louder, but she doesn't protest as I manhandle her, throwing her over my shoulder and smacking her round ass. She shrieks as I walk us into the bathroom, her little hands beating me across the back.

"Theo!"

I drop her onto the counter, flipping on the dial for the heated floor. She gives me an indignant look, her cheeks flushed and red. I do a double take as I flip the shower on. We're both sticky and kind of a wreck — her red hair is matted in some areas and I feel kind of bad about it. I shouldn't have come on her face that one time, she just looked so good with her tongue out.

"You feeling okay?"

June reaches up, pressing her hands against her cheeks, mumbling something under her breath.

I step closer, sliding my hands over her hips. "June?" I lift a hand, pressing it against her forehead. Her eyes look a little glassy as she stares up at me. I curse when her hand reaches for me, brushing my cock, pawing at it with a whine.

Something instinctual makes me pull back.

I've never seen her like this. Not even in the marathon of making her give me every noise I could draw out of her throat in the last twelve hours. Turning to the cabinets, I dig through them and rip open a box for a thermometer. Pushing her hands away from me again, I check her temperature, pausing when I see the readout.

"Fuck."

It's *high*.

It's concerning levels of high, like *this fever requires a doctor* levels. Except it doesn't — because I know exactly what it means. I pull her closer when she tries to get off the counter, holding her to my chest so she can't wiggle away or drop to her knees on the floor. June sighs when her nose presses against my bare skin, breathing in deeply. I let the thermometer clatter to the countertop and swing her back up into my arms, stepping into the shower.

"They should be home soon." Panic sets in as I try to shift her carefully.

She jerks away from the water, groaning, "I feel nauseous, Theo. I don't want a shower right now." Her voice breaks, her eyes turning up to me, filling with tears. "I don't feel good."

"I know, I know." I run my fingers through her messy hair, grabbing a bottle of shampoo and tearing it open. "Let me clean you up, okay? Then I can get you some food and call Arin."

"No food," she whines, her hands going to my chest. They shake as she presses closer to me, "I need *you, please alpha*."

Fuck, why have I *never* looked into how to care for an omega? Why have I spent over thirty fucking years insisting I'd never be in this situation? I rub her back, holding her as I think. I'm already tired — I'm not superhuman — but somehow, in all of this, we must have crossed the line from her climbing me because she wanted to, to her heat setting in.

At some point we went from enthusiastic fucking to her body just giving into me.

Did she even want me?

Nausea rises in my throat.

Blinking hard, I make myself focus as I pull her hands off of me, my voice firm. "No, June." I grab the shampoo, cleaning her hair as best as I can as she fights me every second. Her perfume mixes with the humidity in the air and it makes my head spin.

Bite her. Fuck her. Stuff her full and seal it in with the knot.

I wash her body off, careful as she whines and tries to push herself onto my fingers. Ignoring my alpha is like taking a rusty saw to my arm. I pick her up before she can reach for my dick again, pulling her wrists to the side and binding them in one hand as I swaddle her in a towel with the other. My muscles scream, from holding her upright, keeping myself at bay — and I barely manage to get us out of the bathroom with a clear head.

I climb back down into the nest, switching the towel around her for a blanket. Her forehead is *burning* when my hand brushes it, and I scramble away, trying to find my phone in the mess of clothes we left in our wake.

From behind me, June's hands run over my sides, her voice soft and heart-breaking. "Do you not want me?" Her fingers are warm, her body plush as she rubs against my back. "Don't you want to keep fucking me, alpha? I want you too. I really do."

Closing my eyes, I breathe in, fighting every part of me that *does* want her — but she's not herself. It was one thing to have her consent before, to jump into the nest when she was teasing me, this, *us* — it's another to know she's not entirely herself.

I'm so fucking scared I'll go into a rut and be as mindless as she is.

And I'd never forgive myself if I hurt her. She *asked* me not to.

"I need to go."

I mutter the words as my hand wraps around my phone, jerking away from her touch. I climb up and abandon my clothes, searching for Arin's number as I make a beeline for the door.

I'm not fast enough. Her broken sob haunts me as I slam the nest door shut and walk away from the crying omega inside.

To be continued in

Gold Mine
(Golden Omegaverse #2)

CONTENT WARNINGS

This book contains sensitive content that is suited for adults (18+).

GRAPHIC (throughout the narrative, on page, explicit):

- Ableism / Chronic Illness (omegas are predisposed to chronic conditions and the world treats them as lesser for this)
- Cursing (throughout)
- Mental Health / Mental Illness / Panic Attack / Anxiety (through narrative)
- Sexual content (multi-pairings including: MM, MF, MMF)
  - See spice list for details

MODERATE (on page, appears in a few instances):

- Alcohol (characters drink casually)

- Blood / Medical content (scenes set in hospital-like setting where a character has their blood taken)
- Body Shaming / Emotional Abuse / Fatphobia (some self, in past, and scenes including unsupportive family)
- Confinement (the main character is legally not allowed to leave without approval from an alpha who agrees to take over 'right' of her)
- Misogyny/Sexism (present in world and how omegas are treated)
- Religious Bigotry (of the familial variety)
- Toxic Relationship (some readers might consider Theo and June's relationship toxic)
- Vomit/Nausea (brief scenes of vomiting on page, characters are nauseous from anxiety *only*. No pregnancy of the main character.)

MINOR (in reference):

- Abandonment (mentioned in regards to family)
- Abortion / Pregnancy (mentioned in right to choose, a side character is briefly implied to be pregnant, others imply worthy omegas are fertile ones)
- Abuse (domestic abuse implied, in past of side character — mentions of overarching world containing instances of sexual assault by alphas misusing their power)
- Stalking (implied)

SPICE LIST

This is omegaverse, therefore, there is mention of knots.

- 17: MMF — Voyeurism, exhibitionism, anal sex, female masturbation
- 18: MF — begging, cunnilingus, fingering
- 19: MM — Blowjob, cum tasting
- 24: MF — semi-public sex, fingering, cum tasting
- 25: MMF — face-sitting, voyeurism & exhibitionism, blowjob (mild gagging), cum tasting/swapping
- 26: MF — semi-rough sex, use of bark to force orgasms (consensual)
- 27: M — Male masturbation, unintentional voyeurism
- 29: MF — exhibitionism, teasing, marking

GOLDEN OMEGAVERSE GUIDE

This novel takes place in an alternate universe similar to our's. Much of the world remains the same, except every human also has a **designation**.

Designations fall into three categories: alphas, betas, and omegas. This book does **not** contain shifters and/or werewolves. See below for an overview on each designation, then a more detailed list organized by term.

DESIGNATIONS:

Alphas are humans who are generally more respected and seen as leadership types.

- Alphas can be any gender.
- They have heightened senses, and are stronger physically than other designations.
- Each alpha has a scent, that can either be alluring or off-putting to others.

- Biologically alphas are fine without having an omega, though lonely, as they often want to care for someone. (Even if they have no desire to have children)
- Biologically male alphas have a **knot**, a continuous round of muscle, at the base of their penis. Biologically female alphas have the inverse, a stronger muscle inside the vagina that can **lock** during penetrative sex. Both of these biological traits are meant to aid in breeding.
- Alphas make up 30% of the population
- Alphas bleed red, but it has a silver tinted/oil-slick sheen to it.
- Alphas make up a **large** portion of people in power in the world, as culturally it's seen that they are the "better" by default, which leads to much abuse of power in the case of alphas.

Betas are humans, as we would understand them in this world.

- They have no extra qualities.
- Betas are the majority of the population, at around 65%
- Betas in the *goldverse* have very faint scents when not around their scent match, though there are products that can (and do) enhance these scents to the levels of alphas or omegas. It always has a slight chemical tang, though, and is easy to spot.
- Their blood is red, and has no sheen to it.

Omegas are humans that are often associated with meek, submissive, and calm characteristics.

- Omega designations typically emerge anywhere from the ages of eighteen to twenty-five during a second puberty.
- Omegas are increasingly rare, making up **less than 5% of the total population**.
- Omegas are owned, by law, by their parents, until their ownership is "transferred" to an alpha or pack.
- Biologically female omegas are often not given the choice to prevent pregnancies, with strict rules requiring an alpha signing off on them being provided birth control.
- Biologically male omegas, while unable to get pregnant, are incredibly virile, and often their sperm results in a pregnancy. They are also refused birth control.
- Omegas have red blood, but it has a golden/oil slick sheen to it.
- Omegas are generally seen as weaker, which culturally, has meant that omegas, while being sought after, aren't really treated seriously in any capacity. They're said to be too prone to whims, and it's socially accepted that any and all omegas are too emotional for any serious or leadership positions.

LIST OF TERMS:

Bark/Commands —

- Alphas have a bark, or built-in command, where their word is obeyed. The bark has to be used with intent to make it work, and doesn't work on everyone at all times.
- Varying alphas might have a stronger bark than others, leading to a hierarchy within the designation where one alpha might be stronger than another. This is also true in pack systems, where there is a pack alpha, this alpha is often the most well-respected, and likely has the strongest bark.

Bonds —

- Bonds occur between any alphas and any designation, though most common are alphas leaving a claim bite on betas or omegas that are their life partners.
- Bonds from an alpha open up a neural pathway between the alpha and the bonded, where they can feel the other person's emotions and general state of being. It's a way for alphas to check on their bonded and care for them.
- This neural pathway isn't a way to read thoughts, but more intent and general mood. They can tell if their bonded is stressed/in heightened states of emotion. The bonds can be dimmed and dulled with various medicines.

Blood — *unique to the **goldverse***

- As previously mentioned, alphas have blood that, when viewed from an angle, will appear silver. The same can be said for omegas, who's blood will appear golden. Betas have red blood that carries no sheen.
- Though it has been attempted, there is currently no chemical way to replicate the sheen on the blood of alphas or omegas, making a blood test the one true, trustworthy way to ensure a person's designation.

Claim bites (also called ***bond marks***) —

- Alphas will get the urge to mark, or bite, their partners. These bites are binding and scar.
- Bites made by alphas appear silver in color when healed, while omega bites have a golden hue.
- Bonding bite marks heal faster than other injuries, by biological design.

Designation Centers —

- Centers exist where alphas are paired with omegas, or where an omega's guardians place them with a pack for life.
- Culturally, there are many who do not agree with packs and think every alpha should have a single omega. It often has to do with religion believing that every alpha is "owed" their own omega, and to share one is to share your right.

(Making an omega an object, rather than an actual person with wants and desires)

- In the same manner, many believe that female alphas shouldn't claim female omegas, because it, biologically, cannot result in a child. The same can be said for male alphas and male omegas, or any cross-pairing that does not want children. Breeding and population continue to be hot topics.

- Designation Centers are often government affiliated, though independently run ones do exist. Alphas can buy memberships to centers to have their pack and scents listed as an option for omegas to choose from.

- There are groups that speak out for Omegas and against designation centers, choosing to say that a person's designation should be their right to disclose, and that omegas shouldn't be the "property" of their parents until sold to an alpha (often in an exchange that contains money or other collateral).

Heat (or *heat cycle*) —

- A hormonal cycle that occurs in omegas, after their designation emerges with puberty.
- The heat cycle happens roughly every three months, or four times in a calendar year (though changes have and do occur when hormones are tampered with).
- Heats last for a week (five to seven days) and are a state of heightened sexual desire and activity,

where the omega will both want comfort and sexual satisfaction.

- For biologically female omegas, a heat will coincide with ovulation week if the omega is currently fertile and menstruating.
- For biologically male omegas, a heat will occur roughly three to four times a year, and coincide with testosterone spikes, making the omega want to seek release.

Heat-sickness —

- A flu-like precursor to a first heat, that makes omegas weaker and often accompanied by a fever. Some omegas are unlucky enough to get it multiple times/before every heat, especially if they have unbalanced hormones or are stressed prior to a heat.
- Heat sickness is one of the major signs that someone is about to emerge as an omega, and is often tested for every few months.
  - First signs include elevated heart rate and body temperature.

Heat Spike —

- When an omega is approaching their upcoming heat, flu-like symptoms will begin to present. Tiny "spikes" of symptoms will mimic a heat, often resulting in greater arousal and other various symptoms associated with the omega's regular heat.

- ○ **Symptoms that might be present include**: dizziness, pain in the body, cramping, headaches, fevers, excessive sweating, chills or shaking/trembling, nausea or vomiting, heightened arousal, heightened emotions/mood swings (whether anger, anxiety, or other), sleepiness or insomnia, appetite changes, general fatigue

Knot —

- A ring of muscle at the base of a biological male alpha's penis. This muscle swells and enlarges during intercourse, with the intent to lock the penis in the vagina during sex, to keep semen inside and higher the chance of pregnancy.
- Knots vary in size, shape, and the time it takes for them to go down. When flaccid, the knot is still present, but not as prominent.

Lock —

- A ring of muscle inside the vagina of a biologically female alpha. This ring tightens and locks when aroused and during intercourse, keeping the penetrative object inside to higher the chance of pregnancy. Locks vary in size, shape, and rigidity.

Mannerisms —

- Alphas and omegas often display animalistic mannerisms like: barking, growling, whining, whimpering, and more.
  - **See bark** for more information on commands.

Nests/Nesting —

- A uniquely omega urge to build a small, enclosed space, full of warm and comforting objects.
- This urge is often associated with heats, though it's more of a comforting room that can be kept year-round of omegas to retreat to and enjoy. It's simply a safe place for them to be.
- Many packs will have a nest room or space for their eventual or current omegas to personalize, and it varies from omega to omega.
- Nests normally are reserved for the omega to use, with it being common to ask permission before entering an omega's nest, as they might not want things shifted, or scents to change.

Perfume (*scents* or *pheromones*) —

- Biologically all humans exist with their own natural perfume or pheromones, regardless of designation.
- Scents bloom and become more potent when experiencing heightened emotions, often arousal or fear.
- Omegas have the most powerful perfumes, while

alpha perfumes are secondary and beta perfumes are very subtle.

- The scent is unique to each and every individual. Though there are certain scents that will appeal to specific individuals, these are called **scent matches**.

Packs —

- Because the number of alphas is so high compared to the number of omegas, some alphas will "pack up" with each other, to satisfy their need to caretake and want to be surrounded by like-minded people.
  - This doesn't mean they are all romantic with each other, as the relationships might be familial or platonic as well as romantic.
- Packs will also tend to choose one alpha as their **pack alpha** or **prime** who is the decision maker and leader of the pack. They tend to be the strongest of the group, whether physically, or in the case of their bark.

Rut —

- All alphas might be subject to entering a rut, triggered by an omega in a heat cycle.
- A rut is a biological response to a heat, where the alpha goes into a similar haze of desire to mate. It doesn't occur every heat, nor with every alpha and omega pairing, and is largely up to biological chance when tending to an omega in heat.

- Alphas in a rut become *highly* territorial and single-minded. They are generally seen as more dangerous during this time because they have a lack of control over their own reactions.

Scenting —

- Scenting is objectively one of the first ways to lay claim on an omega. An alpha will rub themselves on an omega (or imbue them with their signature scent) to show to others that they belong to an alpha before a bite.
- Scenting has no permanence and products exist to suppress scents or wash them free.

Scent matches —

- Scent matches are another way to describe fated mates or soulmates.
- Scents will match, or pair well with each other, and in turn connections and attachments between individuals will form faster.
- Scent matching is used in designation centers to find potential matches faster than meetings and interviews, because if a scent of an alpha is off-putting to an omega, it is highly unlikely they will be a match romantically.

Slick —

- Slick is a natural lubricant produced by all genders of omegas that make it easier for penetration of any kind. It's produced during a heat in excess, but is naturally existing in all omegas year round.

ACKNOWLEDGMENTS

First and foremost, it's very strange to be writing acknowledgements that others will actively *read* because so many of my other stories have never made it this far.

I'd like to extend my sincere gratitude to every single person who hasn't given up on me or has offered me even a passing word of encouragement — every single one of them has meant the world to me. I'm sure I will forget names and that will keep me up at night. (I'm already nervous as I type up this list because I *know* I will miss someone.)

Specific thanks to Anne-Marie, who was an incredible alpha reader and really believed in this story from the beginning. And thank you to my editor, Kai, I promise to eventually learn how to use a comma correctly!

Thank you to Silvy (Sarah) and Nikita Navalker, who both beta read this book in an early form! Your early feedback meant the world to me! Other cheerleaders included: Amalia, Ana, Ash, Chey, Emily, Jean, Julia, Michaela, Robyn, and Sarah B. — sorry I stole some of your names (and the names of your partners), it will happen again.

There are two people who always read my work before anyone else: LJ Kobzina and Katie Neel. Thank you, endlessly, for every ounce of love, support, and kindness you've given me in all the years we've known each other.

I'm also incredibly grateful to call Allegra Hall a friend!

Thank you for pushing me to just go for it and get my work out in the world. (And thank you for the voice notes assuring me that all the stress will be worth it) As an aside, I want to shout out Kathryn Moon, Eliana Lee, and CM Nascosta — three incredibly talented writers in the monster romance community who inspire me. I am as much of a reader as I am a writer, and many other stories were devoured before I could write this one on my own.

Thank you to my family who watched me work day in and day out. It is exhausting to do, but so rewarding to craft stories that feel like a reflection of my heart. I wouldn't be able to do it without the support you've given me. If you are related to me and read this book — please don't bring it up as casual dinner conversation. I'm allowed one rebellious act and I'm cashing it in by writing spicy little romance books.

Also — thank you to **me**. I put in the work, and I'm proud of myself. If you've read to this point, you should be proud of your own accomplishments too. <3

ABOUT THE AUTHOR

R.L. Randolph is a mildly feral human woman who just wants to write about people kissing for her day job. She lives near the mountains, but, ironically, has grass and tree mold allergies so she never leaves the house.

 instagram.com/rlrandolph

ALSO BY R. L. RANDOLPH

Golden Omegaverse

June's Duet

Gold Rush (#1)

Gold Mine (#2)